THE RETURN OF THE WOLF

A JOSIAH WOLFE, TEXAS RANGER NOVEL

THE RETURN OF THE WOLF

LARRY D. SWEAZY

THORNDIKE PRESS

A part of Gale, a Cengage Company

LIBRARY OF CONGRESS CIP DATA ON FILE.
CATALOGUING IN PUBLICATION FOR THIS BOOK
IS AVAILABLE FROM THE LIBRARY OF CONGRESS.

ISBN-13: 978-1-4328-6895-6 (hardcover alk. paper)

Published in 2021 by arrangement with Cherry Weiner Literary Agency

Printed in Mexico
Print Number: 01   Print Year: 2021

To Rose, Cherry, Tiffany, and Hazel
for making it happen

"Charged with the mission of operating beyond the boundaries of civilization with minimal support and no communication from higher authority, they lived and often died by the motto, Order first, then law will follow."

—Thomas W. Knowles

CHAPTER 1

October 1875

Josiah Wolfe sighed with relief as the cabin came into view. He drove a simple buckboard, led by a nameless black draft horse who had proven to be reliable on the trip from Austin to Seerville. Clipper, Josiah's trusted appaloosa, had been relegated to the rear of the wagon, pulled along like an angry donkey. The horse had no tolerance for being a follower; he was accustomed to being in the lead, charging into battle, not being dragged back to the farm and put out to pasture.

"Whoa," Josiah said, pulling back on the reins. The black horse obeyed and the wagon came to a slow stop. No dust kicked up as the hard wagon wheels came to rest on the firm, brushy trail. Seerville sat northeast of Tyler in East Texas, and Josiah's family land was north of the little town that had been his home since birth. A perpetual pine forest, with some hardwoods scattered in among the towering green trees, surrounded the place. Oaks, hickories, and pecans showed signs of the season change from summer to autumn, adding a splash of yellows and reds to the unchanging backdrop. The treetops glowed like celebratory candles accented by the golden rays of early evening light.

Josiah took in a deep gulp of the earthy air, then held it in his mouth and throat like he was dining on a long-savored meal. It had been a long three years since he'd left the cabin, and at the time, he wasn't sure he'd ever see it again. Coming back to the place he'd started was not his original plan. "Looks like we are home," Josiah said, exhaling the taste of familiar air.

"*Sí,* so we are." A blank expression hung on Ofelia's round Mexican face. She sat next to Josiah, with Josiah's three-year-old son, Lyle, wedged between them. Ofelia had left Seerville with Josiah, a wet nurse to the boy then, but was now a valued housekeeper and mother-figure for Lyle. She was the one person whom Josiah felt he could trust no matter what happened.

"You don't sound too happy about that," Josiah said.

Ofelia shrugged. "I liked living in Austin."

10

A scowl stayed on her face a little longer than it should have. She was in her early thirties, but the expression and her natural no-nonsense demeanor made her look years older.

"But you have family here," Josiah said.

Lyle, sandy-haired and blue-eyed, sat staring at the cabin. He was calm, at least for the moment, which was unusual for him. His eyes were filled with curiosity.

"*Niño* is my *familia*. You, too, when you are with us," Ofelia said.

Josiah looked away from her. He had been hoping for a different response. "There was no place to go once I decided not to ride with the Rangers anymore."

Ofelia didn't respond, she stared at Josiah unsatisfied with his explanation. She would come around. He was sure of it.

"What about you?" Josiah said to his son.

The boy broke his gaze away from the cabin and looked up to Josiah. It was hard to tell if Lyle understood what Josiah was saying. It wasn't that there was anything wrong with the boy. Lyle was smart enough, a male version of his mother, the most intelligent woman Josiah had ever known, but the boy had been an infant when Josiah had packed him up so he could join the Texas Rangers. The unreadable emotion on Lyle's face was nothing more than a lack of memory. He had no recollection of the cabin, or what had happened there when he was born — or before.

Lyle looked back to the cabin, and said, "We live there?"

"Yes, from now on," Josiah said. He looked over to Ofelia. "You stay here. The place has been empty for three years as far as I know. No telling what kind of critters have made a home for themselves inside." He wasn't only talking about the four-legged kind. Anyone could have come along and staked a claim for themselves on his property. There'd been no one to look after it when he'd left.

Josiah leaned behind the seat and grabbed his rifle, a Winchester '73, that he'd carried with him when he'd ridden with the Rangers. A Colt Single Action Army, called a Peacemaker by some, sat holstered on his right hip. His belt was fully stocked with cartridges, and Josiah's cool summer blue eyes were forever on the hunt for trouble. Ofelia and Lyle were his gold, and he'd die protecting them if something gave him cause.

Certain of his next task, Josiah stepped down from the wagon. "Scattergun's on your side."

12

Ofelia didn't acknowledge Josiah's directive. She knew where the scattergun was and knew how to use any firearm around. Josiah had taken care of that long ago. Lyle had been left in Ofelia's care for months at a time while Josiah was away on one campaign or the other.

"You know what to do if there's trouble," Josiah said.

"No habra problemas." Ofelia looked past Josiah, then back to him.

He knew Ofelia well enough, and had picked up enough Mexican to know that she'd said there wouldn't be any problems. Lyle spoke more Mexican than he did, which had never bothered Josiah — but it didn't settle well with some Anglo folks. Anything Mexican was looked down on.

"I hope you're right." Josiah walked away from the wagon at a slow pace. He dropped his vision to the ground looking for any sign of human presence. The crunch of hard dirt echoed upward, mixing with distant bird songs; chickadees, blue jays, cardinals, foraging for their early evening meal, joyous in their cause. Josiah didn't share the birds' enthusiasm. He didn't feel any joy. Only dread. There were a lot of reasons he'd left the only house he'd ever known, and none of those reasons were good ones.

■ ■ ■ ■

Ofelia stood over Lily's lifeless body and shook her head. "She is dead, señor." There was no blood, no struggle. Lily didn't have the strength to bear a child. She had battled for days between the labor of childbirth and the onset of influenza. She lay flat on the bed, her belly protruding, beads of sweat still on her forehead. A bowl of steaming hot water sat next to the bed, and the room was filled with an odd, sour odor.

Josiah struggled to breathe. He staggered to the bed, past Ofelia's helper, a scrawny young thing with saucer-shaped brown eyes rimmed with tears, that the midwife referred to as niña, girl, and never by name.

Lily's skin was still warm to the touch.

He closed his wife's dull eyes and kissed her forehead without fear of contracting the sickness. Life was too painful. He was willing to die at that very moment himself, willing to join his wife in the land of heaven, even though he was not much of a believer. Not now. Redemption and resurrection seemed to be nothing more than a folk tale. The sickness had showed no mercy, a devil that could not be fought. Where was God's hand in all of this? Josiah had wondered more than once,

14

especially after the preacher man from Tyler had refused to come to the house out of fear for his own health and well-being.

Josiah Wolfe had never felt so empty, or so angry, in his entire life. It seemed that death was everywhere he looked. He ran out of the house screaming his rage into the darkness of the night.

A coyote answered, mocking him.

He fell to the ground in a bundle of tears and spit, and began to pound the dirt. He didn't know how long he was there, how long it was before someone laid a hand on his shoulder. It was only minutes, but seemed like an eternity.

"The baby lives, señor, but we do not have much time." Ofelia stood over him, staring down with the eyes of a sad mother. "I cannot reach the feet."

Josiah caught his breath, filled his lungs, but he could not speak. Everything seemed so hopeless — even the suggestion that life somehow still existed did not, could not, touch his heart.

"I will need a butchering knife to save the baby," Ofelia said. "Can you get it for me?"

Ofelia's voice sounded like it was coming out of a well. The wind had whipped up, pelting his face with dry Texas dirt. In a stupor, he pulled himself up, staggered to the barn, and found his skinning knife. *Ofelia grabbed the knife from his hand and disappeared back into the pine cabin that once held his dreams and love, but now only held the lifeless body of his one and only Lily.*

By the time he returned to his marriage bed, there was blood everywhere.

The niña *could not take the sight of Ofelia cutting open Lily's belly — she had run from the foul-smelling room in a panic when she saw the midwife's intent. Josiah couldn't stand the sight himself. He stopped and hunkered in the corner, his eyes glazed with tears, his stomach in tatters.*

Candles flickered on the table next to the bed, and Ofelia muttered under her breath as she slit Lily's pure white skin. It took Josiah a minute to realize that the woman was praying. "Perdoneme, Dios . . ." *Forgive me, God.*

After making a long cut down the center of the stomach, Ofelia motioned for Josiah to come to her. "I will need your help, señor."

Josiah's knees and hands were trembling. He could not look at Lily's lifeless face, or bring himself to speak. The words "I can't" were stuck in his throat.

"Pronto, señor."

Ofelia shook her head with frustration and mumbled a curse word under her breath. The knife tumbled to the floor. Josiah had never

16

seen so much blood in his life. He wanted to scream at the Mexican woman to stop — but he knew she was doing the right thing. The baby deserved a chance to live. Lily would want him to fight, to do whatever was necessary to save their child.

Josiah made his way to the side of the bed. Ofelia took his hands into hers and guided them to Lily's belly. "I am sorry, señor, this must be done to save your baby. You must pull back the skin with all of your strength."

Josiah took a deep breath, fighting back the bile that was rising from the depths of his throat.

In a swift motion, Ofelia thrust her hands deep inside Lily, tussled and turned her arms, and just as quick pulled a nearly lifeless baby up and out of the body. She placed the baby, covered in blood and dark blue as a stormy summer sky, on the bed and cut the cord.

Josiah staggered back as Ofelia swatted the baby on the behind. Nothing happened. It looked dead. She swatted again. And again, nothing. She blew into the baby's mucus-covered mouth and smacked the baby on the back, just between the shoulder blades. The baby coughed and heaved, and began to cry.

"You have a son, señor. You have a son."

Josiah stopped at the cabin's door. An

17

overhang covered the front porch. It had protected Josiah and Lily from gentle rains when they'd sat and watched the sunset more times than he could count. Simple times, taken for granted, that neither of them thought would ever end. There were no chairs now, and a few good-sized holes had been punched through the roof, like a raccoon, too heavy from whatever theft it had committed, had fallen through the rotted shingles. Twigs and branches littered the floor of the porch in layers. It didn't look like a broom had been taken to the planks since Josiah had left. The buildup of debris gave him hope that no one had taken up residence inside the cabin.

He put his ear to the door, listened for a moment, then prepared to push inside. But before he did, he looked over his shoulder to Ofelia and Lyle. Lyle waved. Josiah waved back.

He stiffened, didn't want to go inside the cabin any more than he had wanted to leave, and shouldered his way inside, pushing through a thick spiderweb. The creature was either gone or hiding, but evidence of its successful hunts, white moths in tidy woven cases, hung in the web like hams hanging in a larder. Josiah had to push the silky threads out of his face and off his worn brown felt Stetson, once he was inside. "Anybody here," he said, coming to a stop inside the threshold.

Nothing living answered him back, but the voices of ghosts screamed back at him. Josiah ignored the voices the best he could. Lily, the three girls, Elizabeth, Clara, and Maddie, the one who could only cry in discomfort or gurgle with delight, all wanted his attention. Maddie had never uttered a word. Not momma, daddy, or help me. She hadn't lived long enough.

Josiah saw his family everywhere he looked. His eyes glazed over with tears, and he sucked in a deep breath in an effort to ward off the sadness, to banish the ghosts, but the effort couldn't rid him of the feeling. The air was as stale and moldy as a forgotten tomb.

The interior of the cabin looked like it had when Josiah left. Downstairs was nothing more than an open room. Josiah and Lily had cordoned off the back section with blankets to give their bed some privacy, but in a cabin so small, with three children, one on the way, and two adults, there was no such thing as privacy. Maddie slept downstairs while the older girls, Elizabeth and Clara, shared a bed in the loft above, accessible only by a ladder.

Josiah glanced over to where the ladder once stood. It had fallen, making the upper floor inaccessible from the inside. Holes in the roof gave entrance to the weather and critters of all kinds. There were signs of animals everywhere; residue, scat, and gnawed wood. It was going to take some doing to make the place livable again, but there was nothing that Josiah couldn't repair or Ofelia couldn't clean up. Nothing but the past, and the ghosts who seemed real. A wispy image of Elizabeth and Clara caught his eye, sitting at the table under the window, playing checkers. When he blinked, they had vanished, along with the table. All that remained were the shreds of hand-sewn cotton that once served as curtains. A cardinal sang outside the window, signaling the coming of darkness.

After seeing the state of the cabin, Josiah was in no mood to linger. He'd gotten what he'd come for. No one was there, and no one had been there for a long time. With night falling and the cabin uninhabitable, Josiah had no choice but to camp outside one more night. He didn't mind. He was accustomed to being on the trail with a battalion of men, but Ofelia preferred a roof over her head. Most women did.

Josiah wasn't sure how he was going to

start a new life inside the house without sweeping the old one away. It had been easier to leave the girls and Lily on the edge of memory when he was a hundred miles away from home. But he was going to have to face them again now. Or what was left of them.

His presence had kicked up three years' worth of dust. Every time he moved, he breathed in more of the past than he wanted to. He coughed, and his throat had started to dry up. His eyes were still glazed with tears. His entire body felt as though it was about to shatter from a pain he didn't want to identify. He knew of no ointment that could rid his heart of grief. Josiah had to get out of the cabin. He couldn't breathe one more breath of the past. The ghosts had distracted him, so he was surprised when he turned to leave and found a man hulking in the doorway, pointing the long end of a rifle at him.

"You make another move, mister, and I'll blow your fool head off."

CHAPTER 2

Josiah stopped and dropped his hands to his sides. His right hand grazed his sidearm, but he continued to let it come to rest. The other hand held a renewed grasp on the Winchester. The barrel was pointed to the floor, and he kept it there. He was not a "shoot first and ask questions later" kind of man. If killing was on the intruder's mind, he'd already had the opportunity to kill Josiah. Better to see what this was about rather than come to regret shooting a man without reason.

Josiah couldn't get a good look at the man's face; a deep shadow graced the inside of the doorway. Outside the afternoon light had evaporated, replaced by the grayness of the coming night. The man's girth blocked a good deal of light from entering the cabin. There was no other way out unless Josiah chose to dive through one of the open windows. It was an option that he didn't want to have to use.

Given Josiah's condition, choked up by the past and all of the dust he'd kicked up, he wasn't sure if the man was real or not. He could have been another ghost come to pay him a visit. "Who are you?" Josiah said.

"I might ask you the same thing," the man said. He was at least a hundred pounds heavier than Josiah, making him around three hundred pounds. He was tall, too, and would have had to duck to poke his head inside the doorway. The rifle was unwavering. It was clear that the man meant business. "But I know who you are, Josiah Wolfe. I had to come and see for myself if it was true, that you had the courage and nerve to show your face around here again."

Josiah licked his lips and blinked his eyes clear. Someone must have seen the buckboard on the trail. That wasn't a surprise. Josiah wasn't being sneaky on the trip. With most of the Comanche pushed north into Indian Territory, there was little threat on the trail other than scurrilous highwaymen.

The man's voice sounded familiar, as was the man's stature. "You're a Langdon," Josiah said. It wasn't a question. Josiah knew he was right about the man's identity. He didn't have to question himself. There were eight Langdon boys. Seven still lived that he knew of. He'd had trouble with one of them, Charlie, not long after he'd joined up with the Rangers, and before, when he was the marshal of Seerville and Charlie was one of his deputies.

"That's right, I'm Morris Langdon. What's the matter with you, Wolfe? City life make you soft in the head? You don't recognize me? I've knowed you your whole life."

"Wasn't expecting any company today is all, Morris. My apologies. It's been a long time and the light's not so good in here."

"Smells like something died in here."

"Something did."

"This ain't no social call."

"I didn't figure it was."

"You killed my brother."

"That's not how I remember it."

Morris Langdon stepped fully inside the house uninvited. He kept his aim with the rifle.

Josiah had a clear view of Morris now. Morris was three or four years older than his brother, Charlie, and they shared a lot of the same features: thick black hair, beady snake eyes, unkempt beards, and chests the size of a German beer barrel. Morris had a scar cut across his right cheek that had come from a hard-fought battle in the War Between the States. He was a big man, but he wasn't fat. Morris had the muscle of a young bull, which was no surprise since most of the Langdons worked in the blacksmith or farrier trade.

"I figured you'd say that," Morris said.

"A hangman saw to Charlie's end, not me." Josiah gripped his Winchester as tight as he could. He was surprised that Morris hadn't challenged him to drop it.

"You put him on that scaffold. Might as well have been you that slipped the noose around his neck."

Josiah shook his head. "I was miles away. You know that. Besides, Charlie put himself there. He killed a Texas Ranger captain. And that was the last thing he did. What'd you expect?"

"I heard it was self-defense."

"Sneaking up on a man and shooting him without warning is not self-defense."

"That captain must of deserved it then, is all. Rangers are hooligans and thieves like the rest of us, you ask me. Exceptin' we don't have the governor's blessings for killin' innocents and takin' other people's land."

"There are bad men in every outfit, but Captain Fikes wasn't one of them. He fought for the good of this state like you and I did. He didn't deserve to die the way

25

he did."

"You would know."

"I guess I would." Josiah drew in a deep breath, could feel Lily's presence in the house, standing behind him, urging him to remain calm, not to do anything rash. Lyle needed his father. "What do you want, Morris?"

"You're not welcome here. You should get in that wagon, turn it around, and take your sorry ass and that Mexican woman back to Austin where you belong."

"I belong here. This is my home. I was born in this house."

"And if you stay here, you'll die in this house."

"I hope you're right."

Morris wasn't expecting that kind of response. Confusion crossed his face, then anger resettled in his eyes like the emotion lived there unrepentant throughout every hour of the day. "A lot's happened since you been gone, Wolfe. I'm going to urge you to reconsider your plans to stay here." He eased his finger onto the trigger in an oversized way so Josiah was sure to understand his intent.

"I don't imagine there's much you could say that would change my mind, Morris."

"You were born a stubborn sort."

26

"I'm glad you think so."

"You're not in a good position to get smart with me, Wolfe. You got the blood of my brother on your hands. I'm here to avenge his death as much as anything."

"You best take up your grudge with the state of Texas or Charlie himself. Like I said, he nailed his own coffin shut. I was one of the men who brought him to justice is all."

"Justice, is that what you call it?"

"That's what the law calls it."

"Men in Austin make laws to suit themselves, not serve folks like us."

"That might be the truth." Josiah stopped speaking, drew in a breath, then dropped the hardness and volume of his voice so Morris would have to lean in to hear what he had to say. "I did no wrong to you or your family, Morris. I'm sorry Charlie is dead. I know what it's like to lose someone you care about. Like you, I served with Charlie in the First Texas Infantry. We saw battle together, Morris. We saved each other's life more than once. All of us did. Charlie couldn't lay down the war once he came home. He had to fight with someone even after the country said there was no reason to battle. You know Charlie had a wild streak. He liked the killing and the chaos more than the discipline of the infan-

27

try. Once he got a taste of blood and power, he couldn't stop himself from chasing after it."

"You got a lot of nerve talkin' bad about a man's kin while he's got a loaded gun on you."

"I figured if you were going to shoot me you would have come in with guns ablazing. I wouldn't have had a chance. No, you came here to tell me what you told me. Now, for old times' sake, let's say you did what you had to and you can be on your way, because I'm not going anywhere. This is my home. I'm not leaving because you told me to."

"You've been warned, Wolfe. Remember that. You've been warned," Morris said.

Before either man could say another word, a voice came from outside the door. It was Ofelia. "You need to leave, *señor. Vamoose.* Go away. *You* have been warned. It is you who has a gun on your back now. You move a whisker, *te mato.* I kill you. You understand?"

Ofelia stepped inside the cabin with a scattergun aimed at Morris's back. Her face looked like it had been carved from solid Texas granite.

"You best call off your Mexican, Wolfe," Morris said. His face had paled a bit, surprised and concerned about Ofelia's intent.

"I think you need to take her serious, Morris. You're outgunned. You do anything stupid, you're not getting out of this house alive."

"That'd be two Langdons you'd done kilt."

"I didn't kill Charlie. I'm hopin' you'll come around to my way of thinking on that, Morris."

"Not going to happen."

"Drop the barrel of your rifle and you can walk out of here with no trouble. Ofelia will let you pass, then you can be on your way. Go back to where you came from and leave us alone."

"That an order?"

"No, a statement. I don't want any trouble," Josiah said. "I want to get on with my life is all."

Morris glared at Josiah, unsympathetic in every way, then looked over his shoulder. "I ain't never trusted a greaser, and I ain't about to start now."

"Like I said, drop your barrel and you can pass. You have my word."

"I ain't never trusted a Wolfe, either."

"I'm sorry to hear that."

"You remember what I said. You're not

29

welcome here. You'll understand soon enough. Trust me. It won't be long and you'll be taking a trip in a pine box or headin' west to somewhere new. You wait and see. I'll be right. I always am." With that, Morris let the rifle slide under his armpit with the barrel pointed to the floor. If he could have bit Ofelia on his way past, he would have. Morris eased his way out of the cabin like a snarling, whipped dog.

Josiah raised his Winchester as Morris went, and Ofelia followed the man with the barrel of the scattergun drooped a bit. Neither of them moved until they heard the pounding of horse hooves hurrying away from the cabin.

"What took you so long?" Josiah said.

"The niño had to *pipi.* I saw the Langdon ride up, so I stayed back so he wouldn't see me."

"Lyle needs to learn how to wipe his own ass. That could have got me killed."

"*Lo siento.* How was I to know the man meant trouble?"

"I think we should assume every man means us trouble until we get on our feet and figure out what's what around here."

Ofelia relaxed and agreed with Josiah, maintaining her silence.

"I knew the Langdons could hold a

30

grudge, but I hadn't thought about them blaming me for killing Charlie."

"It is not your fault, *señor.*"

"I should have thought about it, been on the lookout. I will be now, so I guess Morris did us a favor."

"We need more than one," Ofelia said, looking around the cabin. *"Huele como si algo hubiera muerto."*

Josiah shrugged. He didn't understand a word.

Ofelia read his expression. Confusion on Josiah's face was common when she spoke Mexican. "It smells like something died."

"We have some work to do."

"It will get done."

Josiah allowed himself to relax, though he was still on edge, still unhappy with himself for not thinking about the Langdons or any kind of threat they might bring. "Tomorrow," he said. "We'll start tomorrow."

"Sí, mañana."

Josiah made his way to the door and Ofelia followed. They stopped on the edge of the porch, both of them looking out over the land with their weapons at their sides. Josiah had dreamed of home so often he couldn't believe he was back. It was different. Run-down. Overgrown. Lacking any care at all, but he knew getting the place

31

back in shape would take a little time.

Evening held on with all of its might. Grayness covered everything. Only the occasional bird sang; a redbird or robin announcing to the world that the day was over and all was well. At least, that's what Josiah thought the bird was saying. He hoped the chirps weren't a further warning, that something else was amiss.

Josiah looked across the empty paddock to the wall of tall pines that closed it in. There was a small cemetery opposite the barn, inside a little clearing. He knew he'd have to pay the gravestones a visit sooner rather than later, but that could wait until tomorrow, too. Then he allowed his vision to follow the broken fence all the way back to the buckboard. It sat right where he had left it. Full of all of his belongings. All except one.

"Ofelia, where's Lyle?" Josiah said, as panic rose up from his toes and exploded into his heart. "Where's Lyle?"

CHAPTER 3

"Lyle!" Josiah called as he ran toward the wagon. "Lyle!"

Ofelia struggled to keep up with Josiah. She was stricken with panic. Labored breathing echoed across the paddock. "I told him to stay put. I told him to stay put," she kept saying over and over.

Josiah ignored her and focused his eyes on the wagon. The light was almost wrung out of the sky. It was the deepest shade of gray it could be before it slid into full black. No stars had chosen to show themselves. If they had, the tall pine trees obscured their glow. Darkness ate at every inch of Josiah's line of sight. He wanted to see movement somewhere. Something, anything, to tell him that Lyle was okay. But nothing stirred. Beyond Ofelia's mumbling, the air was still as the aftermath of a hanging. The whole world seemed to be holding its breath. All of the songbirds had gone silent. Even the owls waited to announce their presence. Josiah's heartbeat raced, and it sounded like thunder in his ears drowning out everything but his fear. *Please don't let anything happen to my boy . . .*

He reached the wagon and found it to be empty.

"He's not here?" Ofelia said.

"No." The response was tinged with anger, but it wasn't directed toward Ofelia. Though it could have been interpreted that way, Josiah was angry at himself for leaving Ofelia and Lyle in the wagon to fend for themselves.

"Lo siento," Ofelia said. Her voice cracked, and it sounded as if she was about to start weeping. "I'm sorry. I'm sorry."

"No, don't be. It's not your fault. Where did you go into the woods the first time?"

Ofelia looked to the right, then to the rear of the buckboard, past Clipper. The appaloosa stood silent, white against the early night. His spots looked like holes in the night.

"Lyle!" Ofelia called out again. "Where are you?"

Josiah heard a rustle of leaves behind the wagon. He wasn't sure if it was Clipper, annoyed and moving, or something else. He gripped the Winchester, readying it to aim and shoot if he had to. Morris Langdon had put him on alert, and Lyle's disappearance propelled him into a dangerous place. He slipped his finger on the trigger.

"Right here," a small voice said.

It was Lyle. They both ran to the rear of the buckboard. Clipper snorted with displeasure. Ofelia reached the boy first, and before Josiah could say a word, she'd lifted him off the ground and into her arms. "*Te dije que te quedaras.* I told you to stay."

"I was afraid of the *mal hombre.*"

"The bad man is gone. Your papa sent him away. You do not have to be afraid."

"I don't like it here," Lyle said. "The trees are tall. I don't like the dark."

Josiah caught his breath, regulating the fear and anger coming out of it. "This is home. You'll come to love it like I did."

"You lived here?"

"Yes," Josiah said. "When I was a boy like you. This is our home. It has been for a long time, and I hope we never leave it again." He relaxed his shoulders and took a good look around. The ground before him had disappeared, at least any detail of it, and all of the shadows had joined together to make one giant curtain over the sky. A barred owl hooted with restraint in the distance, while a few crickets joined in, offering a little night chorus to announce to those who depended on darkness that it was time to move about. "I best get to starting a fire."

Ofelia agreed, still holding onto Lyle as tight as she could without squeezing him to death. "It is time for some *cena.*"

"I'm hungry," Lyle said. "Down. Let me down."

"You stay close to Ofelia," Josiah said. "I don't want to have to come looking for you again."

"I'll stand right here," the boy answered, grasping Ofelia's long travel skirt.

"Good." Before Josiah launched in search of firewood, leaving Ofelia and Lyle to themselves, he looked to the cabin, then around the property, to make sure that Morris Langdon, or any other threat, was gone. He saw nothing that gave him cause for concern. With that, he trudged off, happy as he could be to be on family ground, pursuing a menial task. The real work would start when daylight graced the world again.

The flame of the fire was low and steady, after Ofelia cooked some beans and fried some jerky for dinner. Lyle laid across Ofelia's ample lap with a blanket over him, asleep. Josiah sat next to them, satisfied, staring into the flames. His Winchester, in a situation like this, was within reach.

"You're worried," Ofelia said.

"Concerned. I didn't think about the Langdons giving us trouble, and I should have."

"You can handle that bunch."

"Maybe, but I'm a little outnumbered."

"I won't let anything happen to Lyle."

"I know that, but you have nothing to do with this. I'll work it out if I can." At that moment, Josiah wished he'd taken up the habit of smoking tobacco. He could use something to calm him. Tobacco or alcohol had never been a vice for him, and he wasn't about to start now, but it would have been nice to have something to take the edge off.

"Maybe he is, how you say, a blowhard?" Ofelia said.

"Morris Langdon doesn't make simple threats, then walk away. And, he said things had changed around here. That I'd see. I don't know what he meant by that, but it concerns me. It seems that there might be more trouble here than I bargained for."

"We do not have to stay here."

"If I don't feel safe on my own land, where can I go?"

Ofelia looked to Lyle and wiped a stray

37

piece of sandy blond hair from across his eye.

"I know this land better than anywhere else in the world," Josiah continued. "I don't want to start over. I want to be home. I want to know the ground I'm standing on for once. I didn't feel about Austin the way you did. Everything was moving all hours of the day. It was loud and unsettled. I never had a good night's sleep there. Not one."

"Then you will stay here."

"As long as I feel we are safe." Josiah looked to the wall of pine trees that reached for the sky. At night, even in the glow of a fire, the trees looked like an impenetrable wall, but Josiah knew better. "It's been a little dangerous here ever since I can remember."

"What do you mean?"

"When I was a boy my father got sick so my mother gave me my father's long rifle to go hunting. He never let me touch that gun, but there was no choice. We needed food. My mother feared letting me out of her sight those days. You remember the story about the Parkers?"

"*Sí*, the *niños* that the Comanche took away."

"Yes, Cynthia Ann and John Richard. That happened about fifty miles from here, but years before I was born. It had an effect on the settlers around here, and that story served as a source of fear for a long time. Anyway, I went hunting deep in these woods and encountered a Comanche. A lone Comanche with war paint on his face. If I close my eyes, I can see him like he was standing before us here and now. He took the long gun and knocked me in the head with it. I woke up happy to be alive, and hightailed it home. Without the gun, and without food. I was afraid and ashamed. It was a long time before I felt comfortable in these woods. But I kept an eye out for that Comanche. He took my father's gun and my pride with him."

"How old were you?" Ofelia said.

"I was twelve."

"A *niño*. It wasn't your fault."

"No, it wasn't, but that doesn't make it any easier to forget. That Indian has to be dead and gone by now. Another ghost in these woods. I wasn't prepared for any trouble with the Langdons. I hadn't thought about facing the sad memories I'd left behind. Lily, the girls, my ma and pa. They're all here. Everywhere I look. I know they're at rest under their gravestones, but I see snippets of their lives on every inch of this ground. I couldn't breathe inside the cabin. It smelled of death and days gone by. I knew it was a dead raccoon decayed somewhere, but even with that, I swear I smelled a hint of Lily's toilet water. A sweet tincture of violets and happiness, mixed in with the dust and scat."

Ofelia shifted Lyle so he was lying alone on a pile of blankets. She stood up with ease, then made her way over to Josiah and touched his shoulder with her hand. It was a rare touch between the two of them. Each of them had their roles, and there was little affection, or reason for contact to be shared. "You are alive, *señor.* Pardon me, but they are all lost to this world. Lyle needs you to be here for him, but maybe you can heal, maybe you can get on with your life now that you are home. You are here, and I am glad of that."

"Thank you, Ofelia, you're right. I know I'm lucky to be here. I've had some scrapes over the past few years that I was lucky to get out of. I guess I went looking for danger to feel alive."

"Duty fueled you."

"That, too. You're right. Maybe being here will be a good thing. Once I figure out what's going on so we can feel safe and get everything back in shape. But that has to

40

wait until tomorrow."

"*Sí, mañana.* We will live *mañana.*"

Josiah sat on the back of the wagon, keeping watch, staring into the night. Ofelia and Lyle slept and the two horses were comfortable, tied to a straight line between the closest trees. The sky had cleared of clouds and a swirl of stars pulsed overhead. The moon hung between the trees to the east, its glow reaching upward, aching to provide some light in the darkness. All of the owls and insects had gone silent, and the fire was down to its last flame. The wood below it breathed orange; the coals would stay warm through the rest of the night. The air was cool, but not cold. October could be comfortable, or a burst of wind could sweep down from the north, bringing with it a shiver that lasted for months. Lucky for them it had been a mild autumn. One more night outside would do none of them any harm.

Josiah was relaxed, but was aware of every noise. He was to wake Ofelia when he got tired. She was going to take watch. It would be that way until they were in the cabin. Morris Langdon wasn't going to pull a surprise attack without facing the consequences. But as it was, Josiah didn't mind

41

staying awake. It reminded him of the nights with the Rangers and the partner he rode with most of the time, Scrap Elliot. Scrap was a young man full of fire and bluster, half-cocked with anger and confidence that had almost got them both killed more than once. The two of them argued as much as they got along, but to Josiah's surprise, he missed having Scrap around. The boy was a crack shot and a talented horseman, and he could be trusted to keep a good watch and make a good pot of Arbuckle's coffee.

Josiah hadn't thought he'd need backup once he came home, but it seemed he needed it now more than ever.

CHAPTER 4

The wagon was unloaded by midday. A table and four chairs sat on the porch of the cabin. It had been swept clean for the first time in years. Two large chests sat on the ground next to the front step, ready to be lugged inside. A pile of dust and dried leaves sat on the ground opposite the chests, along with the rotted carcass of a possum. It was all hair and bone, deflated, all of the muscle and flesh gone. Something had chewed off one of the hind legs. Josiah picked the creature up by the tail, walked it to the tree line, and gave it a good toss. One more thing to disappear into the woods.

The sky was sapphire blue, clear of any clouds, allowing the sun to warm the ground to a comfortable temperature. Josiah wore a sweat-stained linen work shirt, with the sleeves rolled up, and his ever-present brown felt Stetson. He wasn't whistling, but the look on his face suggested that he was satisfied with the progress they'd made so far. One by one, the chore of moving in was getting done.

He made his way back to the porch and stopped. He decided to take a short break from unloading the wagon and consider what else needed his attention. Cleaning up the barn was a priority. He needed a place to shelter the two horses. After that came fence mending, so the horses could wander free.

At some point Josiah knew he would need to go into town and find a place to buy a cow and some chickens. He'd saved his Ranger pay, twenty dollars a month, and had a decent sum. One that would help him restock the barn, and see his way through winter until he could find a way to replace what he'd spent. Money was the least of his worries at the moment, which made his life a little easier. He needed a couple more hands and twice as many hours in the day to get all of the things done he wanted to.

Ofelia and Lyle were inside the cabin sweeping and cleaning. Lyle was doing a lot of watching while Ofelia was working. She'd scrubbed the walls and floors with hot water and lye soap, not missing an inch of wood as she went. Ofelia was a meticulous house-keeper, which was one of the things Josiah

44

liked about her. He knew how lucky he was that she stayed around. Her heart had been won by Lyle from the moment he'd been born. There was no question about that, but she could have left after the boy'd been weaned. The fact that she hadn't, spoke volumes to Josiah. They had no contract with each other. Ofelia and Lyle loved each other, there was no question about that. Josiah paid her a regular wage out of his own earnings, but Ofelia had never asked for money. Staying with Lyle wasn't about money. It was Josiah's feeling that Ofelia didn't have much family to go home to, that she was as alone in the world as he was, but he didn't know that for sure. Ofelia skirted talks about her life before Lyle. All Josiah knew was that she'd been a midwife for a long time; she'd birthed his three girls, too. However it had played out, the three of them made up all of the family that Josiah and Ofelia had, and that was fine with him. He didn't care that she was Mexican. She was Ofelia to him.

The day's weather had cooperated, allowing Josiah to patch the roof to the cabin first thing in the morning. Then after the source of the smell of death had been located and removed, the cleaning and unloading had begun. There was no way everything was going to get done in a day, but Josiah figured they'd have the cabin set up in a couple of days at the most — as long as the weather held.

After a moment of peace, Ofelia and Lyle joined Josiah on the porch.

"The larder is clean," Ofelia said. "I have beans and some *masa,* but we will need more food soon, *señor.*"

"I'd like to get everything settled before I go into town."

"You cannot stay here with us forever. We have spent many days without your presence. We will be safe."

"You know I'm worried. Someone could be watching us right now."

"There is too much *trabajo,* um, work, to do for us all to go into town."

"You don't want to go?"

"When I'm ready."

"All right."

"I do not know what I will find on my return. I have not heard from my *familia* in a long time, my *hermano* and *hermanas,* brother and sisters. I do not know if they are still alive, or if they will welcome me into their home. My choices are not their choices."

Josiah scanned the tree line, looking for a pair of eyes, anything moving, watching. He saw nothing. He didn't know what to say to Ofelia. "All right. I can ride into town and get a few supplies. I'll take Clipper and leave the wagon here. He'll appreciate the ride."

"You both need it," Ofelia said, then turned and walked back into the cabin.

"I do," Josiah muttered under his breath. "Whether I like it or not."

The trail into Seerville hadn't changed much. It edged the Neches River north, then forked right for five miles. Tyler, the biggest town around, was about thirty miles southwest. The trail was traveled by a lot of folks making their way west to Dallas and Fort Worth, and to Shreveport to the east. Nacogdoches was a good ride south, and Austin was a longer journey southwest.

The construction of the railroad had bypassed Seerville, stifling any hope of growth and prosperity for the town. Everyone's fortune would have improved if the train had run through Seerville, but fate had another idea. The town was near death when Josiah had left. He had no idea what he'd find at the end of his ride. He didn't know if there was a mercantile or livery still in existence. At the least, he intended to find out where the open stores were so he could fulfill his needs. He might have a longer ride than he first thought.

As Ofelia had predicted, Clipper and Josiah both were happy to be on the trail. Josiah couldn't help but worry about the Langdons showing up at his place while he was gone, but he had to trust that Ofelia could take care of herself. She was right, he couldn't hover over them forever. It was best to get on with this new life he'd chosen.

It'd been weeks since Clipper'd had a saddle on his back and a bit in his mouth. There were advantages to being pulled behind a wagon, but the appaloosa was eager to have his own head and Josiah was happy to give it to him. The horse paced along aiming his long nose straight down the middle of the trail.

Josiah never left on a ride without being armed. The Winchester rode in the scabbard, the Peacemaker at his right hip, and a Bowie knife hung on his left hip. His belt was full of cartridges, and his eyes didn't wander too far from the trail in lazy delight. He was as concerned about the Langdons lying in wait for him, or gunning for him, as he was about them attacking the cabin. There were other threats to consider. A lone man on the trail was an easy target. The assumption that he was on an errand, stocked with cash to make a purchase, was easy to make for those less fortunate, or those who chose to employ robbery as their means of making a living. Josiah had encountered highwaymen, thieves, and scoundrels on the trail more than once.

The comfortable weather provided an easy ride. It wasn't long before Josiah passed small farms and homesteads. He had known most everyone on the trail to Seerville before he'd left and he was saddened when he realized most of the houses were empty. They looked abandoned, like the owners had packed up and walked away. He had done the same. Even the little country school where he'd taken his learning sat empty, the windows broken, the bell gone. He slowed at the sight, but didn't linger. There were good memories there, too; kissing Lily behind the tall live oak that stood at the rear of the faded red building; fist-fights with one or the other of the Langdon boys in the recess yard to the right; and struggling with his numbers and letters until his teacher, Virgilene Goodnight, made sense of it all for him. He'd liked Miss Goodnight. He wondered what had become of her.

Josiah nickered Clipper into a trot, push-ing past the school, and headed toward town at a faster pace. He had no intention of reliving those moments in his life. Clipper responded with glee. He wanted to run, so Josiah gave the horse his head and let him go.

There hadn't been any other riders since Josiah had started the journey. He wasn't worried about the horse running full out. Trees blurred by. A spray of dust kicked off of Clipper's back hooves as he ran. The wind pushed Josiah's Stetson off his head. The stampede string caught on his throat. He leaned into the run, enjoying the massage of the wind on his face. For a moment the world fell away, and to his joy, he and Clipper were joined in a common cause. They weren't running from something or to something, other than to town, but that wasn't urgent. They were running to run.

Everything was peaceful until the sound of a gunshot cracked to the left of Josiah, thundering into the clear sky. There was no question what the sound was. The question was the intent; a hunter or an ambush? He pulled up on the reins, gathering himself and his senses as he slowed Clipper.

Another shot erupted. This time the shot hit the trail ten feet in front of Clipper. Josiah dropped his hand to the Peacemaker.

There was no way to see where the shot had come from. The river swerved off to the left, while the trail had eased right, to the west. An open field edged the trail, falling back about twenty yards, then the pine forest jumped up to the sky. Bramble twisted across the low branches discouraging the pines, but someone had found their way inside. Josiah couldn't see who.

With the six-shooter in one hand and the reins in the other, Josiah gouged Clipper with his knees and ordered him back to a run, breaking right, off the trail. The land was cut the same way on the right side of the trail as the left — with the exception of a small house that sat before a wall of tall trees. It was a place to take refuge. He guided Clipper toward the house as he fired off a shot to cover himself. There was no movement, and no immediate response, but that didn't mean Josiah had hit anything. It could have meant nothing. The shooter was reloading. Taking aim. Running off. There were a lot of possibilities.

Josiah hunched down in the saddle, matching his profile with Clipper's. That wouldn't stop a good shot from killing him.

He didn't have time to be angry with himself. He was too busy trying to stay alive. The hope was that the house he was heading to was empty, like so many of the others he'd passed — or home to a friend and not an enemy.

Another shot rang out. This one hit closer to Clipper a few feet off to the right. Josiah saw a flash, a quick puff of gun smoke. He was out of range with the Peacemaker, but he fired another shot anyway. Clipper was running as fast as he could, but Josiah relaxed the reins, giving the horse full use of its head. "Go, boy. Go," he said, eyeing the house.

Two men stepped out of the front door — still distant and unrecognizable. Both of them carrying rifles. Called out by the shooting. They took cover behind the posts that held up the roof of the porch and brought their rifles up to aim.

CHAPTER 5

Both men fired at the same time, but not at Josiah. One man, the taller of the two, motioned for Josiah to hurry to the house. The other man focused on shooting across the trail, into the tree line where the unidentified shots were coming from. Once the tall man was sure that Josiah understood that he was offering cover, he returned to firing. A cloud of gray smoke hovered around the men for a moment, then a breeze carried the taste of gunpowder to the tip of Josiah's tongue. He urged Clipper to run faster, guiding the horse toward the back of the house.

More shots volleyed back and forth, missing Josiah, Clipper, and the men at the house. The two men seemed to have the upper hand, able to get off more shots than the shooter across the field. Josiah fired over his shoulder, emptying what remained of the cartridges in his gun. He reined Clipper

53

in as soon as they were behind the house, out of sight of the shooter.

He jumped off the horse, reloaded the six-shooter, grabbed the Winchester out of the scabbard, then ran up to the back of the house. A rain barrel offered him a spot of shelter. He dipped a ladle full of water, gulped it, then made his way to the side of the house. There were no bushes or trees to help hide him, so he crouched as low as he could, and hurried toward the front porch.

The shots had slowed, allowing the men on the porch to reload and take a breath. When Josiah jumped over the rail onto the porch, he recognized both men right away. The tall man was Luke Halverson, and the other, the shorter, older man of the two, was Leland Halverson. They were Lily's brother and father.

"Well, I'll be darned, Pa, I thought that feller looked familiar. It's Josiah," Luke said.

"So it is." Leland glared at Josiah, then turned his attention back to the shooter. "I bet he's done now that you're here. Could of killed you if he wanted to. You showed some skills there, though. Looks like the Rangers might've taught you a thing or two."

Josiah caught his breath, and took a spot behind a porch post. He hadn't expected to see Luke and Leland Halverson. This wasn't their house. At least, it hadn't been when he'd left. "I sure am happy to see you two."

"I'm sure you are," Leland said.

"There he goes." Luke aimed his rifle, a Henry that had some wear on the stock, and fired off a round.

Josiah followed the shot and saw the silhouette of a man disappear deeper into the woods. Light from the clear sky had caught him just right.

"Damn it, I missed." Luke spit off the porch, and pulled the rifle back.

Leland witnessed the same thing Josiah had. "He's hightailin' it home now, but he'll be back."

"You know who it is?" Josiah said.

"Of course we do. It was one of the Langdons. They knowed you was comin' this way. Figured you was meetin' up with us. Though they was wrong about that. We ain't heard that you was back."

"I got in yesterday," Josiah said. "Morris Langdon already came by for a social call, carrying a grudge about Charlie."

"The dead Langdon," Leland said.

Luke let a smile twitch across his face. "The only good Langdon is a dead Langdon."

Josiah scrunched his brow, confused. "You

55

fellas mind telling me what the hell's going on here?"

Luke shrugged his shoulders. "You been gone a while, Josiah. Things have changed."

"So I've been told."

Leland made his way to the door. "That Langdon's long gone. Come on in, Josiah. We'll put a pot of coffee on, if you got time. There's some things you need to know if you're gonna stay around here."

"This is my home."

"It is." Leland stopped and let his shoulders drop. "For the time bein'."

The inside of the house was sparse and lacked a woman's touch. There were no curtains at the windows or pictures on the wall. The furniture, a couple of chairs in front of the stone fireplace, looked utilitarian, unadorned with padding or blankets. The floor was in need of a good sweeping, and the two beds in the back looked like whoever had slept in them had recently gotten up, even though it was late in the afternoon. The air inside smelled stale, closed up with a hint of metal and oil.

Leland set about putting on a pot of coffee, while Luke took a place next to the window, peering out every few seconds. In between looks, Lily's brother reloaded the

Henry. There were crates of ammunition stacked against the wall, and four more rifles stood ready next to the wood boxes. It looked like the two men were getting ready for war.

Josiah stopped inside the door, away from the windows that faced the front. He gathered himself before he spoke, forced his heart to slow to a steady beat, and tried to get his bearings.

Luke was younger than Lily by a few years. He had the same straight-cut jaw as Lily, which grew even sharper in a disagreement. Not that there were a lot of those, but Josiah and Lily had been together for several years, nigh on ten, before she died, and they'd known each other all through their schooling. Boyfriend and girlfriend sometimes, and sometimes not. He and Luke had been cordial enough, but they were never friends or riding buddies. Seeing Luke standing before him was almost like seeing Lily taking a real breath. Their eyes were the same hazy blue, and their hair, fine as corn silk, glistened yellow in any shade of light. Josiah had no doubt that Lyle would grow up to look a lot like his uncle and mother.

Josiah looked away from Luke, to Leland. He was shorter, more rotund from age, and did not share the bounty of hair that graced Luke's head. The old man's hair was thin, balding, unkempt. His face didn't look like it had been touched by a razor in a week, and his clothes were stained with dirt and gunpowder residue. The temptation to ask about Leland's wife, Helena, got to the tip of Josiah's tongue, but he held it there. Leland looked grayer, more worn down, and angrier than he had been when Josiah picked up roots — which Leland disagreed with. Josiah's gut told him that he and Leland shared a commonality that they didn't have before. Josiah's gut told him that Helena Halverson was dead.

"I knew you'd be back," Leland said, standing up from placing the coffee pot over the fire.

"What's going on here, Leland?" Josiah said.

Luke acted like he was ignoring the two men. He'd taken up his post at the window, and wasn't moving.

"How's the boy?" Leland glared at Josiah with his boots planted, ready for battle. No surprise there. Josiah and Leland had had a tenuous relationship from the start — from courting Lily till the time she had died. Leland Halverson had never wanted to give his blessing to Josiah to marry Lily. He had done so at the urging — and demand — of Lily's mother, Helena. Helena was the buffer between Leland and Josiah.

"Lyle's fine, Leland. I was going to get settled before I brought him around."

"Ain't heard a lick from you in three years. You up and left. Didn't even ask us to watch your place, so we didn't. All we got was a couple of short letters from the post, and that's it. The boy's blood, no matter that his mother's feet grace the golden floor of heaven. I got a right to know how he's farin'."

Josiah looked to the floor, admonished. "I have nothing to offer you, Leland, other than an apology. I'm sorry for that. We were living our life. That's the only excuse I can muster, and it's a weak one."

Leland Halverson stiffened, jutted his chin out, like he'd made a wise checker jump that Josiah hadn't seen coming. "You still lettin' that Mexican live under the same roof as my grandson."

"Ofelia brought Lyle into this world and kept him alive when there was no one else who could do it."

"His mother could have if it wasn't for that woman."

"You can't believe that, Leland? Lily had the sickness. She was weak, too weak to give

59

birth, but she didn't have a choice when the time came. If Ofelia hadn't been there, you wouldn't have a grandson." Josiah flexed his fists, then let his fingers fall free. He wasn't going to slug the old man no matter how much he wanted to knock some sense into him.

"I wasn't there," Leland said.

"No, you weren't."

"We'll leave it at that, but you know folks don't take to a widow man livin' under the same roof as a Mexican woman. It ain't right, Josiah. You gotta know that."

"What happens under my roof is my business, Leland. I'm looking out for Lyle the best I can. He's a good boy, and a lot of that has to do with Ofelia. Now, I'd appreciate it if you'd respect that and leave it be." Josiah paused and studied Leland's face to see if he'd made any headway with the man. Leland's expression was as solid as the butt of Luke's rifle, and just as worn. He was hard to read, but deep down, Josiah knew Leland wasn't going to let go of his distaste for Ofelia. "Now, why don't you tell me what the hell's going on here. I found myself in the middle of something that damned near got me killed. I need to know what's what before Lyle ends up a true orphan."

"He's got kin." Leland snorted, then

turned to check on the coffee. He said nothing else as he poured a mug for himself and one for Josiah. He ignored Luke, who was still at the window, keeping watch. That in itself had Josiah on edge.

"What's going on between you and the Langdons, Leland?" Josiah said as he took the mug of steaming coffee. The aroma calmed him a bit, but not enough for him to relax.

"You see a lot of folks on the ride from your place to here?" Leland said.

"Not a soul."

Leland took a drink of the coffee, looking over the rim of the mug with certain eyes. "Empty farms are sittin' to rot. Town's fallin' down around itself since the railroad deal fell through. Man's lucky we've had decent weather to plant and grow by. A drought'd send this place straight to hell. Not that we're not on our way. There's only a few of us left with any means at all, but that's not what this is about. There's a land grab goin' on is what's happenin'. Them Langdons are squattin' on every place there is to squat. We're standin' in their way. That's why we're here. I've laid claim to this place and so have they."

"So, you and Ethan Langdon are feuding over land," Josiah said.

"Call it what you want," Leland answered. "We don't speak that foul name, if you don't mind."

Josiah took another drink of coffee. "You and Ethan have been arguing ever since I can remember."

"You know, you're lucky to have a place to come back to, Josiah. Your land borders the Langdons' place to the south."

"And yours to the north."

"That's right. You're smack-dab square in the middle of this, whether you like it or not. The only reason that cabin's still standin' and your land hasn't been squatted is the fact that you was ridin' with the Rangers. Last thing that Langdon wanted to do was draw the attention of the Rangers. He already lost one son to them."

"And to me. I thank you for your troubles. You might of explained Morris's visit," Josiah said. "Regardless, this is good to know. I'll talk to Ethan and see if we can calm this feuding down."

Luke pulled away from the window and looked at Josiah and Leland. "Doesn't look like you'll have to wait long. There's twelve Langdons coming up to the house, and Ethan's leadin' the way."

CHAPTER 6

Leland sat the coffee mug down and grabbed up the closest rifle. "I'm gonna blow that son of a bitch's head off." He chambered a round, made his way to Luke's side, and peered out the window.

Josiah stood firm, didn't react. He could see the gathering of men from where he stood. "You prepared to die, Leland? Twelve against three is suicide. From the looks of it, those men didn't stop by for a cup of coffee. I don't know about you, but I've got a reason to live. I'd appreciate it if you'd come to your senses and not fire a shot. I'm in no mood to die today."

Leland Halverson's face pulsed red all the way to the top of his bald dome. Sweat appeared where it hadn't been before. "Bad luck for you, Josiah, this has been comin' for a long time."

Something in the tone of Leland's voice concerned Josiah. "You haven't told me everything, have you, Leland? What the hell is going on here?"

"You better tell him, Pa, before things get goin'."

Leland leaned against the wall next to the window and exhaled so deep that Josiah thought the man was going to deflate. "That volley of fire you rode into was a setup. They think they got us cornered."

Josiah squinted and said, "You've got men in the woods behind the house waiting for your signal for them to come charging."

"Everything's workin' to plan except for you bein' here. Damn it, Wolfe, how come it is that every time you show up, you twist everything around and make my life difficult?"

Before Josiah could answer, a booming voice called from outside. "I know you and Luke are in there, Leland. You can make this easy or hard. I got the sheriff of Anderson County here with me and a deed to the property you're squattin' on. No need for this to get ugly, Leland. Not this time."

Leland struggled to keep his mouth shut. Josiah didn't think it was possible for the man's face to get any redder. It had surpassed a raspberry and warmed into a bright red sun. One more second and it was imaginable that his head would explode.

Leland had the reputation of a quick temper, was easy to rile, but this was a whole different level of rage. A lot of things had changed in the last three years.

Josiah looked away. He could see the older man, Ethan Langdon, on his horse through the window. He decided it was best to take himself out of the line of fire, so he stepped back out of sight.

"Son of a bitch," Leland said. "Ethan brought the sheriff." He took a quick glimpse out the window, then brought his gaze back to Luke, whose face had paled. Rage and fear were a bad mix and that made Josiah even more nervous than he had been.

Luke agreed. "Sure as anything that's Sheriff Howard Cliburn. Damn it. And there's some deputies mixed in with those Langdons."

"You said the Langdons were the ones squatting, Leland," Josiah said.

"They are."

"Not if they've got a deed. You can't shoot your way out of this. You know that, don't you?"

"You sure have gone and mucked this up."

"If you say so." Josiah had a strong jaw himself. He set it forward, and glared at Leland and Luke. "I'll do the talking, you

65

understand? One shot goes off, I'm saving my own neck, not yours, you hear?"

Leland twisted his face into a snarl. "I wouldn't expect it to be any other way with you, Josiah Wolfe."

Josiah ignored the snide comment, clutched his Winchester tighter, and walked to the door.

Ethan called out again. "We know you're in there, Leland. Luke, too."

Josiah cracked open the door, and yelled out, "I'm in here, too. It's me, Ethan, Josiah. Josiah Wolfe." He could see Ethan Langdon sitting on a black gelding, a little hunched over, a reaction to age and creaky bones. The man's fingers were gnarled around the horse's reins like twisted tree roots. He wore a black hat, a long duster, and carried a rifle of his own. All of the riders did.

"I heard you was back, Josiah. It sure didn't take you long to get into the thick of things," Ethan answered. A horse behind Ethan snorted and dropped a load of dung.

"I have nothing to do with this. I was riding by is all and got caught between the shooting. I didn't know the Halversons were here," Josiah said.

"That's not the way I heard it," Ethan said. The old man's face looked hard as stone. His eyes did too. "I heard you rode straight to the house."

"To get out of the line of fire. Anything else is a lie or an assumption."

"You need to be careful calling a man a liar, standing in front of a load of trigger-happy men. More'n one of 'em's got a grudge against you. Myself included. You could have turned around and gone back the way you came. A sensible man would have done that. Come to think of it, a sensible man would have stayed in Austin, but you ain't never been sensible, have you, Josiah?"

"I've had trigger-happy days myself," Josiah said. He was focused on Ethan Langdon. He couldn't see Luke or Leland, but he heard another cartridge being loaded into a rifle behind him. Somebody was going to do something to set the wick of war alight. The air was still, like the whole world was listening, waiting for the wrong move, for the show to kick up a reason to fight. That's the last thing Josiah wanted.

"I'm coming out," Josiah said.

Another man pulled his horse's head even with Ethan Langdon's. A glint of sunshine reflected off the five-pointed star on his chest. Josiah knew that it was the sheriff, Howard Cliburn, even though he'd never met the man. Frederich Hikke had been the

sheriff when Josiah had lived in the county.
Hikke was a decent sort, elected by the
people. He had to assume that this sheriff
was a fair, law-abiding man, too, even
though there was reason to question that
with him sitting in front of an armed regi-
ment of Langdons and deputies, ready to
go to battle.

"You need to drop your weapon, sir, and
put your hands in the air." Cliburn stopped
his horse ahead of Ethan, squared himself
in his saddle, and aimed his rifle at Josiah's
head.

"This isn't the kind of welcoming I was
hoping for," Josiah said.

"I beg your pardon?" Cliburn was younger
than the eldest Langdon. He looked to be
about fifty, had a round belly and genial face
that matched. A bushy salt and pepper
mustache puffed forward every time he
spoke. "You need to stop right there, and
do as I told you."

Josiah stopped. But he made no effort to
obey with the order to rid himself of the
Winchester. "Sorry, Sheriff, I can't do that."

"You're in no position to negotiate, Wolfe."

Josiah was surprised at the use of his
name. Ethan Langdon had called him by
name, so the sheriff picked it up — but it
made Josiah look at Cliburn a little closer.

Do I know you? He didn't think he did.

"I'd like it if you'd hear me out," Josiah said.

"I heard what you had to say. You have nothing to do with any of this. I'm not deaf."

"That's right. I returned to my family farm yesterday. Leland Halverson didn't even know I was home until I was forced to take cover inside this house. I was riding down the trail, minding my own business, when one of these fellas started shooting at me for no cause."

"You see that fella here?" the sheriff said.

"I didn't get a good look at the shooter."

"You'd be wise not to accuse a man of something unless you can prove it, Wolfe."

Josiah sucked in a deep breath, readying to defend himself further. The air around him remained still and the sun beat down on his face. He was sweating, too, but not near as much as Leland Langdon. A crow cawed in the distance, then silence and tension returned. Twelve sets of eyes were focused on Josiah. Twelve fingers rested on triggers. More eyes and more fingers on triggers had his attention behind him — in the house, and beyond, waiting on a signal to show themselves.

Josiah knew he had to defuse the situation. He had hoped appealing to the sheriff's good nature would help, but his ploy didn't seem to be working.

He squared his shoulders, and lowered the tone of his voice. He didn't want to sound angry or scared. "I'm sorry, Sheriff Cliburn, but you have to understand, I have nothing to do with any of this. I rode with the Rangers up to a few weeks ago, and was a sergeant to a good group of men. Whatever is going on here is between Leland Halverson and Ethan Langdon. I don't ride with either of them, and I'm not picking sides to their dispute. I have no reason to, now or in the future. So, if you will be so kind, and let me pass. I'll be on my way home and leave this trouble to you."

Ethan Langdon leaned to the side of his steed and spit to the ground as loud as he could. "You'll never ride with us, Wolfe. You're lucky you're still six feet above ground the way I see it."

Sheriff Cliburn glanced over to Ethan in disgust, then back to Josiah. "Your time with the Rangers garners you no respect or position here, Wolfe. Makes no difference to me what you say. My eyes tell me you're in favor of the Halversons' side of this disagreement, and your presence makes you nothing more than a trespasser." The sheriff looked past Josiah and raised his voice. "All of you need to vacate without disturbance, you hear. Now drop your weapon, Wolfe, and the rest of you come out with your hands up."

Those were the last words Sheriff Howard Cliburn would ever speak. Josiah stood stiff in his resolve. He blinked, swallowed, and was about to argue his case more, no matter the peril it put him in. But any rebuttal was cut short by the sudden crack of a gunshot and the thud of a bullet piercing its target of flesh and bone.

The right side of the sheriff's face exploded into a sudden, bloody red mess. A painful, stunned look crossed his eyes as he dropped his rifle and raised his hand to swat away whatever it was that had attacked him. But a swat would do no good. Bullets were not bees. Another shot followed, shattering the man's skull from back to front, causing another bloody explosion that left Howard Cliburn unrecognizable. He was dead before he hit the ground.

CHAPTER 7

The two shots, wherever they had come from, set off an immediate reaction. The Langdons fired while retreating. The deputies stayed put for an extra second, motionless chickens without their heads, or leader, before tearing out for the line of trees at the back of the house. Some men shot straight into the air with uncertainty. Leland and Luke joined in, firing from inside the house through poke holes bored the right size to push their barrels through.

The spark of the first shot brought the remaining Halversons from the woods behind the house. They met the deputies and some straggling Langdons without an offer of explanation. Flying lead did their talking and negotiating. Anyone who rode with the Langdons was the enemy. Aim was taken, skill employed. Most of the men had fought in the War Between the States. This kind of fighting was familiar territory.

Josiah dove off the porch, then scurried under it to take cover. A dense cloud of smoke filled the air and the smell of battle stung his nose: gunpowder and the coppery smell of blood. The stench of death took time, but it would come quick enough. Josiah had his memories of these kinds of fights, too, in the war and after. He thought he'd left this kind of life behind him.

He righted himself, with his Winchester pointed out toward the melee, but he didn't shoot. He watched and tried to identify the good from the bad, the deputies from the Langdons. The Halversons from the deputies. He had taken sides whether he wanted to admit it or not.

There wasn't a clear view of the fighting at ground level; horse hooves danced in and out of the wisps of rising smoke. The rush of the Halverson men had pushed most of the Langdons away from the house, back to the tree line where the original shooter had taken up his sniper position. Josiah figured that was where the shots had come from that had killed Sheriff Cliburn.

It was hard to tell how many men Leland Halverson had stowed away for the battle. They mixed in the fight in a swarming mass. Two men on opposing sides had come off their horses and were fist-fighting, uncon-

73

cerned about being shot, about thirty yards to the right. Josiah had no idea which man was which. He wasn't going to shoot unless he knew for sure who he was shooting at.

The firing from Leland and Luke continued, only at a lesser rate as the fight moved farther away from the house. Josiah crawled to the edge of the porch to get a closer look. He wasn't hiding, avoiding the fight; he was staying alive. Once he was sure that the way out was clear, he crawled out, dragging the Winchester barrel up. His plan was to join Leland and Luke inside the house.

He stood up and felt the ground rumble under his feet. Josiah glanced to his right and saw a black horse raging toward him, nostrils flared, mouth foaming, eyes crazed with purpose and pain as the rider pushed the beast forward as hard as he could. Blood streamed down the horse's haunch. It had been shot, but refused to stop, to fall. The rider, Morris Langdon, had the same crazed determination in his eyes as the horse.

There was no time to react, no time to run, or to raise the Winchester to defend himself. Morris had run out of ammunition. He was holding his rifle by the barrel, heaving it into a strong swing.

Josiah attempted to jump out of the way, but there was no escape. The rifle stock landed on the side of his face with a hard smack. The power of the strike rattled Josiah's teeth and brain. Blood exploded in his mouth, threatening to drown him. Pain attacked every inch of the skin on his body. The last thing Josiah saw before the world went black was Morris Langdon laughing like a maniac, riding off into the darkness. Josiah wondered if this was how he was going to die.

The shooting had stopped. Or, if it continued, Josiah had lost the ability to hear it. He roused from the ground. His face raged with throbbing pain. It felt like he'd been hit upside the head with a boulder instead of a gun stock. Once he got up on his knees, Josiah spit out a mouthful of blood. Small parts of a back tooth followed. He rubbed his jaw with hesitation. Nothing felt broken. No bones, anyway. Everything moved like it should. The movement hurt like hell was all. It had been a long time since he'd felt pain like that.

Josiah pulled himself up on two feet and surveyed the aftermath of the battle.

Flies had already found Sheriff Cliburn. He lay facedown in a pool of blood, his hat or horse nowhere to be seen. The red looked black from where Josiah was standing. There was no saving the sheriff. Urgency had mattered before the shot had been fired, not after.

Two dead horses had fallen not far from the sheriff's body, and there were at least three other men who had met their maker during the battle, that Josiah could see. There was no way to tell if they were Halversons, Langdons, or the deputies.

A few men stood across the field, overseeing one man who seemed to be trying to help another to his feet. A moan caught on the breeze, the pain of the wounded shared, along with the sound of footsteps behind Josiah. He turned to face Leland Halverson.

The old man was whole of body, not hurt at all from the exchange, but his face, which had been filled with anger and rage before the shooting had started, was now pale. He looked exhausted, appalled by what he saw.

"I see you're still among the living, Wolfe," Leland said, anchoring himself to the porch post with his left hand. A Walker Colt with a nine-inch barrel dangled from his right hand. It was an old .44 revolver with six gunpowder loads that shot lead balls. Josiah was surprised that Leland had brought that gun to the fight, but he must have trusted it, or had a sentimental attachment to it. As it was, there was no need for the Colt. The Langdons were gone.

"By a thread," Josiah said, rubbing his jaw. It was tender and starting to swell. He'd be eating soup for a few days. "Nothing broken that I can feel."

"Well, that boy of yours was spared from becoming an orphan one more time. You're either blessed or lucky." There was a hint of disappointment in Leland's tone.

Josiah caught the meaning and didn't respond right away. "This isn't over," he said.

Luke walked out of the house and joined his father. He shook his head as he took in the view. "Hot dang, would you look at this."

Leland shot Luke an angry look that didn't offer a chance of redemption of any kind. "You're right, Wolfe. This ain't over. It just got started. The way I see it, there's at least two dead Langdons out there. Ethan's not gonna let those deaths go unanswered for. He'll take revenge, blame me for those deaths."

"That's right, Pa," Luke said.

"Shut up, Luke . . ." Leland glared at his son.

"You're still standing on his property," Josiah said. "But that's the least of your problems."

"What do you mean by that?" Leland said.

Luke stood back with his head hung down. He kicked spent cartridges off the porch, but none toward Josiah.

Josiah motioned toward the sheriff's body. "If you think your only trouble's with the Langdons, you might want to think again. The county and state governments are not going to take to one of their sheriffs being killed while he was delivering the rightful owner to his property."

Leland puffed up like a challenged rooster. "I didn't see no deed. And besides, my men were in the woods behind the house. Sheriff Cliburn was shot from behind, from the opposite direction. Any dunce can see that."

"I see it, but the truth will be in the telling," Josiah said. "You don't have a Matthew Brady here to prove your claim."

"What the hell are you talkin' about, Wolfe?"

"Proof. You have no proof but my word, and the word of every other man here who's blood kin to you. Brady took pictures in the war, you know those tintypes you see around. Can't argue with what you see in one of those things, but a man's word, well, that colored with favor and blood makes it your word against Ethan's."

"That lyin' son of a bitch has never told

the truth in his life. Everybody in Anderson County knows that. You can't trust a Langdon."

"Says you."

"There's deputies to say what happened here. A starred chest can't be argued with."

Josiah looked over his shoulder, then back to Leland. "Looks to me like there's two dead deputies. That makes your troubles even deeper. I don't see any badges on a living, breathing man, do you? All I see is death. Blood and soil on those silver stars. Somebody's going to have to answer for that, and my guess is, that somebody is you."

The exhaustion that had grayed Leland's face disappeared. It was replaced by the pure red of anger — and maybe fear. There was recognition in the old man's eyes that what Josiah said had merit. Three dead lawmen weren't going to be overlooked by the authorities.

"Them Langdons started the shootin'," Leland said. He stomped his right foot. The sound echoed across the field, causing those who were still alive to look toward the house.

"You best be able to prove that," Josiah said.

"You got standin' with some folks. You'll tell 'em, and that'll be enough."

Josiah cocked his head back. *Now that you need me, my time with the Rangers means something.* He thought it, but didn't say it. Instead, he rubbed his jaw and felt a shock of pain travel across the top of his head, then down his right side to his toes. "I'll tell anyone who asks what I saw, but for now, Leland, I don't want any part of this, you understand. This is your fight, not mine. The dead sheriff and his deputies are your problem, not mine. I came home for a quieter life, and I intend to have that, no matter what you two old fools are fighting about. Leave me out of it, you understand. Leave me out of it."

Josiah leaned down and picked up his hat and gun, and started to walk away.

"Where are you going?" Leland demanded. "Where in the hell do you think you're going?"

"Home," Josiah said, "I'm going home."

Leland Halverson exhaled a load of hot air, stomped his foot again, then turned to Luke, who was watching the exchange between the two as close as a buzzard watches over a piece of rotted meat.

"Go with him. Make sure he gets home, then get your ass back here and help clean this mess up, you hear?" Leland said to Luke.

80

"Yes, Pa." Luke hurried off the porch to catch up with Josiah. "Wait up," he called out to Josiah.

Josiah didn't slow. He was in no mood for an escort home from Luke Halverson. Josiah had had enough of that family for one day.

He rounded the house and sighed when he found Clipper waiting, unhurt. It took all of the effort he could muster to climb up on the horse. Pain careened through him, but that didn't stop him from mounting the appaloosa. He wanted to get as far away from the house and the aftereffects of the gunfight as he could. If there were men who needed tended to, Leland could see to that.

"Come on, boy, let's go," Josiah said, sheathing the Winchester in the scabbard. He settled into the saddle, then took a look around. There was no sign of any of the Langdons. He didn't know what had happened to them, other than they had gathered and ridden off. Defeated in battle, but fueled up for a longer war. Josiah was sure of that. He agreed with Leland on one point. This fight wasn't the end. It was the beginning of an all-out war. A war Josiah wanted no part of. But he knew that didn't matter. Not now. He was in it — as long as he stayed.

"Come on, Clipper, let's go home."
I haven't dropped roots yet. He guided the horse's head away from the house. *Leaving might be easier than staying.*

CHAPTER 8

Luke rode next to Josiah whether he liked it or not. Silence had settled between the two men, not only because Josiah had little to say to Luke, but his face hurt like hell, throbbed like Morris Langdon's gun stock was still taking whacks at him. His vision hadn't been affected. Nothing felt broken, but the pain was almost unbearable.

They rode head to head, alert, both on edge waiting to be ambushed. Josiah wondered if he would be able to ride to town, or anywhere in the county again, without fearing for his life. That was no way to live. He almost said so out loud. He would have if he was alone. But he restrained himself, his eyes focused on the trail and everything surrounding it. He was in no mood to share his regrets or any thoughts about the future after witnessing an unexpected gun battle. He hadn't expected to encounter death on his way to town to buy supplies. Just the opposite. All he wanted to do was reestablish his old ways, find the mercantile open for business, and get on with his life.

"You really think there's gonna be more trouble?" Luke looked at him, then turned back to the trail. "Hurts to talk, uh?"

"Yeah, a little. But you can count on more trouble, or at least the law looking into this dispute between Leland and Ethan. People are going to want to know who killed the sheriff and his deputies. They're going to demand answers, and justice for all their deaths. Somebody pulled that trigger. Someone started that battle knowing full well what they were doing. That won't be let go of easy."

"Kind of hard to prove, though."

"Maybe, but that won't stop them from asking and holding the rightful person accountable."

"You're smack-dab in the middle of this."

"Don't want to be." Josiah rubbed his jaw, then watched a squirrel dart across the trail ahead of them and scurry up an oak tree, out of sight.

"Doesn't matter. You shoulda known the Langdons would make your life difficult when you came back. They owe it to Charlie. They're gonna make your life a misery."

Luke's words felt like another slap to the

face. "Charlie Langdon was as bad as they come. You know what he did, you know how that ended. After he shot Captain Fikes, he came here and took Lyle hostage. My Ranger friend, Scrap Elliot, took the shot that put an end to that ordeal. Charlie hanged for his crimes. Justice was served whether his family wants to believe it or not. I'm not owed anything other than what every man ought to be owed: the right to live on his land the way he sees fit. I didn't ask for a feud with them."

"I didn't mean to rile you."

"It's okay. Besides, the fact that my head feels like it's about to explode and a swarm of wasps have taken up residence inside it, I keep running face first into the Langdons. I thought all of this was put to rest three years ago."

"Some folks carry a torch for a lot longer than that," Luke said. "Besides, you was gone. They been savin' up, is all. I don't know how you make peace with that bunch. You saw what happened with Pa."

"Yeah, well, I've got questions about that."

"Pa's got the answers for all that. I only do what I'm told."

"I guess you do."

They came to a fork in the trail and eased north, toward the cabin. It was still a few

85

miles away. The horses kept a steady pace, unaware of any threat that might be lurking behind a bush or in the forest that edged both sides of the trail. Daylight was muted, and the shadows were long. Birds flittered about and more squirrels showed themselves, unconcerned about the men's rifles. Josiah figured the little creatures knew the difference between riders and hunters. He wished he did.

"You could have lived anywhere. Why'd you come back here after all that's happened?" Luke said.

"This is my home. I don't know why I have to defend that decision. Wouldn't you come home if you had the chance?"

"I'm sorry, I'll shut up," Luke said.

Josiah didn't encourage Luke to do anything other than that. He could use some silence, not only because of the pain, but to think things through. There were a lot of reasons to question himself. Every second seemed to push him toward the fact that he'd made a bad decision by coming back to Seerville, not only for himself, but for Ofelia and Lyle, too.

Luke stopped his horse, garnering Josiah's attention. He followed suit.

Luke pointed to the sky. "What the hell is that?"

Josiah followed Luke's finger and saw a rise of smoke billowing in the distance.

The smoke reached above the treetops and had started to float to the east, coloring the sky black with a heavy cloud that promised not to have an ounce of rain in it.

"Looks close to your place," Luke said.

"That's what I was thinking," Josiah said, as a wave of panic washed over him, wiping away any pain he might have felt. He gouged Clipper with his knees, and commanded him into a full, breakneck run. "Come on, boy, let's go. Let's go." He didn't bother to see if Luke was joining him. That was the least of his worries.

Every inch of the cabin was engulfed in a fury of red and orange flames. Smoke roiled from what was left of the roof. It hadn't collapsed yet, but it wouldn't be long before it did. Crackling fire roared out of the windows like a dam had been let loose, sending sparks high into the air to dance inside the smoke. The air smelled of burning wood and ash.

Ofelia was in front of the cabin with a bucket in her hands, trying to douse the flames, but it was a hopeless cause. There was no saving the structure. Josiah worried that the fire would catch in the trees and start a forest fire. If this were a drought season that would have already happened.

A dead man lay on the ground, face up, toes pointed to the sky, about twenty yards from the cabin. The man's horse, an unknown paint gelding, had wandered back to the fence that ran along the barn, and stood there, saddle on.

Josiah and Luke rode into the cabin's clearing and dismounted at the same time. Without saying a word to each other, both men grabbed their rifles out of the scabbards, checked them, then hurried to Ofelia.

The roar of the fire was loud as the flames continued to build. Josiah had to yell to get Ofelia's attention. "Ofelia! What happened? What happened?"

She turned to Josiah with her face covered in black ash, streaked by rivulets of tears. "Two men rode in shooting, and threw *antorchas*. We were in the house. They tried to come in, but I shot them. One of them. He's dead. I killed him. The other ran off."

Luke exhaled and looked over to the dead man. "More trouble, Josiah. That sure does look like a Langdon from here."

"I bet you're right." He returned his attention to the house, to Ofelia. "Where's Lyle?"

"I put him out the window and told him to go hide where he went *pipi.* To stay until I come get him. He understood, but he was *muy* scared."

"And he's okay?"

"I have tried to save the house. Lyle is a smart *niño*. He will do what I tell him. *Lo siento, señor.* I know this *casa* means much to you. It is too much fire and the water is too far away."

"I'm relieved you're alive, Ofelia," Josiah said, then turned back to Luke. "Go make sure that fella is dead. See if you know who he is, and keep an eye on Ofelia. I'm going to get Lyle."

"What about the cabin?" Luke said.

"Let it burn."

Josiah made his way into the forest. The smell of the smoke overwhelmed the smell of pine. The raging fire lit his way, providing sight in the graying light. Even on the most perfect blue-skied day, the floor of the forest fought for light of any kind. It was brighter in the winter when the leaves were off the hardwoods. Even that wouldn't help light the way with competition from the smoke. He found a deer path and started calling for Lyle, unconcerned if he might attract the attention of a Langdon, or any other foe who might be lurking in the trees.

The strength of the smoke faded as Josiah walked inside the tree line. His eyes and lungs burned. His lips tasted charred, even though he hadn't gotten near the fire. He hoped Lyle had been smart enough to cover his mouth. That was a lot to expect of a boy Lyle's age, but it was a hope more than a possibility.

Josiah found his way to the spot where Lyle was supposed to be. There was no sign of the boy.

"Lyle!" Josiah called again as a different level of panic rose up the back of his neck. He tried to shake off the fear like he had the pain in his face. He had almost forgotten that, though it was still there, still troubling him. Numbness mixed with a state of uncertainty and absolute panic. It was hard to breathe. He had to find Lyle.

The deer path wound down a ravine and Josiah worried that Lyle had wandered too far into the forest. The Langdons' land butted up on one side, and the Halversons' on the other. Josiah wasn't too encouraged by either family, but the Langdons troubled him the most. Hard telling what they would do to a boy on his own.

Lyle, Josiah reasoned, could have been scared by the shooting, by the fire, by anything. The forest was a foreign place to him. He knew more about the city than he did the woods.

Josiah watched the path for any sign of the boy. A footprint, a broken branch, something caught on a twig, but there was nothing.

A few more steps down the path Josiah saw something that brought him to a stop. He kneeled and looked at a set of animal tracks. They weren't deer or anything with a hoof. Too big for a fox. Pads like a dog. A medium-sized dog. Josiah thought there could be loose dogs in the forest. People could have set them free when they abandoned their farms. That in itself gave him reason to be more concerned. But something in the back of his mind, something buried deep in his memory, made him stand up and look all around, searching for anything that moved. There were wolves in this forest. Or there once were. A long time ago. Red wolves. They were about the size of coyotes, maybe a little larger, and like all wolves, they ran in packs.

Lyle wouldn't stand a chance against a pack of wolves in this forest. No three-year-old boy would.

"Lyle!" Josiah called again, moving on the deer path with more urgency, following the paw prints.

Every time he called, he was answered by silence.

Josiah gripped his Winchester tighter and pushed deeper into the forest, farther than he had been in a long, long time.

CHAPTER 9

The wolf's tracks veered off the deer path and disappeared in the leaf litter and undergrowth of the forest. Josiah thought about following the creature, but there was no evidence that it was tracking Lyle. There was no sign of the boy. No footprints, nothing to offer Josiah any hope of finding him. *Where are you, Lyle?* he screamed inside his head. *If I had known this was going to happen, I would have stayed in Austin.*

He knew second-guessing himself wouldn't do any good, but he couldn't help himself. Not after everything that had happened. He moved on, leaving the wolf to itself. Any explanation of the beast's presence, perhaps in search of a mate, or pushed out of the pack, would have to wait until later.

The light was dim and gray, and growing grayer as the day pushed toward evening. The towering pines made it even darker inside the forest. His jaw ached. His face hurt from a decent amount of swelling, but discomfort wouldn't stop him. He couldn't. Life without Lyle would be unbearable. It would be a complete sever of his tie to Lily. One more ton of grief to weigh him down. No one could control sickness. What happened to Lily and the girls was the way of the world. People got sick. But if anything happened to Lyle, then Josiah would blame himself for the rest of his life. He'd brought Lyle back to the cabin, and then left him there with Ofelia. It would be Josiah's fault, not Ofelia's. She'd killed a man protecting the cabin, protecting Lyle, but not everyone was going to see it that way.

He eased down the ravine, then back up, discouraged by the lack of clues to Lyle's whereabouts. The view from where Josiah stood was thick and dark. The forest blended together to make it almost impossible to see anything with any clarity.

The deer path was growing harder to see. Between the diminishing light and the narrowing of the trail, it was becoming difficult to follow. He could go deeper in, hoping to stumble across the boy, or he could turn around and go back to the cabin — or what was left of it — and hope like hell that Ofelia or Luke had already found Lyle.

■ ■ ■ ■

It was lighter outside of the trees, but the smoke still made the day seem darker. The cabin fire continued to burn, only now the flames were lazy and in retreat. The roof had collapsed, and the fire ate away at the outside planking and what was left of the interior. Nothing could have survived the inferno; no furniture, mementos, nothing that Josiah had lugged from Austin. It was all gone.

Beams flittered with flames. Sparks spiraled into the air. And where the fire had forgone itself and burned out, only black scars remained on the exterior. It was easy to see that the cabin would be a heap of ashes and nothing more.

The dead man lay where he had fallen, and the horse stood in wait next to the barn. Ofelia and Luke took sentry before the cabin, watching the fire, out of the way of the stream of smoke that pushed out, then upward. There was no sign of Lyle.

Luke looked up and saw Josiah coming. He shook his head, then looked to the ground. Ofelia followed suit, looked up, but she pulled away from Luke, from watching the cabin burn to the ground and made her way to Josiah.

"Any sign?" she said.

It was Josiah's turn to shake a forlorn head. "Not a footprint. Nothing. Is there any way he could have gone across the paddock to the other side of the woods?"

Luke joined them, but said nothing.

"It is possible," Ofelia said. "But I do not know for certain. Once I put Lyle out the window, the bad man kicked in the door. I only had time to grab up the scattergun and shoot him before he shot me. I do not know what Lyle did. I know what I told him to do and that is all." She bit her lip, looked away, and forced back more tears. Her face was still blackened by the ash. She was as upset as Josiah.

Josiah reached out and steadied Ofelia's quaking shoulders. "It's okay. We'll find him. Don't worry. He couldn't have gotten far."

Ofelia looked to the sky, then back to Josiah. "It will be night soon."

"I know." He wasn't going to mention anything about seeing wolf tracks in the forest. "It's Gordy Langdon," Luke said. "That fella there."

Josiah looked at him, uncertain. "One of the brothers?" He withdrew his hand from Ofelia's shoulder, then turned his attention

96

to Luke.

"No, a cousin. Lives on the land, though. More than one of the cousins do."

"I was hoping it wasn't a Langdon. I knew it wasn't Morris. He was at the house."

"Most of the brothers were."

"These fellas must have been second tier, sent to take care of the cabin while I was away. They weren't expecting to come up against Ofelia," Josiah said.

"Or maybe they were."

"Could be. She showed Morris to the door. Revenge or redemption, either way, that seems to be what the Langdons hang on to."

Ofelia stiffened, then said, "I should have shot him when I had the chance. Morris is *loco.*"

Josiah was worried that Luke was right. "You think they aimed to kill Ofelia and Lyle?"

"Hard to say about the boy. I've never known them to hurt a child," Luke said. "But Morris was faced down by a Mexican. That's the story going around, anyway. That embarrassed him. He isn't going to let that stand. I can tell you that. No offense, ma'am," he said to Ofelia.

The expression on her face had changed.

97

She had gone from scared to worried to angry.

Josiah looked to Ofelia. "You're going to have to answer for this."

"I did nothing wrong. I was protecting Lyle," she said.

"I know that. But the sheriff is dead. Killed in a shootout in a house not far from town. That's why I came back."

"He told me," Ofelia said, motioning to Luke.

"I don't know who the law is around here, but we need to get to them as soon as we can so you can tell them your side of the story. It was self-defense and nothing more."

"*Sí,* I had no choice."

"Josiah," Luke said, tugging on his shirt-sleeve. "Look." Then he pointed toward the barn.

Josiah turned to see what Luke was pointing at. His heart almost leapt out of his chest.

A woman wearing a simple white linen dress that looked more like a shift than a proper dress had walked out of the woods. Her hair was long and as black as the inside of a coal bin, while her skin shimmered pale white. She looked to be young, maybe in her early twenties, but the most important thing about this woman was that she was walking with Lyle, hand in hand, at a slow, easy pace. Lyle wore a wide smile on his face.

Josiah took a long stride forward, but Luke pulled him back, stopped him before he was able to break into a full run. "That's Eva Langdon, Josiah." There was a warning tone in Luke's voice that Josiah hadn't heard before, not even before the shooting started at the house.

Josiah's eyes were fixed on the woman and Lyle. He had to wipe them clear to make sure he was really seeing the two of them.

"Eight Langdon boys and one Langdon girl. You even look cross-eyed at her and the whole gang of Langdons will rain down on you so hard and so fast you'll wish you were dead before they arrived. It ain't gonna be a pleasant death, I can tell you that."

"I don't care who she is. All I care about is that she has Lyle and he's safe. He's home."

CHAPTER 10

Eva wore a warm expression on her face as she walked across the paddock. When she was about twenty yards away from Josiah and Ofelia, Lyle broke free from Eva's grasp and ran straight to Ofelia's outstretched arms. Josiah took no notice of the boy's preference to Ofelia's comfort; he was used to the direction of Lyle's affection.

He remained focused on Eva, trying not to stare, not to be obvious that he couldn't look away from her. All of his pain vanished in an instant. The tragedy that continued to burn behind him was of no concern. Even the dead body, drawing flies, couldn't sway the sudden heart-stopping, lump-in-your-throat feeling of seeing a beautiful creature for the first time. It didn't matter to him that Eva was a Langdon or younger than he was. Her presence took his mind, and heart, away from all of the troubles that had befallen him since he'd returned home. She was a beautiful sight in an ugly place and time. Her presence changed everything.

Ofelia fussed over Lyle more than usual. She kissed his forehead, wiped his bangs from his eyes, then pulled him in and out of a deep bear hug. *"Me asustaste,"* she said, then looked to Luke, who had stepped back, more from discomfort than respect. "You scared me," she added in English.

"Estoy bien," Lyle said, telling Ofelia that he was okay. She picked him up as he looked over his shoulder. "The bad man is dead."

"Sí," Ofelia said.

"Good," Lyle said.

"No, no, we mustn't take pleasure in a killing. It is not good." Ofelia's ash-covered face dropped into sadness as she glanced over to the dead Langdon cousin.

Josiah stepped forward as Eva approached. He searched her face for some kind of recognition. He had to know of her existence, had to have seen her in town before he had left, but he couldn't place her, not even in all of the eight grades he'd attended. Maybe she didn't go to school, or was that much younger than him. Maybe Ethan didn't let her out much. That might explain the blank Josiah was drawing. He would have remembered her if he had seen her.

Maybe. If she were a little girl at the time, he wouldn't have noticed her in the same way as now.

"Thank you," he said to Eva. He stood with his hands at his sides, not sure whether it was proper to shake hands, to touch her, or to abstain altogether.

A slight breeze wound around the two of them, pushing the smoky smell of burnt timbers and boards away from them, allowing a sweet feminine vanilla scent to take the place of destruction.

Eva smiled, then let the expression fade away. "I looked up and there he was, standing out in front of the house. I saw smoke and knew he was in trouble. I know all of the children around here. I've never seen him before." Eva's voice was a little husky, like all of the Langdon men, and her hair color and facial features did not betray her lineage, but her eyes were different than her brothers. They were a soft green. At least that's how they looked in the fading light.

"I'm Josiah. Josiah Wolfe," he said.

"I figured as much." Eva looked past Ofelia and Lyle to the man lying on the ground, toes up. "That looks like cousin Gordy."

"I'm afraid it is," Josiah said.

Eva dropped her head. "The troubles never end. He set the house on fire?"

"Yes, with Ofelia and Lyle inside."

"They won't see that as cause for his death." She stared at Josiah's face. For a second he thought she was going to reach out and touch him on the cheek. He didn't recoil. But she restrained herself. "I'm Evangelina. Evangelina Langdon. Everybody calls me Eva, though." She extended her hand for a shake. Josiah did not hesitate to take her hand into his.

"I'm sorry, I don't remember you," he said.

"I know who you are," Eva answered.

Lyle, Ofelia, and Luke stepped back. To Josiah, the world all but disappeared — other than Eva. He expected her to say she knew that he was the one that killed her brother, but that's not what she said.

"Your little girls died one by one, and then your wife, Lily. My mother and your mother were friends when they were girls. You can't imagine such a thing now, can you? A Halverson friends with a Langdon, but it's true. They were friends. It was sad that you lost your family. All but the boy. He looks like his mother. I remember you, yes. I don't blame you for leaving, but . . ."

"Why did I come back?"

"Yes, how'd you know?"

Josiah didn't find Eva shy, or unapproachable, which made Luke's warning even more perplexing. He figured it was related to the feud, and the fact that Eva was the only girl in the family. It made sense that Ethan would be protective of her.

"I didn't know what I was coming back to," Josiah said. "I didn't know there were troubles or a grudge against me."

"Because of Charlie?" she said.

"Because of Charlie. I had nothing to do with his death."

Eva stared at Josiah. Her eyes penetrated his. He shivered.

"What happened to your face?" Eva said.

"More trouble. I met the butt end of Morris's rifle."

"I can't apologize for my family." She looked away, scuffed her bare foot against the ground, then looked Josiah in the eye like she was seeing him for the first time.

"I appreciate it that you brought Lyle back to us."

"I should be getting home. It's almost dark. Father will be worried."

"I'll need to deliver your cousin," Josiah said.

Eva looked to Gordy again. "I'll take him home. It's the least I can do."

A wave of relief washed over Josiah. He shrugged, then made his way to Gordy's patient ride. By the time he got to the body, Luke was there to help him load Gordy onto the saddle.

Gordy Langdon was a skinny man — not too far from being a boy. Feathers of whiskers grew on the side of his face, and fuzz still existed above his lip. He didn't look like he was even twenty years old. Josiah felt sad that his life had been cut short, but he couldn't conjure too deep a regret. You don't set a man's house on fire without expecting some kind of retribution.

Gordy's stomach had a hole blasted in it. Ofelia must have been close. It was her or him.

Luke looked at the Langdon boy with a blank face. "We was in school together, me and this one. He never said much, hung out in the middle of the gang like a tiny bird in the flock. Can't say that I knew much about him." He glanced over to Eva, who stopped about ten feet from the body. She wore the same emotionless expression as Luke.

"There's no sense of anyone dyin' because of where they live or who they was born to," Eva said.

"A lot of men died today. Good men who did nothing to deserve what they got. It was their duty to be here and nothing more," Josiah said. He looked past Eva to Ofelia

105

and Lyle. They stood in front of the cabin. The diminishing fire gave off enough light to see them clear enough to see their forlorn faces.

"I feared that was the news," Eva said. "What of my family?"

"I don't know for sure. Morris lives. Your father lives. That's all I really know. There was wounded and then there was the dead. I didn't stay around to take account of the casualties," Josiah answered.

Eva lowered her head. "It will be a sad day for the mothers who have to bury their sons. There was plenty of that in the war. Now there's this. For what I ask? For what?"

"I have no answers for you," Josiah said. Eva trembled and Josiah was tempted to reach out to comfort her. He wanted to, more than anything, but fear and manners stopped him. The last thing he wanted was to give Ethan Langdon another reason to be angry, another reason to rage against him. Besides, he had just met the woman. It would be wrong to offer such a touch. He might be interpreted as fresh, and that's the last thing he wanted. "I can only hope that your mother does not suffer a loss."

Something crossed Eva's eyes that concerned Josiah. Pain. Anger of her own. She looked him straight in the eye and narrowed her eyelids. "My mother is dead. She died giving birth to me."

"I'm sorry, I didn't know," Josiah said in between breaths. "And if I did, I've forgotten. My humble apologies. Yours is a pain that I see every day in the eyes of my son. He will never know his mother. Only the stories he hears of her. I wish it were different, but it's not. I know it is hard for you."

The anger, or pain, on her face fell away as quick as it had arrived. "Thank you," Eva said. She looked to Lyle and smiled. "He is a good boy. You have done a good job with him."

Josiah forced a smile. "Thank you." He knew that statement wasn't true. Ofelia had raised Lyle. She'd seen the boy through sickness and happiness. Josiah's job was to teach him how to be a boy — when he was around.

Eva made eye contact with Josiah and held it there. "I should get Gordy home. I fear the news of his death has already touched the ears of my father. It was his brother Cal who was riding with him. They always rode together. Perhaps, I can calm father. There doesn't need to be any more trouble on this night."

"No, there doesn't," Josiah said. He looked to Luke, and they both moved toward the

107

body in unison, picked it up, and hung it over the saddle.

Eva stepped in, grabbed the horse's reins, and started to walk off. The horse eased on like it knew the load it was carrying was sacred. She stopped, a few feet away, and said, "It was nice to meet you again, Josiah Wolfe. Please give Lyle my goodbyes. It is time for me to go."

"I will," Josiah said, as he watched her walk away. Her feet seemed to float across the ground. She made no sound at all. "It was nice to meet you, too," he offered.

Eva headed toward the woods unaffected by his words. She disappeared into the darkness the same way she came. Josiah watched after her until he could see her no more.

"She's a Langdon," Luke said, almost in a whisper, but, with the same warning all over again.

"She's a kind woman who returned my son. That deserves some gratitude."

"Not around here."

"Well, it should. Maybe things would be a little different than they are now if people showed a bit of decency when trouble shows itself."

"I should be getting back," Luke said. "I'll tell Pa about the cabin fire. You'll be all right?"

"I'll be fine."

"Pa will be worried about that boy," Luke said.

"You make sure and tell him about the kindness Eva Langdon showed us. Tell him she brought Lyle home, where he belonged, unhurt and unafraid. You make sure and tell Leland that," Josiah said, with a clenched jaw.

"I'll tell him, but it won't matter none." Luke shrugged and walked off, leaving Josiah to stand there alone to stare after the darkness, and the woman who was no longer visible, but he could still see in his mind, and still smell the remnant of vanilla. He hoped he would see Eva Langdon again, regardless of what Luke or Leland thought, or anyone else for that matter.

Chapter 11

Night fell fast, covering the land with an oppressive blanket of darkness. Clouds hid the stars and moon, threatening to bring rain and cooler temperatures to the October night. The cabin had burned to the ground, and it continued to smolder. A timber would fall every now and then, sending a shower of sparks upward, causing a flame or two to flare up. The fire would die out almost as fast as it arrived. Even so, there was warmth to be had from what remained of it, orange breathing coals, but Josiah was opposed to staying too close to the cabin. He'd moved Ofelia and Lyle, and what remained of their belongings, to the barn. They would shelter there — from the weather and whatever else that came for them in the night.

Two coal oil lanterns lit the inside of the barn. It was as neglected as the inside of the cabin had been. Spiderwebs occupied every corner the spiders could stretch their web to and from. The cooler weather had tempered their activity; only a few insects skittered out of sight when Josiah entered. There were old harnesses propped up in the corner, and a dull, rusted plow sat useless at the rear of the building. Empty barrels and crates littered the rest of the stalls inside and out.

Josiah mucked out a stall for the three of them to camp in until he could figure out what to do next. With that done, he poked the straw that remained to ensure that no snakes had settled in for the coming winter season. He didn't see any, but there were a few holes burrowed into the dirt. Owl pellets littered the floor in the far corner, but that didn't bother Josiah. He was comforted that something was keeping the rodents under control. He'd heard mice scattering while he made the stall as livable as possible, but he hadn't seen any of those pesky creatures, either. Texas-sized rats had once made their home in the barn, providing hours of target practice over the years. He wondered if they had moved back into the barn in his absence.

There had been some blankets in the buckboard, and Ofelia had managed to salvage some jerky and beans, but that was all they had. The precarious situation Josiah found himself in confronted him as the night grew deeper; there was nothing left of his life before or after joining the Rangers. This was not how he had planned for things to go once he got home.

A cookfire burned outside the barn door. Ofelia tended to a pot of beans, while Lyle sat on a blanket in the stall with his eyes fixed outside. He jumped at every new sound, uncertain of where he was, or what was coming next. When Ofelia was close, he hung on to her like a leech on a fish. There was no escaping the uneasiness for any of them.

Josiah paced back and forth from the door to the stall. His face had stopped swelling, but it felt twice its normal size, and was tender to the touch. His head could have been on the receiving end of an anvil in a smithy shop the way it felt. Every noise irritated him, and he wanted nothing more than to sleep. But a real rest seemed impossible, considering the threats at hand. The cover of darkness offered opportunity, not a reason to cease fighting. He expected another raid any second.

Ofelia walked into the barn, carrying the beans. "We will have some dinner, then sleep," she said. She had washed the ash off her face, cleaned herself up, but she still looked ragged from the day.

"I'm really not hungry," Josiah said. He wondered if Gordy Langdon had been the first man Ofelia had ever killed. He'd never asked, never seen her do such a thing. Her action was warranted, but that didn't make the act of killing any easier. Killing had never come easy for Josiah.

"You need to eat." Ofelia stopped in front of him. The smell of the beans did nothing to change his mind.

"You need to take care of Lyle and yourself. I'll keep watch." He headed toward the door, then stopped. "Are you all right?"

Ofelia looked at Josiah with curiosity set in her moon-shaped brown eyes. "What do you mean?"

He took a step toward her, then stopped again. "You killed a man today. Are you all right?"

"It was him or me. I had no choice. Like you say, shoot to kill, not to wound. I had to stop him. That sent the other one running."

Josiah agreed, and turned to head back outside. "You did the right thing," he said over his shoulder.

Ofelia started to say something, but restrained herself. The look on her face suggested she had more to say, but didn't know how to say it.

The fresh air agreed with Josiah. He stopped a few feet outside of the barn as his face was caressed by a steady, cool breeze. It was a momentary relief. Pain was never far away.

He still wore his gun belt and had his Peacemaker on his side. The rest of the weapons were in the stall, close at hand if he needed them. He scanned everything before him, looking for anything out of place, for anything moving that shouldn't have been. He was betting that the Langdons would come back sooner rather than later. Or maybe someone else. He had no idea who was friend or foe in Seerville. But he knew one thing for certain. There would be fallout from the shooting between the Halversons and the Langdons. Whatever came from that wouldn't hold a candle to what Ofelia had done. A Mexican woman killing a white man wasn't going to go unanswered, no matter whether the cause was just or not. There was a lot to be on the lookout for.

No matter, I'm outmanned and outgunned. He looked back inside the barn to Ofelia and Lyle. He felt incapable of protecting them, but more than that, he felt like a fool for bringing them back to Seerville without considering the consequences.

When Josiah looked at what remained of the cabin, his regret transformed to anger. He wanted retribution. He wanted the Langdons to pay for what they had done to his life. They had destroyed what remained of his life with Lily, with his parents. Josiah had been born in that cabin. It had withstood storms, sadness, and happy days. The memories of the lives of all the people whom Josiah had ever loved existed inside that cabin. Now his memories were nothing more than a charred pile of ash.

He wanted to jump on Clipper and ride into the Langdon compound shooting, without hesitation or regret. But that would be a suicide mission. Lyle didn't deserve to be an orphan — or raised by Leland Halverson. Josiah didn't want his son to be an underling to a power-hungry man. That would be a tragedy all unto itself.

Josiah sucked in a series of deep breaths, trying his best to calm down as he came to the realization that his anger was at both men, at Ethan Langdon and Leland Halverson. He realized that he was no different, and wouldn't show his son anything different if he let his emotions rule him.

Eva Langdon was the cause of the change.

He couldn't hate her because of her name, because of her family. He wanted to know more about her, to see her again. But that seemed as impossible as one man standing up to an army of Langdons.

As Josiah was about to relax, two men on horses rode onto his land, past the smoldering cabin, then veered toward the barn, riding fast. It would have been easy for them to see that the barn was occupied with the cookfire and the lanterns burning inside. There was no escaping the target he had placed on himself.

Josiah reached for his Peacemaker, but stopped pulling it out of the holster once the riders drew close enough to see. He recognized one of them. It was Luke Halverson. The other rider was about the same age as Luke, but Josiah didn't recognize the man.

Luke reined in his horse and edged up alongside Josiah. The other rider, on a midnight black horse that looked like it was built more for pulling a plow than carrying a rider, hung back. He carried a rifle and his eyes, reflected in the fire, were on alert.

"Didn't expect to see you again this evening, Luke," Josiah said. "Is there a problem? You came in in a hurry."

"I was hoping you wouldn't start shooting."

"I'm ready if I have to be."

"Pa sent me. This fella here's Clyde Laine. He's been working on our place for a while. We're keeping watch on your place. Two more men are already out there. Wanted you to know in case one of us shows ourself and you get a little edgy with that Peacemaker there."

"I can handle my own land," Josiah said.

"Pa don't think you can. Besides, we're here to watch over that boy in there, not you. Pa said to not let him become an orphan, though, so he kind of scratched out what he said. Don't worry, we ain't gonna let nothin' happen. Not tonight, or any other night as far as that goes. Not now that that boy's returned home to his kin."

Josiah started to tell Luke that he didn't need the help, but that wasn't true. All it took was one glance inside the barn to know that.

"The womenfolk," Luke continued, "are gathering up some clothes and supplies. I told 'em about the cabin burnin' to the ground, and the Mexican shootin' Gordy Langdon to keep Lyle safe. Pa figured we should keep watch. I'd 'xpect the supplies to come 'round at daylight tomorrow."

117

"I'll express my gratitude the next time I see your pa."

"Shoot in the air if you need us. We'll come runnin'. Until then, it sure looks to me that you need some rest, Wolfe. That face of yours could use a visit by a doctor."

"I've been in worse shape than this. I'll be okay."

"All the same, if the Langdons step foot on your property, they can expect hellfire to rain down."

Josiah wondered if Luke had told Leland that Eva Langdon had returned Lyle after the boy had run off. He wasn't going to ask. Leaving Eva out of this seemed right.

"I'll call if I need you," Josiah said. He turned and walked inside the barn. Luke and Clyde Laine rode off as fast as they rode in. Their thundering horses' hooves entered one ear and bounced around the inside of Josiah's head like a hammer. He passed up another offer of beans from Ofelia, and stumbled back to the corner of the stall, found his bedroll, made himself as comfortable as he could, and fell straight to sleep.

CHAPTER 12

Morning light crept into the barn like a stranger unsure of where he was at. Fingers of soft sunshine reached to Josiah's face and stopped searching until Josiah stirred awake. The smell of coffee was strong, and Ofelia was puttering around outside of the barn. Lyle was nowhere to be seen, which at first was cause for panic, but Ofelia came into focus after a couple of strong blinks, and she was not worried about anything. Robins and sparrows chirped outside the barn, adding to the perception of calmness.

Josiah propped himself up on his elbows with caution. Pain from his head traveled through every bone and muscle in his body. He gasped, but held in what he could of the discomfort. His head and face throbbed, and for a second he didn't know if he could stand up. But he had to move; he couldn't lay on the ground the rest of the day, even though he wanted to. A good dip in the cold

119

creek at the bottom of the ravine would wake him up, and help get the day before off him — if he could make it that far.

He teetered upward without grace or confidence. Once on two feet, Josiah made his way to Ofelia. He had to shield the sun from his eyes as soon as he stepped outside. The light was brighter than he'd anticipated. His eyeballs burned from the inside out. "What time is it?"

"Midmorning," Ofelia said. "I let you sleep. Lyle has collected firewood for us."

Josiah looked down to a pile of twigs next to the cookfire, then to Lyle, who had appeared and was standing next to Ofelia, clutching her long skirt. "He didn't go far, did he?"

"Those men, *Señor* Luke and the other, they showed themselves to let me know they were still here, that we are safe — if that is *possible.* But I did not let Lyle out of my sight."

Josiah looked past Ofelia to see the scattergun propped up against the barn. It was close by if she needed it. He relaxed the best he could. It felt like he was on the backside of a week-long drunk. He could only imagine that pain and discomfort because he'd never experienced such a thing, but he was sure this was what it was like — save the heaves.

Ofelia poured a mug of coffee and handed it to Josiah. He took it without hesitation.

"You need whiskey," Ofelia said.

"Not going to happen."

"No, I know it is not. It is the wrong time of year for me to collect *heirbas* for *medicina.* You need a salve on your face. Are you sure nothing is broken. You look like a *mapache.* "

"Raccoon!" Lyle shouted. "You look like a raccoon!" Then he broke into a giggle.

Josiah grimaced. *Great,* he thought, though it was nice to hear laughter for once.

Ofelia shushed Lyle. "Papa's head hurts."

Lyle stopped giggling. "I'm sorry. 'Felia will make it better. She makes everything better."

Josiah forced a smile, but said nothing. He wished that was true. He wished she could conjure some magic and make their life better. They had some trouble to face.

"My head will be fine in a couple of days. Until then, I'll do what I can."

"We need *huevos* and milk," Ofelia said. "I am low on beans." She glanced over to the buckboard. "I will go and fetch some."

"No. None of us stay alone until we know that it's safe to travel or leave."

"Fine," Ofelia said. "We all go."

121

Before Josiah could object, the clamor of a team pulling a wagon sounded to his ears. He looked to the opening by the cabin and caught sight of a pair of Springfield mules making their way toward him. The mules were tall and proud, their coats shiny in the sunlight, black as mirrors, or the surface of water on a moonless night. They were beautiful.

A stout woman sat in the driver's seat of the wagon wearing a bonnet that covered most of her gray hair. She wore a pink and gray gingham dress. Her cauliflower arms fell through the short sleeves. Two more women rode in the wagon bed dressed alike with bonnets on their heads, too. Josiah knew the woman driver. She was Leland's sister, Sarah, the matriarch of the family, if Josiah's assumption of Leland's widowhood was correct.

Luke Halverson and Clyde Laine followed close behind the wagon. Both men carried rifles, ready to fire. They were protectors, overseers, there to see that nothing happened to the women. Josiah wondered if the perimeter was safe with the two men away from their posts. It was a Ranger habit he couldn't break.

"Luke said the women were putting together supplies for us last night," Josiah said to Ofelia. "I didn't think much of it."

"I hope they bring *huevos,*" Ofelia answered. Lyle eased behind her, trying to hide, though his curiosity got the better of him as he peered around Ofelia's girth every other second to look at the women in the wagon.

"Eva is not there," Lyle whispered.

Ofelia shushed him again. "You don't say that name."

Josiah didn't react to the correction. He ignored it, because she was right. These were not the people to mention a Langdon's name in front of.

Sarah brought the mule team to a stop a few feet in front of the barn, and clambered down off of the wagon. "Troubles still followin' after you, Josiah Wolfe. Nothing ever changes, does it?" She had a no-nonsense manner about her, curt and to the point, when she chose to speak to you. Nothing had changed from what Josiah could tell.

"Good to see you, too, Sarah."

"Where's the boy?" she said, looking past Ofelia, trying to catch a glimpse of Lyle.

"He's shy," Josiah said.

"No call for that," Sarah said, almost in a growl. "We're family. Though he wouldn't know it since you took him away from us."

"Leland's already had his say about that,

thank you very much."

Ofelia stood, minding her own business. She knew her place.

"You think you've heard the last of it?" Sarah said. "You're mistaken if you do. I got an earful for you."

"Can you save it for another day?" Josiah said, rubbing his jaw, taking his attention from Sarah to the other two women who had climbed out of the wagon, and had come to a stop next to the stout woman. They were her daughters, smaller versions of Sarah — only both of them wore a kind of understanding in their eyes as they looked over the land, and then to Lyle. Ruth and Esther. Cousins to Lily, both in their early thirties like she should have been. They looked nothing like her, but that didn't matter. There was no question that they were kin.

"You look near beat to death," Sarah said. "Heard Morris Langdon took a couple good licks to you. A mean one that Morris. He'll get what's coming to him one of these days. All them Langdons will. You wait and see."

"Morris is the least of my problems."

"I can see that." Sarah looked behind her to the remains of the cabin; a pile of black ash with a stone fireplace jutting up from the ground like a giant gravestone planted

124

there long ago. "You can rebuild," she said, turning her attention back to Josiah.

"If I stay."

"You can't turn around and leave 'cause things are a little rough."

"A little rough?" Josiah protested. "Lyle was in the cabin when the Langdons came at it with fire and bullets. If my son's not safe here, I'm not staying here. Simple as that."

"Leland will have something to say about that."

"Good for him." Josiah crossed his arms and planted his feet.

Esther, the younger of the two daughters, stepped forward and touched her mother's elbow with gentleness. "Maybe it's not the time for that, Momma. Josiah's had a bad spell. We brought 'em some goods to ease his needs, not tell him how to live his life."

Sarah shot Esther a look that would have caused granite to crack, then pulled herself back when Lyle looked around Ofelia again, this time holding his big-eyed gaze on the woman.

Luke and Clyde eased off their horses behind the wagon, put their rifles on the rail, then stood and waited for instructions on what to do next.

"There you are," Sarah said, forcing a

smile at Lyle.

She only held the expression for a second, long enough for Lyle to see that she didn't mean it. He disappeared behind Ofelia again. "Go inside," he whispered.

"Be nice."

"I see you still associate with that one," Sarah said, nodding toward Ofelia.

"Good thing," Josiah answered. "She killed a man yesterday to save Lyle."

Sarah let out a harrumph, then looked away. "I heard about that." She turned to Luke, and said, "You best start unloading. We ain't got all day."

Luke stepped forward and directed his attention to Josiah. "We've got blankets, a couple of chairs, some feather pillows, and a bit of food. Where you want it?"

Josiah studied Luke and Sarah. If he chose to be honest, he would have told them that he didn't want their charity. But he couldn't do that, reject their claim of kin to Lyle and the kindness they were offering. He didn't want to be obligated to them, to any of the Halversons, not even Leland or Sarah.

"In the barn," Josiah said. "Ofelia will show you where to put things. I'll consider this a loan until I get on my feet, and decide what I'm going to do."

"It is no such thing," she said.

126

Luke joined Clyde and the two women followed them to the rear of the wagon. Clyde climbed in and started handing blankets to Esther and Ruth. Luke pulled a chair off, and headed toward the barn. Ofelia made her way inside with Lyle in tow, leaving Josiah and Sarah to stand alone, facing each other.

Josiah didn't care to argue with Sarah. To him the goods were a loan, and that was the way it was going to be whether she liked it or not. He still ached with pain, and the last thing he was in the mood for was an attitude he couldn't abide. It took all he had not to be rude to the woman.

Josiah waited until Lyle and Ofelia were out of earshot before he said anything else. "Tell me of Helena, Leland's wife, Lily's mother. I get the feeling she has been lost since I was away. Leland didn't say when I saw him. Not that we had much of a chance to share niceties. He didn't mention her, and well, I know the look and tone of a widower man, and he looked to fill those gray, dirty clothes like they were tailor-made for him."

"Helena died two years ago. That'd be that boy's grandmother, and he was nowhere to be seen when they put her in the ground."

"I didn't know."

"You didn't have to leave."

"Yes, I did."

"You didn't have to take him with you."

"Yes, I did." Josiah looked to the ground as Luke, Clyde, and the women came back for another load. He straightened and made direct eye contact with Sarah, to convince her he was serious. "I can't change the past, and neither can you. I understand the entire Halverson family is upset with me for leaving, but that's not helping anything now. Considering how things are around here."

"We're afraid you're gonna leave again is what we are," Sarah said, focusing on Josiah with as much shoulder into her look as his. "That boy looks like Lily. He is a breath of fresh air, hope for our future here. We want to know him, and him to know us, is all, Josiah Wolfe. That boy can lighten an old man's grief. Leland's not been the same since Helena died."

"I'm sure he hasn't," Josiah said.

Before Sarah could say another word, a distant gunshot cracked from the west, garnering everyone's attention.

"Take cover!" Josiah yelled. "Take cover, now!"

CHAPTER 13

The gunshot was cause for sudden alarm. Josiah hadn't strapped on his gun belt, and the Winchester was inside the barn. Panic careened through his veins as he hustled Sarah inside, out of harm's way. "Go back to the corner and stay there until I tell you it's okay." Ofelia and Lyle were already there, their cover plan already put in place.

Sarah started to protest, but shook her head and did as she was told. Ruth and Esther followed, looking over their shoulders, trying to get a glimpse of the unseen invaders.

Josiah grabbed up his rifle, then joined Luke at the barn door. Clyde was on the east side of the wagon, opposite where the gunshot had come from. Both men were ready for a fight, for an attack. They all had known it was coming, not when.

Luke aimed his rifle at the entrance to the clearing with his eye on the sight and his finger on the trigger. Clyde, too, took the defensive stance. Josiah stood in wait, not convinced an attack would come from such a predictable place. "Anything?" he asked Luke.

"Nothing," Luke answered. "Sounded a good distance away. My cousin, Vance, is on the main road along with his brother-in-law Billy."

"The shot sounded like it came from the woods."

"Did, but that don't mean nothin'. Langdons like to fight like the Indians, use silence and their knowledge of the land to pounce. Wild cats, they are. Angry wild cats. They's a lot of them, too. Can't drain that swamp and be rid of 'em, but I sure would like to."

Another shot, from the same direction, interrupted the conversation. Luke and Josiah refocused, but it made no difference, they couldn't see through the piney forest. It was a solid wall of green unwavering branches.

The echo of the shot faded away and silence returned. The women remained at the back of the barn; they took turns giving Lyle attention, much to Ofelia's discomfort.

"That doesn't sound like an exchange to me," Josiah said.

"You can't trust what you think you know. Like I said, the Langdons are dirty fighters."

"I know that."

"They've got dirtier since all of this kicked up."

"Well, trust in what I know is all I've got. It'll have to do." Josiah winced, feeling the weight of the rifle in his hand. He had fought Kiowa, Comanche, Juan Cortina's cattle rustlers, and men as bad or worse than the Langdons — like Liam O'Reilly, the Badger, who came to a bad end after a long campaign of dirty tricks and unfathomable violence. Those battles had ended with Josiah standing, all because of the trust he felt in his skills, in his experience. There was no use explaining that to Luke. It wouldn't make any difference.

Luke glanced over at Josiah. "You taken a good look at yourself in a mirror?"

Josiah held his gaze at the forest steadfast. He wasn't going to respond to Luke's bait.

Birdsong and the sound of normalcy returned with a flourish to the sunny morning. It was too normal for Josiah, but he didn't say so. His attention was drawn away from the distance by a cloud of blackbirds, fleeing into the sky along the trail. The birds had Josiah's full attention. If a hawk appeared in a breath or two, giving chase, it would explain the reason for the birds to erupt into the sky like they had. If not, then something roused them. A predator, or a man — or men — on the trail, heading toward the farm.

The sound of thundering horse hooves reached all of the men's ears. Recognition registered in their eyes.

"Company's comin'. Wait on me, Clyde," Luke called out to his partner.

Luke steadied his aim at the opening. Josiah did the same, raising his rifle to greet the visitors. The women went silent behind them. Birds and insects ceased communicating, too, fearful of what was to come, or anticipating more noise, smoke, and disruption.

The horses were in a hurry, and that struck Josiah as odd. The Langdons were either bold, had more men coming from different directions, or the riders weren't on the attack at all.

As it turned out, Josiah was right. Vance Halverson and his brother-in-law, Billy, rushed into the clearing — both men waving their arms, yelling, "Don't shoot!"

"It's Vance and Billy," Luke announced as loud as he could, calling off the reason for concern.

Vance, who bore a striking resemblance to Luke, led the two men and rode hard toward the barn. His weapons were holstered. He had one hand gripped hard on the reins, while the other carried two dangling squirrels. A smile lit across his face as he came to a stop shy of the barn door. "Brought you some breakfast," he said, thrusting the squirrels outward.

Billy, whom Josiah knew to be a member of the Pike family, stopped short of Vance.

"That was you doin' the shootin'?" Luke said.

"Yup, sure was. We had to slip away this mornin' with no food on our stomachs. Thought we'd share," Vance said.

Luke's face drew tight with anger. "Who's watching the trail in?"

"Billy's brother. Told 'im we'd be back soon. He's a crack shot and has a keen eye."

"He's out there alone." Luke settled his rifle to his side.

Josiah wasn't too concerned about squirrels for breakfast. He was glad he didn't have to defend his life again.

Vance picked up on Luke's attitude quick. "He's top-notch, Luke. Besides, you know those Langdons don't climb out of the bed until noontime."

"They do when one of their own has been

133

killed and there's revenge to be had. This is a war, Vance, we can't let our guard down." Luke stood firm, his eyes narrowing so much that Josiah wondered how he could see out of them.

"I was with you on Sherman's march, Luke," Vance snapped. "That was war. This ain't nothin' but a skirmish."

"Tell that to those whose kin are diggin' graves today," Luke said. "It's war, and this won't be over until all them Langdons are dead, or hightail it out of Anderson County. Ain't none of us gonna get any rest 'til that happens."

Both men stared at each other, unwavering, until Vance took a chance to speak. "Are you gonna take these squirrels or not?"

Luke reached up and took the dead animals. "Wolfe'll take 'em." He handed the squirrels to Josiah, who then walked them back to Ofelia. By the time Josiah had returned to the barn door, Vance and Billy had rode off in a huff. They were halfway out of sight, leaving a trail of dust in their wake.

"Vance ain't never taken anything serious in his life," Luke said. " 'Bout got me killed in Chickamauga when he wasn't payin' attention to his flank."

"Why's he on post?" Josiah picked up his

Winchester, preparing to put it away.

"Pa says who goes where. I don't have nothin' to do with that. If I had my way, Vance Halverson would be on a long trip to Abilene, not here shootin' squirrels for breakfast."

"Well, you'll have your day," Josiah said.

"I ain't in no hurry for his problems, if you know what I mean."

"I do," Josiah said, looking into the barn. "Of course, I do." He turned his attention to Sarah, who was barreling her way toward the door. "Much ado about nothing," he said to her.

Sarah ignored Josiah and directed her wrath toward Luke. "We are done here. It's time to leave."

Josiah, beyond being relieved that he wasn't in the midst of a gunfight, still had his injuries to deal with. His head pounded, and his face ached. But more than that, he was confused by Sarah's obvious anger, or distaste, or whatever it was. "What's wrong, Sarah?" Josiah called, as she hurried to the wagon.

Sarah stopped, planted her feet, put her hands on her hips, and glared at Josiah. "That boy called that Mexican *mamacita. Mamacita,* mind you. An Anglo boy calling a woman like her his momma. That ain't

135

right. Josiah, no matter how you paint it. It ain't right. No Halverson boy should ever call a Mexican his momma. Leland will be tied in knots about this when I tell him."

Josiah dropped his shoulders, looked to the ground, then behind him, to the inside of the barn. Ruth and Esther were heading his way, readying to join their mother with the twisted look of disapproval plastered across their faces. Ofelia hadn't moved from the back of the barn. She stood holding Lyle to her waist with a horrified look on her face.

Josiah didn't acknowledge Sarah. Instead, he turned to Luke. "Looks like you better get these women home, Luke. A storm's coming."

Luke looked to the clear blue sky. "I don't see a cloud."

"It's coming. You wait and see."

Sarah stomped her foot. "This isn't going to stand, Josiah Wolfe. You hear me? It won't stand."

Josiah turned to walk away, but stopped and said, "Tell your cousin thank you for the squirrels. I appreciate his thoughtfulness." Then he made his way to Ofelia and Lyle, ignoring Sarah and the difficult air they'd created. He didn't speak until they were long gone.

"Don't worry about them," Josiah said to Ofelia. "Don't you worry about them women. This is your home as long as you want it to be. But you might teach Lyle another word to call you." He looked down to the boy, who looked sad and lost.

"I did not teach him that word to call me. He asked me what he would call his momma in my language, that is all. I tell him *mamacita*. That was a long time ago. I would never ask him to call me that. I am not Miss Lily. I am only his *vigilante,* um, his caretaker. That is all. I tell him that someday he will have another momma, that you will bring another woman into his life."

"I don't know about that," Josiah said.

"When the time and the person are right. You will, you must. I am not his *mamacita.*"

Josiah kneeled down to Lyle, and looked him in the eyes. "Do you understand that, Lyle. You can't call her *mamacita.*"

"I want her to be," the boy said.

"I know," Josiah answered, "but that is not the way it is. Ofelia is Ofelia, okay?"

"Okay."

"Promise?"

"If I have to."

CHAPTER 14

Josiah fell asleep after Sarah and her daughters departed, leaving Ofelia to keep watch and prepare the meal of squirrels. He needed time to heal, to work the aches out of his head and allow the swelling to go down. Worry beyond the paddock was there, but the Halversons had taken it upon themselves to watch the perimeter. Regardless of Luke's lack of trust in his cousin, Vance, a man on the post was better than no man at all. It allowed Josiah to rest, to fall asleep with only a hint of concern. The meal came and went, and the more Josiah slept, the more he seemed to want. Ofelia didn't push him. She kept watch over him, saw that he was covered up, had water, and was nearby when he woke. The next time he stirred, night had fallen, and it didn't take him long to realize he had lost a whole day.

A lantern burned with a dim flame at the

front of the barn, and the cookfire was nothing but a glow of coals. Ofelia was at Josiah's side before he could prop himself all the way up.

"I slept all day," he said. His throat was dry. Before he could say anything else, Ofelia had a mug of water in front of him. He took it and drank it down without taking a breath.

"How do you feel?" Ofelia said. Lyle was asleep in a bundle nearby. She spoke in a soft voice.

"Like I was run over by a train."

"It will take some time to heal."

"I fear we do not have time."

"You have no choice. Are you hungry?"

"No, not really."

Ofelia offered Josiah another mug, only this one was not full of water. It had a strong alcohol smell to it. "*Señor* Luke gave it to me for you, for the pain, to help you sleep. Go on, drink."

Josiah hesitated. He'd never acquired the taste for whiskey like some men, but he'd found that the drink had its uses over the years. Cleaning wounds, calming a cough, helping to sleep when the troubles came. He took the drink and drank it down. It burned all the way to his stomach.

"*Más?*"

"No more."

"I will save it for tomorrow."

"You need to get some sleep, Ofelia."

"Don't worry about me. I am fine, as you say."

The sun beat into the barn like it was the middle of summer and everything was right. Brightness and noise caused Josiah to wake with a start. Ofelia was puttering around in the next stall, her eyes to the ground as if she had lost something. She had an iron poker in her hand, weaponized for some uncertain action. Lyle sat atop the stall rail, his feet dangling, watching with intent, but without fear or concern. He wore an amused expression on his face.

Once Josiah was able to stand, he looked to his feet, and confirmed they were planted on the ground. When he touched his face, he found that the swelling had gone down. Now it was tender to the touch. When he blinked again, Ofelia was standing before him, with Lyle at her side. They both looked at him like they were seeing him for the first time.

"You are hungry, *señor*?" Ofelia looked him over like he had returned from battle.

"I don't know. Thirsty, maybe," Josiah said. "What day is it?"

"You have been asleep, in and out for almost three days."

Lyle stood by Ofelia's side. "And no trouble?"

"Not a peep," Ofelia said. "*Señor* Luke has come by to check on you a few times. Brought us a chicken. I have it in the pot. Are you hungry?"

"Yes, maybe, of course. Three days? Are you sure?"

"*Sí,*" Ofelia answered. "I gave you water, helped you when I could, but let you sleep. It has *te ayudó mucho.*"

"Helped you a lot," Lyle said, translating for Josiah.

"And no trouble, you say?"

"No."

"That's odd. I really expected some retaliation from the Langdons by now."

"*Señor* Luke said the same thing. The quiet makes him uneasy. He don't trust those Langdons."

"Me, either," Josiah said. He started to go outside to take care of himself, but he stopped midway and turned back to Ofelia.

"No, even the owls have been *tranquilo,*" Ofelia said. "Maybe the danger is gone."

"You don't believe that, do you?"

"No, but I can hope for us that it is that way."

"Hope's all we've got. Hope and each other," Josiah said, grabbing up his Winchester as he made his way out into the bright sunshine.

CHAPTER 15

Luke Halverson rode in as the sun tilted past noon. He was alone, riding with ease, no guns showing other than what was secured in his holster and scabbard. The afternoon light was bright and the air was cool. October waned and winter would reach down from the north soon enough, forcing jackets over shirts and fires burning all day. But on this day, nothing was needed to ensure warmth of any kind. It was as perfect a day as Josiah could hope for.

He walked out to meet Luke. "Filled the trough with fresh water."

Luke climbed off his horse, a tall gray gelding with relaxed eyes, and tied it to a fence post next to the trough. "Good to see you up and about, Josiah."

"I lost some days."

"I know. I checked on you and the boy from time to time."

The horse was eager for a drink of water.

It lapped a good gulp, then shook its head, spraying Josiah and Luke with tender drops. They both chuckled.

"Ofelia told me." Josiah looked to the barn and caught sight of the Mexican sitting on a stool talking to Lyle. The boy sat at her feet, rapt with attention to whatever she was saying. Where there was one, there was usually the other. "I appreciate it, Luke. I wasn't up to much of anything other than sleeping."

"You look like it don't hurt too bad to stand."

"I'm better." Josiah paused, looking toward the trail that led away from the farm, his Winchester down to his side. "You carrying news?"

"Wish I could say I was. Everything's silent as a church on Saturday night. Not a word from the Langdons, or anyone else as far as that goes. No retribution or retaliation for those that they lost. Nothin'. It's makin' Pa more nervous as the days go on. He knows they're up to somethin'. He don't know what."

Luke looked rested himself. He had on a set of clothes clean of trail dust and his boots were wiped clean of mud. It didn't bother Josiah to stand downwind of him, either. It looked like everyone had taken advantage of the lull in fighting.

"And there's no news of Sheriff Cliburn and the deputies that were injured or killed?" Josiah said.

"Not yet. Pa went to the funeral to pay his respects. He's makin' plans for an attack on the Langdons if they don't do somethin' soon. That's why I'm here, to let you know what's comin' so you're ready, so you're stocked up for more than a few days. None of us expect you to ride with us when we go."

Josiah didn't indicate whether he'd ride with the Halversons or not. He remained stone-faced. "He's not going to let this rest, is he?"

"No, not until he runs the Langdons out of the county."

"That's not going to happen."

Luke shrugged. "Tell him that. He blames all the ills of his life on the Langdons. Pa's been carryin' that grudge for as long as I've been around. Don't know the whole of it, but this ain't gonna stop until he's dead or Ethan's dead, or packed up and moved out. Simple as that. I can't talk sense to the old mule, and you won't be able to, either, if that's what you're thinkin'. Nothin' is gonna change that old man's mind."

"You don't want to fight?" Josiah said.

"What am I gonna do? I've gone from one battle to the next, either wearin' the gray, or chasin' my pa's shadow. It don't matter. It's the life I've been given to live."

"I need to talk to Leland."

"I told you, you'll be wastin' your words."

"Maybe, but I don't want Lyle to live the life you've described. I don't want him bouncing from one battle to the next because he's kin to you Halversons."

"He'll say he's doin' all this for the boy."

"That's not true, and you know it."

"Maybe, but suit yourself. You can go talk to 'im if you think it will make a difference. I'm sayin' it won't make a damn bit of difference. You best hurry, though. You got a day at the most before we ride against the Langdons."

"I need supplies. Doesn't matter if I stay or go." Josiah looked to the barn, to Ofelia and Lyle. "Then I'll go talk to Leland."

"You up to ridin' into town?"

"I am. But I'm not leavin' those two behind. Not this time. They're coming with me."

"Fine with me," Luke said. "If that's the way you want it."

Josiah didn't answer. He was already two steps toward the barn, readying himself to go.

146

The ride to Seerville was uneventful. Josiah drove the wagon with Lyle sitting next to him. Ofelia was on the other side of the boy. Weapons were loaded, reachable if needed. Luke Halverson brought up the rear, while Billy Pike led the way. Both men had their rifles out, fingers on the trigger, eyes peeled for a Langdon. They'd all expected trouble, but it never came.

Josiah was sure of Luke's skills, but he knew little of Billy Pike. The Pikes were river people who kept to themselves — but Billy was related to Luke by way of Vance, being his brother-in-law, so it was pretty clear how Billy had got caught up in Leland Halverson's feud with Ethan Langdon. There could be more to it for all Josiah knew. Who knows why a man jumps into a fight that isn't his? Life in Anderson County, and Seerville, had been difficult before the railroad decided not to cut alongside town, and it was more difficult after that decision was made. There was little to know of life on the river, but Josiah imagined that it was given over to the fickle nature of the seasons like anything else. One year was better than the other. Droughts. Floods. Lack of fish.

Bounty and depression. They were frequent visitors no matter the toil of a man's life. All he could hope for was that Billy Pike was a good aim and was true to the side he'd chosen to ride with.

Vacant cabins dotted the ride to Seerville, but as they drew closer to town more and more of the places were occupied. Luke had told Josiah that the mercantile in town still existed, but that was about the only business that had held on. The Langdons had the corner on smithy work, so if the need was there, then they would have to be dealt with on their terms, or the repair or purchase would have to be made elsewhere, like Tyler.

The road to town widened and as the first few two-story buildings came into sight, a wave of sadness fell over Josiah. There had never been an outright sense of optimism emanating from the town, but even from a distance, the place looked defeated. It had struggled since its founding, by Jonathon Seers, a man who had come from Yorkshire, England, and bought up the land in the river basin as it became available. It reminded him of home, or of a place in England that he loved. Josiah couldn't remember which, but he knew times had been hard for Seers, unaccustomed as he was to the hard life in the West, dealing with raiding Indians, fierce weather, and the uncertainty of each day. Seers took ill with consumption ten years into his life in Texas, and died not long after. No more had been added to the town after that.

Now, the Western Union office stood empty, along with the marshal's office next to it. Ragged curtains pushed in and out of the opened window unhindered. Critters occupied the place where Josiah once worked and slept, where he wore the badge and Charlie Langdon rode with him as a deputy. Seerville needed the law then — not that it didn't now. But the desire for order had been lost and given over to the county. Which, as it was, had found itself without a sheriff. Lawlessness bred like mosquitoes on a stagnant pond.

The boardwalk was still intact, but precarious to those who took to it. Some of the boards looked rotted, about to shatter into splinters under any weight. Like the Western Union office, the hotel and livery were gone. The buildings were shells of what they once were. Anything useful had been carted off long ago. No one was out and about, the street and boardwalk were empty, except for a buggy and a tall black mount tied up in front of the mercantile.

The mercantile looked like the rest of the buildings in town; ready to fall in on itself, uncared for, lacking whitewash, or any adornments. Even the name arched above the doorway was faded, hard to read. The place used to be run by an old German, Hugo Dansker, but Luke told Josiah that Hugo had died and left the store to his son, Axel, and his wife. Neither of them, from what Luke had said, were too enthusiastic about life behind a counter selling needs to a small population, but so far, they'd made a go of it.

Billy Pike reached the mercantile first. He jumped off his horse, tied it up, then stood in wait for Josiah and Luke. He scanned the rooftops for any movement, but didn't act like there was anything to be concerned about.

Josiah rolled the wagon to a stop, and Luke rode up beside it, eyeing the buggy and black horse. "We need to see who's inside before you go in," he said.

Josiah looked at Luke, curious, then to the door of the mercantile. "We don't have to," he said, nodding, motioning for Luke to have a look.

Morris Langdon walked out the door carrying a crate of goods, not expecting to see anyone. He stopped with a rattled look on his face. "Wait," he said over his shoulder.

But that didn't stop Eva Langdon from exiting the mercantile. She was wearing a black dress, not quite widow's weeds, but she was in mourning from hat to button-up shoes.

Lyle jumped up at the sight of Eva. A wide smile crossed his face when they made eye contact. "It's Miss Eva!" he said with glee.

Morris's face went from concern to confusion. "How's that Wolfe boy know who you are, sister?"

"Don't you worry about it, Morris." Eva made her way past the eldest Langdon, and walked up to the wagon.

Luke, who had been present when Eva had walked Lyle home, held his horse steady and let Josiah do the talking. Billy looked nervous, but held fast where he was, cradling his Henry rifle with Morris close to sighting; predator and prey stood staring at each other.

Josiah remained sitting, and still held the reins in his hands. "We're not looking for trouble, Morris. Coming to town for a few supplies, like you."

Morris glared at Josiah, then turned his attention back to Eva. She was at the side of the wagon, looking up to Lyle with a matching smile on her face.

"If I had known you were coming, I would have bought you some rock candy. Mr. Dansker has a new batch," Eva said to Lyle. "Would you like that?"

"We have to go, Eva," Morris said.

Eva ignored him, keeping her gaze on Lyle.

It was almost like the air had been sucked out from around the earth, taking with it the sounds and smells that were common to the decaying town. Not one bird sang or whistled. The only thing Josiah could hear was his own heart beating.

"I think that's what we should do, Lyle," Eva said. "Go back inside and get you some rock candy. Would you like that?" she paused, looked to Josiah, then said, "If it's okay with your pa?"

Josiah glanced over to Morris, who was growing more agitated. The last thing he wanted to do was get into a shootout with Ofelia and Lyle caught in the cross fire.

"It's okay with me, if it's okay with Morris," Josiah said.

"Morris doesn't mind, do you?" she said to her brother, offering her hand to Lyle. "He could use some candy himself. Maybe it'd wipe that hateful look off his face."

Lyle took Eva's hand, then climbed over Ofelia and down off the wagon.

Eva didn't wait for Josiah or anyone else to join them. She walked right by Morris, holding hands with Lyle, smiling.

Lyle was transfixed by Eva. Nothing else mattered but her and the promise of candy inside the store.

Morris didn't say a word to Eva, but Josiah was certain he heard the man growl with disapproval as the two passed by. The tall Langdon brother turned and followed after his sister, unhappy about being over-ruled, but unwilling to do anything about it.

Ofelia started to shuffle about, preparing to follow. Luke caught her eye, and said, "Ain't no Mexicans allowed in this store these days, ma'am."

"You wait here," Josiah said to Ofelia. "Billy, you stay out here and keep an eye on things."

"You mean her?" Billy said.

Josiah squared his shoulders, grabbed his Winchester, and climbed down from the wagon. "You have a problem with that?"

"No, sir, I don't." Billy steadied his horse and looked down the empty street, away from Josiah and Ofelia.

"Good. Come on, Luke, let's go inside, get what we need, and get out of here as quick as we can."

"Sounds like a good plan to me, Josiah,"

Luke said. "But it sure does seem awful strange that there's only one Langdon lookin' out for Eva, all things considered."

Josiah stopped, looked around, and saw nothing that concerned him. "I agree, but I don't see anything out of place, do you?"

"Don't mean there ain't eyes on us, though."

"Then why not shoot?" Josiah said.

"That woman is why," Luke said. "You know that as much as I do."

Josiah looked to the door of the mercantile. He'd lost sight of Lyle. "All right, let's get in and out. Billy, keep your eyes peeled and holler if you see anyone coming."

"Sure thing," Billy Pike said, tapping the brim of his hat.

CHAPTER 16

Axel Dansker stood behind the counter, nervous as a bird cornered by a cat. There was no questioning his German roots, or that he was Hugo's son. He was built like a short bull with a trimmed bushy mustache that rested on his lip like his father's had. A bald patch graced the top of his head, and he wore a crisp white apron across his broad chest. His wife, whom Josiah had never met, was nowhere to be seen. Axel's eyes widened when Josiah and Luke walked in the door, and what blood had pooled in his red face vanished as it became apparent that a Langdon and a Halverson were in the store at the same time.

"How can I help you?" Axel said with a quiver in his voice to Josiah and Luke.

Josiah and Luke filled the door, blocking any quick exit. "We're only looking," Josiah said. "Thanks." It was a lie, he was there for supplies, but stocking up for the future was the least of Josiah's concerns.

Axel looked to Morris, preparing to ask him the same question.

Morris jumped in and said, "The same. Only looking. You worry 'bout her. That's all." His hands rested at his sides within an inch or two of the guns in his belt. He wore a Peacemaker on each hip with a full accompaniment of cartridges riding across his waist. With Josiah and Luke carrying one six-shooter apiece, they were a matched pair.

The mercantile was well-lit with the aid of two large windows that fronted the street, and another that sat behind the counter Axel stood at, filling the back of the store with sufficient light. A pair of water-driven ceiling fans spun overhead, circulating the smell of new linen, iron nails, and a slim assortment of vegetables and grains throughout the store. The right side of the store was dedicated to clothing needs, though the shelves were stocked with slim pickings. There looked to be one or two pair of man-sized Levi Strauss pants on the shelf, and the women's dress form stood bare. Reams of material, gingham in various colors, blue, green, and pink, sat on shelves — all free of dust — that were understocked, too. The left side of the store held cooking utensils;

pots, pans, skillets, along with kegs of nails and tools of all sorts. Needs for horses and work animals sat kitty-corner from the nails and hammers. A harness hung on the wall, with a few lengths of leather to be cut into reins dangling from hooks driven into the walls. Soaps and brushes filled out the shelves on that side, while the middle of the store held barrels of grain, rice, and crates of late-season tomatoes and peppers.

The candy aisle fronted the sales counter, and it was there that Eva stood with Lyle, hand in hand, with Lyle trying to decide what he wanted. Josiah was tempted to interfere, and tell the boy to mind his manners, but he restrained himself. There was no sign of any other living creatures in the store other than the humans, but Josiah imagined there was a cat and a family of store mice hiding close by.

Morris stood on the left side of the store, close to the keg of hammers. His position concerned Josiah, and Luke, too, but neither of them worried out loud. They kept Morris in their sight, watching him like he was a rattlesnake sunning himself on a rock. Neither of them was going to provoke a wild creature like Morris. Not with intent, anyway.

Josiah turned his attention to Lyle and

Eva. He stared at her from behind. Even though she was dressed all in black, there was an air of lightness to her. Maybe it was her voice, her gentleness with Lyle, but her presence was a distraction from the discomfort he felt with Morris Langdon in the room. Without Eva there, Josiah would have been inclined to give Morris back what he had given him — a rifle butt in the face. But that kind of behavior wouldn't do in front of a woman, not even a woman named Langdon. Not in front of Lyle, not in front of Eva, no matter how much he wanted retribution.

"I'll have those," Lyle said, pointing to something Josiah couldn't see.

"That's perfect." Eva stood up tall. She had been leaning down to Lyle's height. She opened her bag and produced a small coin purse. "We'll have a nickel's worth of the rock candy, Mr. Dansker."

The man didn't object or try to sell Eva anything else. He hurried to a shelf on his left, pulled out a small bag, then returned and filled it with candy. He didn't weigh it on the scales behind him before handing her the bag. There was no question that he wanted Eva out of the store quickly.

"Go on," Eva said to Lyle, as she dug in her purse, "take it. It's yours."

Lyle didn't need to be told twice. He swiped the bag out of Axel's hands like a hungry little bird taking a desired bit of food from its mother. "Thank you," he said to Axel without having to be prompted.

Axel and Eva said, "You're welcome in unison." Then Axel said, "Will that be all, ma'am?"

"Yes, for now." Eva handed a nickel to Axel, and smiled. She turned to Josiah, preparing to say something, but she was cut off by Morris.

"It's time to go, sister. We should have been home by now."

"Wait a minute, Morris," Eva said.

Morris stepped forward. "No. You've had your fun, for what it's worth." He didn't stop until he was next to Eva, close enough to grab her by the arm. "We're leaving, now."

Angered, Josiah stepped forward, but Luke pulled him back. "Easy there, cowboy," he whispered. "Another time. That's family business."

Josiah relented because he knew that Luke was right. Instead of getting involved, he motioned for Lyle to join him. "Come here, boy. We need to go, too."

Lyle stood looking at Josiah, then to Eva, then back to Josiah. "We just got here."

159

"I know. You can go out and sit with Ofelia while I get the things I need."

"But what about Miss Eva?" Lyle said.

"She has to go home."

"I don't want her to."

Eva put her foot down and made Morris stop. He had dragged her halfway to the door. "I'll see you another day, I promise," she said to Lyle.

"Not if I have anything to do with it," Morris said under his breath, then exited the store, pulling Eva with him.

Josiah hurried to Lyle and took his hand. "Come on."

They followed Morris and Eva out the door, much to Axel Dansker's obvious relief. Bright afternoon sunlight blinded Josiah for a brief second. He shielded his eyes and watched as Morris helped Eva into the buggy. She was red-faced. Josiah didn't know if she was angry, embarrassed, or a little bit of both. Then, much to Josiah's surprise, Morris climbed into the buggy himself, taking a seat to drive. There had been a lone horse and a buggy parked outside of the mercantile when they'd arrived, but the horse was gone.

Lyle tugged on Josiah's sleeve. "Pa?" he said, continuing to tug.

"What?" Josiah said.

"Where's 'Felia?"

Josiah looked to the wagon and found it empty. Billy Pike was gone, too.

He looked around and saw nothing moving, or alive, in the deserted town. Nothing. Not even a crow in the sky. Josiah felt a rush of panic, felt his throat go dry. He looked back to Morris, who was smiling as he urged the horse pulling the buggy into a full run. Panic turned to dread, then fear.

"I think we might've walked into a trap," Josiah said to Luke, who was at his side. "We have to find Ofelia and we need to find her fast."

Chapter 17

Josiah looked to Lyle, then down the empty street. He didn't like being out in the open with the boy. He took Lyle back inside the store and beelined it straight to Axel Dansker. "I need a favor," he said. "I need you to watch my boy for a minute."

A horrified expression crossed Axel's face, then he looked to the right side of the store where a door led to somewhere unknown. Josiah assumed the door was to the living quarters, or where Axel's wife was.

"He's no trouble," Josiah said, then waited a beat. "I don't think it's safe out there. The Langdons are up to something."

Axel's expression changed from horror to uncertainty, like he needed to ask his wife's permission.

"Look," Josiah continued, "I know you don't know much of me, but I knew your pa and I did a lot of business over the years. I trusted him and I'm hoping I can trust you, at least for a short while."

"I remember you, Josiah Wolfe, of course I do, it's just that . . ."

Josiah cut him off. "Please. Guard him with your life. I need to find Ofelia." He didn't give Axel a chance to object. Josiah was to the door before the storekeeper could utter another word.

Josiah stood at the door, taking in the sight of the town, getting his bearings, feeling guilty for leaving Ofelia in Billy Pike's care. Not one of them had been safe since arriving home. Beyond the rifle butt he took to the face, losing the cabin to fire, and now, contemplating life without Ofelia, any anger that Josiah felt exploded into a rage. Once he had Ofelia back safe, they were packing up and heading out. Enough was enough. The thought of losing Ofelia, of raising Lyle without her, would be impossible. An unbearable heartbreak neither of them could withstand.

Josiah spotted Luke a block up the street, looking down alleys, and inside buildings. Not knowing if there were Langdons on the roofs or not, Josiah hugged the side of the buildings until he caught up with Luke.

"Anything?" he said to Luke.

"Not a sign of her or Billy. It's like a giant

bird came out of the sky and picked them up."

"Been better for us if the street was muddy. Make it easier to track them. I don't like this. I don't like this at all."

"I can't say that I do, only 'cause of what that Mexican means to Lyle."

"And to me."

Luke shrugged. "We knew the Langdons were up to something."

"They were waiting for us to make a move."

"And watching. You was bein' watched the whole time you recovered. They're like snakes in the grass, those Langdons. You don't see them 'til you're upon them, 'cause they been waitin' there the whole time, and then it's too late to do anything. I had a bad feelin', but I didn't think they'd take that woman. I thought Billy'd be able to handle anythin' that came his way. At least shout out if he was in trouble."

Josiah stared at Luke, judged his face as he formed a question to ask. One that had to be asked. "You don't think Billy Pike double-crossed us, do you? I know nothing about him, only that he comes from river people. They tend to stay to themselves, not get involved in other folks' troubles, like this feud."

Luke took his hat off and ran his hand through his thick straw-colored hair. Like Lily and the rest of the Halversons, Luke had soft blue eyes, but they hardened at the question. "If he's ridin' with us, we trust him. That simple."

"Sorry," Josiah said, acknowledging the tone in Luke's voice. "I had to ask."

"Look here, I've knowed Billy Pike since he was a schoolboy. Pikes are good church-goin' folk who take readin' and writin' serious. They's not idiots 'cause they live on the river. Anything but. Billy comes from good people. He wouldn't betray me or Pa. Besides, they got their reasons to rise up against the Langdons. They been beat up and stole from like the rest of us. Ethan Langdon wants a piece of the river trade as much as he wants the land we're standin' on."

"Every penny counts."

"As long as they don't have to work for it."

"Okay," Josiah said. "If Ofelia's in trouble, so is Billy. I should have known better. She killed Gordy. The Langdons got a good reason to want to harm her."

"For their kind of justice."

"If you want to call it that. If they're the judge and jury, Ofelia won't have a chance.

165

We have to find her," Josiah said. "Damn it, I should have known something was wrong. I assumed the horse was Morris's and that Eva was driving the buggy. Somebody was hiding, holding back."

"I told you, they knew we were coming."

Josiah almost disagreed. He did not want to believe that Eva was part of a setup. But if he was being honest with himself, he didn't know Eva any more than she knew him. All Josiah knew was that she was good with Lyle, and that the boy liked her. Lyle wasn't old enough to be a fair judge of character. "I think you're right," he said, keeping his disappointment to himself.

"We should split up," Luke said. "I'll take the streets, if you want to start checking the buildings. I don't think they're far."

"Agreed."

"I'll whistle if I come across something."

"Same here," Josiah said.

He watched Luke disappear across the street, then ease out of sight down the alleyway, between the livery and the old smithy shop.

He pulled his Peacemaker out of the holster, then made his way back to the vacant hotel, keeping his eyes on alert for anything that moved. His mind, though, turned back to Ofelia. He couldn't imagine life without her. Lyle would be bereft, and Josiah would be lost. He had come to depend on the Mexican woman far more than he had realized. If he were a praying man, this would be time to appeal to a higher power, but any belief beyond the real world, what stood in front of him, able to be touched, had been lost when the preacher man from Tyler wouldn't step foot inside the cabin when Lily was sick.

Josiah made his way to the hotel without seeing anyone, or anything, move at all. At one time, the Seer House had been a decent hotel, one of a handful in this part of Anderson County, but like everything else, it had gone downhill once the railroad deal had fallen through. To make things even worse, the stagecoach route carrying mail and passengers had been changed, too. With no influx of outsiders bringing commerce of any kind to the town, it was no wonder that all but the essentials had dried up.

Josiah swept the doorway of the hotel with the Peacemaker. A foul smell assailed him. Something had crawled inside and died there. A raccoon, or maybe a whole colony of mice. He looked around, but didn't see anything obvious. The main hall of the two-story building had never been grand. It was meant to be more functional than anything else. A clerk's desk stood empty at the forefront, and a staircase with broken newel posts and missing spindles ascended each side of the open room. Doors to the guest rooms overlooked the entry. Some stood open, but most of them were closed. A chandelier hung from the ceiling in a tilt, with most of the crystals gone, or so dirty that they looked like black diamonds. Dust and cobwebs covered everything — which as it turned out, made it easy to see a fresh pair of boot prints that had stumbled and scuffed across the floor. Drops of fresh blood gave a hint that someone had entered the hotel.

Josiah raised his weapon, a cartridge already in the chamber, and started to follow the blood trail. A groan from behind the clerk's desk stopped his trek. He listened and looked around again, aware that he could be walking straight into another trap. Even the cries of a hurt man couldn't be trusted.

There was nothing to see that gave Josiah reason to pause any longer, so he made his way to the desk with caution. The blood grew brighter, and pooled into a puddle.

"I'm coming around," Josiah said, as he opened the gate to let himself behind the desk. It only took a second to see a man, balled up in the corner, seeking shelter, holding his stomach. His shirt was blood-soaked, and his face and eyes were pale. It was Billy Pike, suffering from a stab wound.

"Wolfe," Billy whispered. "Where you been?"

Josiah kneeled next to the man, almost certain that there was little he could do to help him. "Looking for you. Are you alone?"

"They snuck up on me, pulled me off my horse and stabbed me on the way down."

"What happened to Ofelia?"

"They carried me inside here and left me for dead."

"They?"

"Langdons. Two of the brothers. Earnest and Forrest."

"Ofelia? What happened to Ofelia?"

Billy coughed and grabbed his stomach like he had been stabbed again. A spittle of blood dripped out of the corner of his mouth. "I don't know. I didn't see much after I got stabbed. I heard 'em talking though, heard 'em say they were gonna give her what was comin' to her for killin' Gordy."

"Did they say what that was?" Josiah said.

"Yeah," Billy answered. "They said they were gonna hang her."

CHAPTER 18

Billy Pike died wide-eyed with a painful gasp, followed by a short wheeze that Josiah had heard more times than he cared to count. There was nothing left for him to do but lay Billy out on his back, and close his eyes. Getting the body home to the Pike family would have to come later.

How many more people have to die? Josiah wondered to himself as he doffed his hat in respect. He made his way to the door without looking back, anxious to leave the sight of death behind.

He checked that the street was clear, his gun ready. A quick glance to the mercantile told him nothing had changed there. No new horses or wagons had arrived. He worried about Lyle inside with a stranger, but he had to hold on to the hope that Axel Dansker and his wife were good people. His stomach was tied up in knots with worry, but that was a chronic ailment of late.

There was no sign of Luke, so Josiah whistled twice and waited for a reply. It only took Luke a second to respond. A similar two-note trill came back to Josiah like he was a bird of the same feather with Luke. It was a relief to know that Luke was okay.

Josiah stayed put inside the doorway of the Seer House, eyeing the distressed buildings close by, on alert for anything that looked out of place. While he waited for Luke to join him, images of Ofelia hanging from a tree turned his focus inward and terrorized Josiah's mind. He couldn't help but wonder if she was already dead, if there was no saving her. It wasn't long before Luke popped out of an alleyway two blocks down the street, then made his way to Josiah, wary all the way. Nothing puts a man on edge like knowing the next breath he takes might be his last. A gunshot could come from anywhere, at any second.

"I got bad news and more bad news," Josiah said, as Luke stepped into the outside foyer of the Seer House.

"I don't like the sound of that."

"Billy Pike's dead. They stabbed him, then carried him inside the hotel so he'd be out of sight."

"Damn it. He was a good man. His momma's gonna be heartbroken. He still inside?"

Luke asked as he flicked his head toward the door.

"I didn't figure we could do much for him," Josiah said.

"You're right. What's the rest of the bad news?"

"They've got Ofelia. They're going to hang her."

Luke looked away from Josiah for a second. "I was afraid of that. They were waiting for an opening. Now, I'm worried about Pa. I bet they've got more plans than hangin' that Mexican woman. They might be attackin' the home place right now. We're distracted here, makin' Pa two men short."

Josiah could have objected to Luke's count. He hadn't committed to riding with the Halversons. It was an assumption on Luke's part, and Josiah understood why — but Luke was making a mistake thinking that sides had been taken. That discussion could come later.

"No way to know what's going on beyond here," Josiah said. "But we've got to find Ofelia before it's too late. There have to be tracks out of town. There's no way they could have carried her off without leaving some sort of a sign."

"They had this one thought out," Luke said. "We didn't hear a thing while we was inside Dansker's store."

Josiah agreed, even though he didn't want to. He still wondered how Eva played into all of this. It was looking more and more like she was involved, or at the least, had to know that something was going to happen. He hoped he was wrong, but his gut told him different.

"If you were going to hang someone close by, where it would be, Luke?" Josiah said. "Is there anywhere that you can think of where they might run straight to? I don't think they're going to wait around to do this horrible deed. No trial. No waiting for a judge to convict her to the gallows for killing Gordy. I think they're going to want to get the deed done as soon as they can. We might already be too late the way it is."

"They had a rope ready. I don't know where, though. The river's not too far away. There's a couple of old live oaks that sit off the road south of town. Some tall sycamores stand closer to the water. Those ol' sycamore limbs could hold a person on the end of a rope, and they'd be more out of sight than the oaks along the road. I'd say that's where we need to ride, 'cause I think you're right. They're not gonna go far. The need for revenge for Gordy's death is strong, and once they got her, hangin' her'll be all that matters."

They both holstered their six-shooters at the same time and hurried to the horses. Josiah took Billy's ride. He considered diving into the store and telling Axel Dansker what his plans were, but there was no time to spare.

The mercantile sat at the south end of town along with a few other buildings. A rise in the land provided some safety from the Neches River as it cut past Seerville. Beyond town, the land eased down into a flat plain of useless ground that caught the floodwaters in the spring.

Jonathon Seer had put some thought into the location of the buildings that he'd bet would attract settlers and commerce, but the wisdom of placement wasn't enough to ensure the town's success.

Josiah and Luke sped out of town on their horses, knowing full well that they were moving targets. They were betting that all of the Langdons had gone off to the hanging once Ofelia had been abducted.

Both men focused their eyes on the ground in search of a sign of passage. It wasn't long before they came upon the deep running tracks of two horses, followed by the obvious tracks made by a buggy. A pile of fresh horse apples gave away the riders' presence, though at this point, it didn't look like they were too concerned about hiding themselves.

Josiah brought his horse to a stop, jumped off, and examined the tracks. Luke stayed on his horse. The horse tracks veered off the road into the floodplain, but to Josiah's dismay, the buggy tracks kept on going.

"If we keep going, we're riding straight to our deaths, Wolfe," Luke said.

"If we don't ride after those tracks, Ofelia dies. Looks like there's two men. We can handle them."

"What makes you so sure that the Mexican ain't already dead?"

"Nothing but hope."

"I guess you've got to hold onto something."

Josiah looked to the sky as a gathering of crows lit into the air out of the tops of a tall stand of hardwoods. "We might not be too late," he said.

"I say we ride back to the house and get Pa to man us with some reinforcements."

"There's not time." Josiah turned his focus back to Luke. "You don't have to do this if you don't want to. I understand. Ofelia's not your charge, but she's mine. You can go on home. This is my problem. I'm willing to die trying to save Ofelia. You don't feel the way I do about her. There's no way you can."

"Runnin' off ain't that easy. My job's to keep you alive. No matter how much of a grudge Pa holds again' you, he don't want that boy of yours to grow up an orphan."

"I should be grateful for that." Josiah stood up and looked after the tracks. The ground wasn't rock hard, but it wasn't soft and wet, either. Still, tracking the two horses shouldn't be too hard. The horses were riding hard, not doing anything to cover themselves. It looked like the riders didn't have a second to spare. Neither did Josiah. He jumped onto his horse's back and urged him into a full run, without saying another word to Luke. He could stay or go, it didn't matter to Josiah. He was going after the riders, regardless.

The floodplain was filled with small trees bare of leaves, and some taller birches that could tolerate the occasional flood. It was a fifty-yard ride to the stand of taller trees, pines with a grove of oaks mixed in the glade, along with the sycamores that Luke had mentioned. Josiah looked over his shoulder and saw that Luke was following him.

Josiah slowed his horse once he got to the

edge of the forest. He could still see the tracks, but something caught his eye that made him stop. He didn't need to jump off to clarify what he was seeing. Luke eased up alongside Josiah. "Looks like a lot of men," Luke said.

Josiah agreed. "They came in from the north, behind the town. We wouldn't have seen them." There were so many horses' tracks that the ground was mashed into a grassy pulp. "I'd guess it's the rest of the Langdons, come to see the hanging."

Luke held a worried look on his face. "They've added to their numbers, then."

"I'm still going in," Josiah said.

"They got us twenty to one. Even on a good day those are a dead man's odds."

Josiah wasn't going to tell Luke, again, that he didn't have to come along. He nickered his mount and followed the tracks at a cautious, steady pace.

The October air had pushed a lot of leaves to the ground, but the tracks were so plentiful that there was nothing that could have obscured them. Josiah tracked the group of horses without any trouble, staying alert with his rifle in hand, ready to defend himself at any second.

There were no birdsongs close by. The crows had flown off and left the place to silence. Not even a cricket chirped. Man and beast were about, which meant that most creatures had gone into hiding. A thousand pair of eyes watched the two men ride toward the river, both of them looking for the tracks to stop, or a sycamore that looked to be a good hanging tree.

It didn't take long for the river to come into view. It was only about thirty feet wide and ran shallow around a slight bend. The trees thinned out, and stands of weeds grew everywhere. All of them were in the process of browning out from lack of sun, and the end of the growing season. Any flowers had already bloomed. The smell of dead fish hit Josiah's nose, and for a minute he allowed himself to consider again that he was too late, that Ofelia had met her maker. The thought was reinforced when he rode around the next bend and the horse tracks stopped in a clearing.

The ground was covered with brittle brown sycamore leaves the size of pie plates. There was no one in sight. The soothing sound of water trickled over rocks as the river moved south. A few birds skittered about.

Like Luke had predicted, a tall sycamore stood lurched over the river. The limbs that jutted out of the tree were the size of a good hog, and the trunk itself looked like it had a ten-foot radius. It was a giant tree, and must have reached well over a hundred feet into the air. It was the biggest tree Josiah had ever seen.

A rope dangled from the lowest branch. It looked strong enough to hold twenty men, let alone one Mexican woman. The noose was empty and there was no sign of Ofelia anywhere.

CHAPTER 19

Josiah sat in the saddle staring at the empty noose. His mount swished its tail without worry and held his head high. A thin cloud of tiny flies drifted past them, offering the first real sight of life since Josiah and Luke had entered the forest. The insects were silent and uninterested in attacking.

The movement drew Josiah's sorrowful attention away from the noose. He watched the cloud disappear into the thickets that pushed deeper into the trees. Birds flittered in the canopy, too high to make out what they were — only that life was returning to normal, even with the presence of men. On cue, the harmonizing saw of a cricket's leg added a subtle hum to the ground.

Luke's face was blank, void of emotion or surprise. "I'm sorry, Wolfe," he said.

"For what?"

"We're too late."

"You don't know that."

"Seems plain as day to me. There's deep tracks under the branch, and the group of riders moved off north, toward the Langdons. Doesn't get any plainer than that to me. They hung her then headed home."

"Where's the body, then?"

"In the river for all I know."

Josiah didn't wait to consider anything else. He moved Billy's horse under the branch, then around the sycamore, looking for anything that would dispute Luke's theory. He found nothing other than the tracks. From there, Josiah made his way to the riverbank.

There were no human tracks beyond the tree. The mud along the river was dotted with raccoon tracks, and an occasional wading bird. The water was clear, and shallow enough to see the sandy bottom. He didn't even see a fish, let alone a body. The current was too slow to whisk Ofelia out of sight. The river ran slow, lazy, wore out by the fury of spring and summer.

With no sighting of Ofelia anywhere, Josiah made his way back to Luke. "Nothing there. They took her with them."

"Why would they do that?"

"I don't know, but I aim to find out." Josiah pulled the horse's reins to the right, and proceeded to ease by Luke, determined to find Ofelia alive.

"You're gonna ride onto Langdons' land and help yourself to a look-see, are you?" Luke chuckled with some spite in his throat. "You're crazier than I thought you were."

"Maybe so, but until I see Ofelia's dead body, I'm not going to believe that she's gone from us." He kept on going, keeping his eyes to the ground, following the heavy, prolific tracks as he went.

Luke followed along even though it was apparent that he didn't want to. He muttered something unintelligible as he rode, adding his voice to the cricket's lament.

The tracks were easy to follow inside the forest. A game trail had been widened to accommodate two horses, side by side, creating a path of tramped down weeds and turned up mud. The riders were in no hurry, moving along at a steady pace, not concerned about being discreet. They didn't seem to care about being found or followed, which led Josiah to believe that Luke was right. It was the Langdons he was after. Maybe it was Morris taking Ofelia's dead body home to show to Ethan as proof that the deed was done. Made sense, but it seemed risky carrying Ofelia out in the open. Maybe that explained why the riders hadn't made any attempt to flee the forest.

Luke rode head-to-head with Josiah, silent as they followed the trail. "There's a sandbar upriver about a quarter mile," he said. "Be a good place for a group this size to water their horses if there's a need."

"They aren't that far from home."

"Just sayin' is all. Our horses could use a sip."

"You're right." Josiah glanced over and caught the dreadful look that hung on Luke's face. "I'm not convinced we're going to die today."

Luke stiffened in his saddle. "I worry about that every day. You should, too, all things considered."

"I've been in worse situations than this."

"You miss your old life?"

"It's not that old really," Josiah answered. "This part of my life doesn't feel new. Something I wasn't expecting is all."

"I thought about leavin' here before, you know. But I couldn't leave Pa after Ma died. He took that loss hard. I know he would have never forgiven me. Hell, it might've killed him off the way I see it."

"So you stay for him."

"Can't leave him to face these troubles on his own. But I got dreams of my own. I know the world's a bigger place than I'll ever see. That don't stop me from wantin' to see it."

"Everything started with the Langdons after your ma died?"

"Pretty much. Things got dicey after Charlie got his due. Langdons blamed you, but you wasn't around to take nothin' out on, so they chose us since you was married to our Lily. It was a good enough reason for them. That was when Pa and Ethan started gatherin' abandoned property, tryin' to get as much territory of their own to keep the others out."

"So Leland blames me for everything bad that's happened to him?"

"Pretty much," Luke said.

"Good to know."

As they rounded a bend in the trail that pulled deeper into the forest, Josiah heard the whinny of a horse. The cry echoed throughout the woods unseen, but left no mistake as to what it was. He pulled up on the reins and brought his horse to a stop. Luke did the same.

"Sounds like your watering hole might be full up," Josiah whispered.

"We're outnumbered. I say we tie up the horses here and take a look to see what we're up against."

"Sounds like a good plan." Josiah dis-

184

mounted, and tied Billy Pike's horse to the closest substantial tree.

It was only a matter of seconds before Luke was on his feet, standing next to Josiah, ready to go.

"You know the way," Josiah said, holding back, allowing Luke to take the lead.

Luke hesitated for a second and loaded his Henry. He pulled a tab up the barrel that opened up the tube, then slid a few rimfire .44 cartridges in and closed the tube. "Guns are ready to go," he said, tapping the Peacemaker on his side. "You?"

Josiah had his Winchester in hand. He gave a quick drop of his chin to answer Luke's question, then motioned for him to move on.

Luke eased into the woods with quiet confidence, easing past a tall dried pokeweed plant, and a small patch of foxglove without knocking off a leaf. Josiah wasn't as adept at such easy movement, but he tried his best to imitate Luke. More flies and mosquitoes seemed to be present the closer they got to the river, making it more difficult to maintain silence and move undetected.

They both crouched low to the ground. The October air was cool, and the sun was distant, as a patch of thick gray clouds covered the sky. That didn't stop Josiah from sweating. He was nervous, they were outmanned, and if he was being honest with himself, he had no plan to rescue Ofelia. They'd have to figure something out once they saw that she was still alive.

Cockleburs attached themselves to his pants and shirt, and swiping at the no-see-ums threatened to give the two men away. They heard a murmur of voices as they drew close to the river, causing them to slow down. Luke held back and let Josiah catch up so they were shoulder to shoulder. It was not long before they could see movement along the river. Men rambling about at the sandbar, watering their horses. Josiah motioned for Luke to drop to the ground, then did the same. They crawled forward as quietly and carefully as possible.

It took longer for them to get a good view of the men than Josiah thought it would. By the time they reached a good spot, the men were starting to pull the horses off the water, preparing them for more riding. Luke drew a bead on one of the men with his rifle before Josiah realized what he was doing.

"Wait," he whispered with authority. "We don't know who these men are. You can't go shooting them for nothing."

"Only good Langdon is a dead Langdon."

"I don't see a Langdon. I can't make out any of the men." With that, Josiah moved a little closer. He blinked sweat out of his burning eyes and focused on the small group of men. But it was more than men. There was a woman standing next to a shorter man, who held himself with some pride and position.

Josiah recognized them both. His heart lightened when he realized that Ofelia was still alive. But more than lightened, he was relieved to realize that the group of men were not Langdons. They were Texas Rangers. Special Forces Texas Rangers. And Ofelia was standing next to Captain Leander McNelly, one of the most formidable men Josiah had ever met and had the pleasure of riding with.

CHAPTER 20

Josiah motioned for Luke to join him, but the man seemed hesitant to breathe, let alone move. "They're Rangers. I know them. Ofelia is alive." There was a relief and joy in Josiah's voice that was hard to contain, but he still spoke in a whisper.

Luke shook his head. "Can't be sure."

"I'm sure. We have nothing to fear." Josiah started to pull himself up off the ground.

"I don't like this." Luke drew back, looking over his shoulder, back to the way they'd come.

Josiah didn't have anything else to say to Luke. He knew what he was seeing. He'd know Leander McNelly from a hundred yards away. The man was short, dressed in as close to a uniform as a Ranger would wear, black riding boots that cupped at the knee, fresh laundered gray trousers held up by a hefty gun belt fully stocked with Colt revolvers, a thick linen shirt that matched the color of his pants, along with a white Stetson squared atop his head. The lower half of his face was obscured by a thick, wavy dark brown goatee, and no matter the situation, McNelly wore serious eyes. He had suffered from consumption as a child, which was what had precipitated a move west by his parents. When the call of duty came to fight in the War Between the States, McNelly took up the cause with vigor. He'd served as General Thomas Green's aide, and never missed a day of battle in four years, even when he was wounded in the Battle of Mansfield. His men held him in high regard for his fortitude, and McNelly had little use for malingerers, or laziness in general. When Governor Coke took over in Texas and created the Frontier Battalion, he'd handpicked McNelly to head up the Special Forces — of which Josiah had been a member until he resigned and came home. McNelly had put an end to the bloody Sutton-Taylor feud straightaway, and then gone after the notorious Mexican cattle rustler, Juan Cortina. It took little consideration to understand why McNelly, and his men, would be in Anderson County with everything that had been going on, including the killing of Sheriff Cliburn. One more reason for Josiah to relax. He stood up the rest of the way, certain of his own action. Luke would have to decide what to do on his own.

The rustle of the weeds drew McNelly's attention to the thickness of the forest. Instinct showed itself in a reach, as his hand swept to the gun in his holster, most likely a Colt Single Action Army — a Peacemaker — from the looks of it. The captain was twenty yards away from Josiah, well within the pistol's range. A man of McNelly's skill should never be underestimated. Josiah knew better. He raised both hands in the air, the right one handling the rifle with the barrel pointed to the ground, showing clearly that he wasn't a threat.

"I mean no harm," Josiah called out. "It's me, Wolfe. Josiah Wolfe."

Every man in the crowd was aware of Josiah's presence, and not only did he have McNelly's barrel pointed at him, there were twenty more that had turned on him. That didn't stop Josiah. He took slow, measured steps forward, hoping to make it out of the weeds to show that he wasn't a threat. A quick glance behind him told him that he was alone. Luke was gone. That disappointed Josiah, but he wasn't surprised. The bet was, Luke was hightailing it home to tell Leland that the Rangers had arrived in the county.

"Stop right there," McNelly countered. "And drop your weapon." His voice sounded weak, and his words were followed by a familiar wheeze.

Josiah obeyed. He was about ten feet from the edge of the weeds. He laid the Winchester down at his feet, then stood tall, reaching to the sky, not breaking eye contact with the captain.

Ofelia's attention had been drawn by the commotion, too, and a look of relief crossed her face when she saw Josiah. She angled her head and uttered something soft to McNelly.

"Come on in, Wolfe," McNelly said, after listening to the woman.

A man Josiah recognized broke from the group and walked over to join McNelly. It was Verlyn "Doc" Tinker, a healer who rode with the company. Tinker had never been schooled as a doctor, but he had the touch and knowledge to restore a man from a snake bite, a gunshot, and a host of other calamities that might befall a Ranger on duty.

Tinker was fifteen years older than Josiah, which made him about fifty, and was tall with stooped shoulders and a narrow face. Josiah had liked Tinker from the day they'd met. The man was as honest as any man he'd ever met, and when solicited, the doc doled out reasonable advice. It had been Tinker who had prompted Josiah to leave the Rangers, citing the obvious, that his heart wasn't in it any longer. "Maybe," Tinker had said, "It is time to go home." At the time, Josiah agreed, but now he wasn't so sure.

Josiah walked toward the captain, who was now surrounded by men. Ofelia and Tinker stood at the captain's side. There were other faces Josiah recognized. It hadn't been that long since he'd ridden with them, all going after Cortina on the Red Raid. Tom Darkson was there. He was a boy no more than twenty, if that, young and impetuous, and had helped Josiah bring his friend Juan Carlos's body back to Austin for burial in the family plot. There were new faces in the crowd, too. That wasn't unusual. Men came and went from the company all of the time. But the one he was looking for was not there. He had assumed that Scrap Elliot was still riding with the captain. There was no sign of him. Josiah had ridden with Scrap on a lot of missions. They'd taken on the Kiowa and Comanche, set about some spying work on the coast, and did their darnedest to capture Cortina. But that hadn't happened. Scrap, whose real name was Robert Earl, could be contrary, stubborn, impetuous, and a whole list of other things that got under Josiah's skin. But Scrap Elliot was the closest friend he'd made while he was riding with the Rangers. They'd worked well together.

The crowd of men swayed and moved as another man made his way through from the back of the pack. Josiah didn't recognize him either. The man damn near pushed Tinker out of the way. He was robust, had a belly shaped like a beer keg, a wily gray beard, and wore a faded ten-gallon black hat that was in tatters. More important was the silver star pinned on his chest. He was a lawman. Maybe the new county sheriff, or something else. Josiah wasn't sure.

Josiah continued to walk toward the captain, then stopped before him and offered his hand for a shake. To his surprise and relief, the captain responded in kind.

"You're the last person I expected to see climbing out of those woods, Wolfe." McNelly's grip was tight and short. He let go right away, but he'd searched Josiah's eyes, looking for something unsaid.

Ofelia stared at Josiah, her eyes warm, with the same kind of relief that he had felt upon seeing her. It was then that he saw a red rash ringed around the Mexican woman's neck. There was no mistaking a rope burn. The captain and his men had arrived in time to save her from hanging. He was curious of the details, but that would have to wait.

"Who is this man?" the man with the silver star said.

"I'm Josiah Wolfe," he said, answering quick so he could speak for himself.

"I've heard of you. You're one of them Halversons." The man looked him up and down, then spit a hefty splat of tobacco juice to the ground. It splashed over the toe of Josiah's boot.

"I'm not a Halverson," Josiah said. "I'm not now and I never have been. I was married to a Halverson is all. She's been dead and gone for three years and I've been away from here as long. I rode in less than a week ago. Now that I've told you who I am, who are you?"

"Chester Busser. New sheriff of Anderson County, thank you very much," the man said. He didn't offer Josiah his hand to shake. Busser sneered at him. His breath smelled sour as he shifted the wad of tobacco from one cheek to the other, and chomped his molars together to show some anger or toughness, Josiah wasn't sure which. He'd never heard of or seen Chester Busser before, and knew nothing of the man's character or standing. For all he knew, Busser was a flunky deputy who had been moved into the empty sheriff's spot to fill a hole. The man looked like he had a lot to prove to the world.

Josiah did extend his hand. "Nice to meet you, Sheriff." But Busser didn't take it. He stared at Josiah's hand like it was infected with some kind of fatal disease. It only took Josiah a second to realize that the sheriff was not going to reciprocate the offer of manners and kindness, so he withdrew his hand, and dropped it to his side.

"You was there when Sheriff Cliburn was murdered in cold blood," Busser said.

"I was, but I had nothing to do with that. I was riding into town and I got caught up in the shooting. I had to take cover in the house is all."

"With Leland and Luke Halverson." It wasn't a question. It was a statement.

Josiah felt uncomfortable. There were twenty pairs of eyes staring at him, hanging on every word he said. It was the same kind of vacuum of silence that came before the shooting started.

"I had nothing to do with that. You can ask any of the men there."

Busser put his fatty, skillet-sized hand up to stop Josiah from talking. "You can save your sniveling for the trial."

"Trial? What do mean trial. Am I under arrest?"

"Now that you mention it, yes, you are. Josiah Wolfe, you're under arrest for the murder of Sheriff Howard Cliburn."

CHAPTER 21

Josiah's mouth went dry as he considered protesting the charge against him. He said nothing though, as a quick look to Captain McNelly told him that he would find no sympathy with the Rangers. A vibration of coughs and discomfort rode a wave through the company of men that stood in wait, watching every move made. Tom Darkson looked away. Doc Tinker shook his head in disbelief, and Ofelia wore a shocked expression on her face.

"Circuit judge is on his way here," Busser stated with a smile. What was left of his teeth were tobacco-stained, but the sheriff didn't seem worried or ashamed of himself in any way. "You won't have to wait long for your judgment, Wolfe."

"You're mistaken," Josiah said.

"I told you, save it for the trial. You'll have company soon. We're rounding up every man in the county who participated in the assault." Busser almost banged his chin against his chest, putting an exclamation on his final word. "We'll worry about separating the wheat from the chaff later. You people need to know there's a new sheriff in the county."

Josiah thought if this man puffed himself up an inch more he'd explode.

"Excuse me," McNelly said, stepping between Josiah and the sheriff. "But where do you plan on housing all of these men you're rounding up?"

Busser looked surprised at the question. "There's a jail in Seerville."

"Excuse me, sir," Josiah said to McNelly. "There are two cells in the marshal's office and the building is in poor repair from what I saw. A man with little skill could escape the confines without much trouble. There was nigh on twenty or so men at the shooting that day. There's not room to hold them all."

McNelly stared at Josiah with thought, then turned his attention back to Busser. "It is our duty to keep the citizenship safe while we're here, and to make sure that the principles in this dispute, Ethan Langdon, Leland Halverson, and the witnesses against them, if those men are duly charged, stay alive until the judge arrives and a trial is put forth. My men are not jailers. If it is your intention to jail every man who was at this assault, then you will have to take that upon yourself, and use county means to do so. Am I clear?"

Busser's face deflated as he turned his gaze away from the captain. No one else offered a word. They knew better than to interfere with McNelly and his handling of the business at hand. The air was still. Only the sound of the slow-running river could be heard.

"I only have a few deputies. We lost three men to injuries and death," Busser said, then stammered as he spoke again. "I'm new at this. I thought since you was Rangers, that you would do as I saw fit."

"We are here to serve the people of Texas, sir," McNelly said. "Not serve as employees of the county. We were asked to be here and I've stated our duty without question."

"You have. I understand." Busser looked like a child sent to a corner for misbehaving.

"One other thing, Sheriff. I know Wolfe as a man of character. He has a fine reputation as a former Ranger and I have ridden with him on various missions. I would suggest that you rethink the arrest, or at the least, place him in my custody. I will be responsible for his actions until he has the opportunity to speak to the judge at the trial. But I do this only after Wolfe himself swears to me that his words are the truth, that he is innocent in this matter." McNelly coughed, then wheezed as he held eye contact with Josiah. It had been a long string of words put together. The captain needed time to catch his breath.

"You have my word, Captain McNelly. I had nothing to do with Sheriff Cliburn's death. I was there by happenstance, and that is it," Josiah said.

"That is good enough for me," McNelly said. "We need to ride. The longer we stand here fiddling around, the more trouble can come to the county. Do you have a mount, Wolfe?"

"Yes, it's not far from here."

"Darkson," McNelly called out.

"Yes, sir," Darkson answered, separating himself from the crowd, making his way to the captain.

"Go with Wolfe to retrieve his horse, then meet back up with us on the main road."

"Yes, sir," Tom Darkson said. "Come on, Wolfe, let's go."

Josiah hesitated, not wanting to leave Ofelia behind again. McNelly picked up on the concern, and said, "She's safe with us,

Wolfe. Go on."

"Lead the way, Wolfe," Tom Darkson said.

Josiah didn't waste a second getting far away from Sheriff Busser.

They walked up the game trail about twenty yards before either man said anything. It was Darkson who spoke first. "Boy, you got lucky back there. Captain steppin' up for you was something. That sheriff's been a pain in his side right off, actin' like he has the power to boss us all around. McNelly ain't havin' that. None of us are. Not even you, Wolfe. Good to see you again, by the way."

"I'm not feeling real lucky of late, but it's a pleasure to lay eyes on you and the entire company — though there seems to be a shortage of you."

"Captain broke us off in thirds. The other fellas are cornerin' the heads of the families."

"Leland Halverson and Ethan Langdon?"

"Yup."

"Makes sense." Josiah was leading the way. He'd stopped and picked up the Winchester. "I'm worried that each unit won't be enough, though."

"Hell comes down in a fury to the man who underestimates the force and will of

201

twenty Rangers. Those fellas that was about to hang that Mexican woman took to runnin' real quick once they realized what they was up against. We showed up just in time."

"I'm happy you did. I wish you would have caught those responsible. Langdons, I'm sure of it. She killed one of their men in self-defense so they've got a score to settle."

"Scrap Elliot and a few other men tore out after them. That fella can make a horse fly like it's got wings. If anybody can catch 'em, Scrap can."

Scrap Elliot rode a blue roan mare that he called Missy. The boy — which is what Josiah continued to consider Scrap, even though he was in his early twenties — was a fine horseman. Even though the captain forbade it, when the boys were bored and had some time on their hands, they raced each other on horseback. Bets were on Scrap when he was in the mix. He had a thick wad of savings from those dealings. Josiah envied the skill Scrap had with horses.

"Well," Josiah said, "that makes me feel a little better. But those Langdons don't fear the Rangers' reputation near as much as the normal man. I'm not sure that Leland Halverson has all his senses about him, either, right now. Both men are stubborn mules and won't stop until the other is dead. Fact is that you fellas are here whether they fear you or not. A company of Rangers ought to calm things down, even if there's little law to be found with the new sheriff."

"You regret walkin' away, Wolfe?" Darkson said.

Josiah pushed through a low thicket of brambles and could see Billy Pike's mount standing right where he'd left it. He wouldn't have been surprised if Luke had taken the horse, or untied it and set it free. But he hadn't.

"I thought it was time to come home," Josiah said. "And maybe it still is. I didn't know what I was walking into, what kind of trouble had flared up since I'd been away. I liked riding with you fellas, but I got a child to rear and most all of you don't have that worry."

"Because it's again' the rules, is why. Men with families are turned away ten to one. I was surprised you rode with us when you did."

"Captain Fikes made an exception for me," Josiah said, thinking back to the time when he'd become a Ranger. He had given up on life, was in a deep, gray mood after the loss of Lily and the girls. Fikes had reached out to Josiah with an offer to escort Charlie Langdon to jail, which as it turned out, was a bad thing for Fikes, since Charlie had killed him in the end. "He shouldn't have," Josiah continued, "all things considered, but it's good that he did. After Fikes died, I stayed on because I liked the adventure and life on the trail. I felt useful in a way I hadn't since the war. And I had Ofelia to watch after my boy. But as things wore on, I could see how hard my life as a Ranger was on Lyle. But, yes, sir, I do kind of regret leaving the company. At least the way things worked out."

"Well, it ain't been the same since you been gone. Elliot's been more contrary than ever. Touchy as a sunburned skunk if you ask me. You kept him in check."

"Good to know." Josiah reached Pike's horse, untied it, and started to lead it out of the forest. Tom Darkson fell behind watching the rear as they went.

For the first time in days, Josiah felt comfortable walking out into the open. It heartened him to know that the Rangers were local now, on duty to set things straight. It might take some time, but there was no doubt in Josiah's mind that life in Anderson County was about to take a turn for the better.

CHAPTER 22

They rode into Seerville three abreast. There was no crowd of people to welcome the Rangers to town, no marshal to see to their needs, no celebration for the promise of peace. The town was as empty as it had been when Josiah had ridden out in search of Ofelia. A lone crow sat uninterested on the roof of the Seer House.

Nothing had changed, which was a relief to Josiah. His buckboard sat in front of the mercantile, with no other horses in sight. There was no sign that any other riders had passed through town in his absence. He could only hope that the Danskers had been able to keep a close eye on Lyle.

Josiah rode next to Captain McNelly, and Ofelia rode on one of the Ranger's horses behind him. A fella named Paul Dobson rode on the other side of McNelly. Dobson was a new sergeant who had come to the Special Forces from Company A. From what Josiah could tell, Dobson was a no-nonsense kind of man, who like him, was older than the rest of the boys, and had accumulated military experience in the War Between the States.

Josiah didn't feel as vulnerable riding into town with the Rangers as he had with Luke and Billy Pike, but he still kept an eye on the roofs as he loped into town on Pike's horse. Most everyone was quiet, minding their own p's and q's, eyes alert, with their rifles in their laps.

The whole company slowed to a stop in front of the mercantile. Josiah eased his horse to the hitching post, dismounted, and secured the gelding. "There's a body in the hotel," Josiah said to McNelly. "I'll need to deliver the bad news to his family."

The captain tipped his hat, and cast a quick glance to the hotel doorway. "Been plenty of bad news to go around from what I hear."

"Too much of it for my taste." Josiah looked over his shoulder to the mercantile. "I could use a man or two to see us home, if you have them to spare, Captain. I have made foes on both sides of this feud, I fear, and I have the safety of my young son to consider."

"We've yet to set up camp, but I can send

Darkson along with you. One Ranger ought to be enough to see you home. I'm confident of your skills, Wolfe."

"Any idea where you're pitching camp?"

"First good place we see that doesn't sit on the land spoken for in this feud."

Josiah considered what the captain said, then offered, "My place sits between Langdon and Halverson land, sir. There's a running creek nearby for water and plenty of room if you'd like to take that into consideration."

McNelly stared at Josiah with contemplative eyes. "We'll take a look. Go retrieve your boy, then we'll ride along to see if your place suits our needs."

"Thank you, sir." Josiah checked that Ofelia was secure. She was already off the horse making her way to the wagon. Satisfied, Josiah headed inside the mercantile.

At first he didn't see anyone, which alarmed him.

Axel Dansker popped up from behind the counter, and a look of relief crossed his face. "It's okay," he said, looking down. "It's your papa."

Lyle ran out from behind the counter and jumped into Josiah's arms. The boy was reticent to show affection to Josiah, but there was no hesitation this time. Josiah responded in kind. He was as happy to see the boy as Lyle was to see him.

"You're all right," Josiah said with as much of a calm voice as he could muster.

"I was 'fraid."

Josiah knew that there had been a lot for the boy to be afraid of since they had returned home. It was another dull mark against his decision to return to Seerville. "Everything will be all right. The Rangers are here." He looked past Lyle, and made eye contact with Dansker, offering to lighten the load of his worry, too.

"Is Scrap here?" Lyle looked to the door with expectation. He liked Scrap Elliot a lot. Scrap doted on Lyle when he was around. Elliot was as good with children as he was with horses.

"Close by." Josiah walked to the counter, carrying Lyle.

"Good. I missed Scrap."

"Me, too." He stopped at the counter. "I hope he wasn't any trouble."

"No, no, not at all," Dansker said. "Though I might have gave him a little too much candy. My wife is asleep with a headache. She has those quite often these days. I think it's the worry over our life here if you ask me. It's precarious these days."

"You're not thinking of leaving, are you?"

"If my wife's health continues to decline, I will have no choice."

"I'm sorry to hear that. Maybe the Rangers will calm things down now that they're here."

"That will help," Dansker said, "but there are only so many wallets around that have any coin in them. My fortunes may be better spent in Tyler or beyond. We are hand to mouth ourselves, and with this feud, times are even worse. No one feels safe to travel the roads to and from town."

There was no use arguing with the man that his struggle wouldn't be over even if the Rangers did quell the feud. Josiah couldn't blame the man for wanting a better life for himself and his family. Seerville seemed to have little to offer anyone.

"Well," Josiah said, "I appreciate you keeping an eye on Lyle."

"He's a good boy. Says please and thank you, unlike a lot of little children these days. He is welcome here anytime."

That made Josiah smile. "The Rangers will be customers if they're here for a long period of time. Maybe that will help you out, and relieve your wife of some worry."

"I can only hope."

Josiah said thanks again, then headed out the door. He wanted to believe that his gut feeling was right, in telling him that the Rangers' presence would improve conditions.

Billy Pike's body was draped over his horse in motionless repose. Walking a dead man home was all too common of late in Anderson County. Word had got out that another death had occurred, flew through the population on the wings of a bird, it seemed, but whispered from one man to the next as they passed each other on the road.

The Pikes knew of the loss before Josiah and Tom Darkson arrived. Two men, one an older version of Billy who Josiah assumed was Pike's father, and another younger man, a brother from the looks of it, met them at a fork in the road as it branched off toward the river. They both carried rifles and had sad, drooping looks on their faces.

Josiah came to a stop, and said, "You Pikes?" Tom Darkson eased his horse, a gentle-tempered sorrel gelding, up next to Josiah. His rifle, a newer Winchester like Josiah's, sat within reach across his lap.

"I hear you's bringin' us sadness, Josiah Wolfe," the older man said. He spurred his horse to a lope and made his way to Josiah. The son stayed put, armed at both hips and a repeater, close in the scabbard, if he needed it.

"I wish it wasn't so," Josiah answered.

Darkson stood sentry, not trusting either man, watching beyond them for anything to move in the brush. Josiah liked that about Tom Darkson. He never let go of the fight he was in even when things were calm.

The older man wore a grizzled gray beard and his face looked like it was covered in worn leather, touched by long hours in the sun. The work of summer still showed on him. A fishy smell rode along with him as he eased to the rear of the wagon to inspect the dead body. "Yes, sir, that there's our Billy. Hate to say it, but I'm not surprised. I warned 'im not to get caught up in Luke Halverson's mess, but he wouldn't hear of it. Said they was friends and friends stuck together. I'm not sayin' we'd a sided with those Langdons. I don't care much for them kind of folks. Never have trusted 'em. I'd jus' as soon be left out of it all." He spun his old mare around and came up the other side of the buckboard, so he was even with Josiah and Darkson. "I knew your pa, Wolfe. He was a good Indian fighter. I heard you was, too."

The other Pike stood sentry, eyeing the conversation with caution.

"My pa never had a bad word to say about

211

you Pikes," Josiah said. "I was surprised Billy was riding with Luke, but didn't say as much. None of my business."

"You been gone," the old man said. Josiah wished he would have moved on downwind. The old man wore more of an unclean smell than a fishy smell. One sat on top of the other. He figured it was how river people were but he wasn't used to the smell. He was uncomfortable. That's all he knew, but he couldn't show it, offend the man, not in a time of grief.

"I thought it was time to come home is all," Josiah said.

"You might want to rethink that."

"I have been, but the Rangers rode in, so I'm hoping they'll put an end to this feud and we can all get back to normal, whatever that is."

"Rangers," the old man said with sudden disgust, "ain't nothin' to be proud of. Wind blows whatever way the government tells 'em to. Thugs can be Rangers, too. I got stories from the olden days that'd have you takin' sides with the Comanche over those no-good Rangers." He glared at Josiah, then urged his mare on with the flick of a knee. "You'll see. They'll take sides themselves. Then it won't be no feud we have to worry about. It'll be a war. I jus' wish people'd leave us the hell alone is all. You, them Langdons, and the Halversons. 'Specially them Halversons. They's all dead to me now." He didn't look back as he rode away from the wagon. "Myron, go fetch your brother. It's time for us to go home and bury the poor boy 'fore darkness comes and stays on us longer than we want it to."

The younger Pike took Billy's horse in tow as quick as he could without jostling the dead body off the horse.

Josiah didn't say anything. A simple mention of the Rangers had set the old man off. Anything else might escalate further, and that was the last thing Josiah wanted. He watched the three Pikes disappear, then motioned to Darkson that it was time to go. Josiah wanted to get as far away from the river as he could.

CHAPTER 23

Tom Darkson and Josiah doubled up in the saddle, and headed back to the main road. The company of Rangers had come to a stop about a mile away from the plot of land Josiah called home. There didn't seem to be anything wrong; no one was running for cover, or seemed concerned with their physical safety. Men stood in clumps talking with ease, no more worried about being shot at than a turtle lazing on a sunny log. The sight of the relaxed Rangers put Josiah at ease as he approached. He could see the buckboard on the road with Ofelia and Lyle still on it.

Darkson eased his horse off the road once they caught up with the company. Both men dismounted and went their separate ways. Darkson joined in a conversation taking place nearby, leaving the sorrel to its own devices. The horse chewed on some brittle grass that was green at the roots. Josiah headed for the wagon to where Ofelia and Lyle waited.

Captain McNelly stood at the front of the company, next to his horse, a solid black mount, tall and proud, befitting the stature of its rider. "We've been waiting for you, Wolfe."

Paul Dobson, the sergeant, stood off to the side with his horse about ten feet away from McNelly. There was no chatting between the two of them. Dobson was waiting for the next order, and nothing else.

There was no sign of Sheriff Busser. Josiah assumed that he had stayed behind in Seerville, or had been called away for other business. Or, the man could have stalked off in a huff angered by Captain McNelly's choice not to jail Josiah. It was hard to know what had happened. All Josiah knew was that he wasn't going to bring the subject of the sheriff's absence up with the captain. If McNelly wanted him to know of the sheriff's whereabouts, he would tell him.

Josiah walked to the captain. Duty called, even though Josiah wasn't in the service of a contract. But the captain was the captain, and when he spoke or called you forth, every man obeyed — out of respect and demand. McNelly wasn't a man to be taken as a fool given the current situation, by civilians or Rangers.

"The Pikes were already aware of the death," Josiah said.

"They didn't cause you any trouble, I presume?"

"No, no, they're river people. They want to be left alone. Which is what I did. They had a burial to tend to and I left them to it." There was no need for Josiah to tell the captain of the Pikes' disdain for the Rangers.

"All right then." McNelly looked to the sky, then back to Josiah. "We better get a move on. We'll need to strike camp soon and settle in before night arrives." He didn't say anything else. He climbed up on his saddle with ease, then settled himself into it with a straight spine. Still, the action brought on a slight cough. Paul Dobson reacted, aping the captain by mounting his horse with the same easiness. Both men kept their eyes on Josiah as he made his way to the wagon.

Ofelia slid over, allowing Josiah his spot on the bench. Lyle rubbed his shoulder against Josiah's arm and smiled.

"Giddy up. Let's go," he said to the draft horse. He heard the company mount up behind him.

There was a calmness to the start of the

ride that made Josiah feel uncomfortable. The Langdons had been quiet since taking Ofelia. He expected them to attack since that had been their way after he'd arrived back home. But, as he thought about it, he knew he didn't know what was happening elsewhere in the county. Scrap and a party of Rangers were making their presence in the county known to the Langdons, and another group was doing the same with the Halversons. There was no way he could know what was going on beyond what he saw in front of his own two eyes. He could imagine, though, and he was pretty certain that Leland Halverson and Ethan Langdon weren't going to take to having twenty Texas Rangers standing in their front yards telling them what to do.

McNelly decided that the farm was as good a place as any to strike camp. He liked that Josiah's land was situated between the Langdons and the Halversons, and all of the company's basic needs could be met from one place. It wasn't long before the paddock was filled with white dog tents. A few larger wall tents sat in the middle of the group, one being the captain's residence and planning tent, while the other served as Doc Tinker's field hospital to treat the sick and injured. McNelly sent a rider to tell the other Rangers where to find them.

The orange glow of easy fires dotted the ground, and the smell of woodsmoke and boiling stews filled the air. Darkness had not yet come on in full detail, but the sky was filtering out all of the gray until there was nothing left but a silky black blanket. There were no clouds to obscure anything from shining, including the evening star, which pulsed overhead.

A perimeter of Rangers had been set up around the camp, replacing Luke Halverson and the rest of the men Leland had sent to look out for Lyle's well-being. They were gone, not to be found once the company of Special Force Rangers had arrived.

Ofelia set about putting the barn in order and preparing something to eat for Josiah and Lyle. She was quiet, hesitant to talk when Josiah spoke to her. He wasn't sure if she was upset with him, traumatized by having a noose slipped around her neck, or both. If there was one thing he'd learned in his life, it was not to press when a woman didn't want to talk. Ofelia would tell him what was troubling her sooner or later.

Now that he was home — as home as he could be in the barn — there was little left for Josiah to do. He was still sore from the beating he'd taken from Morris Langdon. His face was tender and achy, but the couple of days of rest he'd gotten had helped. Still, the day had taken its toll. He was tired, hungry, and still leery of attack — even if he did have a yard full of Texas Rangers.

Josiah sat outside the open barn door, cleaning his Winchester, watching everything. What he was really hoping for was the sight of Scrap Elliot riding into camp. He was anxious to see his old friend and know that he was safe.

Ofelia walked up to his side. "Lyle is asleep."

"Long day."

"*Sí,* a long day. I will wake him when the food is ready to eat."

Josiah kept on wiping the rifle. "I'm sorry. This isn't what I expected."

"What?"

"This," he said, as he set the Winchester down at his side. "All of this. Everything that has happened since we arrived. If I would have known —"

Ofelia cut him off, and said, "There's no way you could have known what was happening here. No one knows the future."

"I would like to sometimes. It would make our lives easier."

"Maybe. Maybe not."

Josiah glanced over to Ofelia and let his eyes linger on the rope burn a little longer than was polite. She looked away.

"I don't know that we can stay here," he said.

"You should not say that. The Rangers are here. They are your friends and they will make things right."

"I'm afraid some things can't be made right. Even if the Langdons and the Halversons come to a truce, I worry about the affect they will have on Lyle. I don't want him to grow up fighting with everyone he disagrees with, or worse, going to war with them. I want him to have a better life than that. That's one of the reasons I came home instead of staying in the city. I thought it would be quieter here. I was wrong about that."

"It is too early to tell." Ofelia adjusted herself, then walked over to the tripod and stirred the stew.

Josiah stood up and joined her. The stew, a *menudo,* made of tripe, broth, and a red pepper base, smelled comforting. He wasn't sure where she'd gotten the ingredients, but his guess was the Ranger cook shared some of his store. "I wasn't finished apologizing to you."

"You have nothing to apologize for, se-ñor."

"I do. I didn't protect you. You were hurt, taken away. If the Rangers wouldn't have shown up when they did . . ." He let the words trail off, then he looked away, out over the paddock full of tents.

There was no gray in the sky now. It was all black. Darkness had won the war over light — at least for a little while.

"I was *asustada,* scared," Ofelia said. "More *asustada* than I ever have been in my life. Those men wanted to kill me."

"Yes, they did. They still do. That's my worry. Even with all of these men here. Langdons don't give up that easy. They'll be back."

"And I will be ready for them. I am not ready to die. Not yet. Not at the hands of a bad man. I want to grow old and see Lyle grow up to be a good man."

"I want you to see that, too." Josiah paused, listening to the crackle of the fire, the boil of the *menudo,* and the soft murmur of voices floating from the tents, then said, "I will protect you until the day I die. I promise you that. I won't let any harm come to you again."

"*Gracias,* but I am a grown woman. You do not need to worry about me." A slight

221

smile crossed Ofelia's face. "I think the *menudo* is ready to eat."

Josiah didn't answer. His attention was taken away by two horses racing into camp. He heard the sound before he saw the shapes. They were clear, as dark as it was, but the fires lit a flickering path to the tents. Other men stepped out, drawn by the sound, too.

The horses stopped short of the larger of the dog tents, and the rider jumped off, shouting, "Where's Doc? I got a wounded man, here. It's Scrap Elliot. He's been shot."

CHAPTER 24

Josiah stood outside the door of the hospital tent, pacing like an expectant father, worried about the delivery. Only in this case, he was worried whether Scrap Elliot was going to live or die. He wasn't alone in his worry. McNelly and Dobson had been roused by the news like the rest of the camp. They waited for the status of Scrap's injuries along with the Ranger that had brought him in, a fella Josiah didn't know who called himself Miguel Santino. He was a blond-haired, blue-eyed, half-breed Mexican boy about the same height as McNelly, maybe twenty years old, if that. Whatever experience Miguel had, he was keeping to himself. He paced back and forth taking the opposite path of Josiah, the leather of his gun belt and holster rubbing against his leg in a dull clap. His normal sun-browned skin looked pale and he was muttering to himself under his breath, adding fret to his chorus of

223

concern.

"Miguel, can you stop that incessant rambling," McNelly said. He stood next to the closed door of the tent. Dobson wasn't that far away, rolling a cigarette from a pouch of Bull Durham, on the other side of the door. He looked bored, like he didn't want to be there.

Miguel stopped. "Sorry. I'm just worried about Scrap."

"We all are," McNelly said.

Josiah continued walking back and forth, listening for any sign of life from inside the tent. There was the occasional clatter of metal tools and heavy footsteps, but nothing else. Not one scream of pain from Scrap. Not even a moan. That was either a good thing, or a bad thing.

Dobson put the cigarette to his mouth, struck a Lucifer, bringing a quick explosion of light to his face, then drew in, taking a deep breath of smoke. He exhaled, then examined the cigarette as if to judge it in some way, good or bad.

Josiah paced his way over to Miguel who stopped muttering. "What?" he asked.

"Nothing, I just think we all want to know what happened is all?" Josiah said.

The question drew both the captain and Dobson's attention, but they didn't object to it. Instead, they lent an ear, waiting for Miguel's answer.

Miguel looked to McNelly, who gave a slight nod of approval. "We rode up with me and Elliot on the rearguard. We was stopped about three hundred yards from the Langdon house by two armed men. Timmons announced our presence and intention, then one of the men rode up to the house. We waited in line. In hindsight, we should have been more concerned, sittin' out there like targets, but we was under orders not to engage unless we was shot at." There wasn't a hint of Mexican in Miguel's words. He spoke perfect Anglo.

"So they started shooting then?" Josiah said.

Dobson smoked his cigarette, paying attention to Miguel only because it seemed to be the thing he should be doing. In between draws on the smoke, he yawned, then looked away into the darkness beyond the camp.

"No," Miguel said. "The man came back with another man, an older man. He told us to get off his property.

"Timmons, who was in charge, agreed that we would, but we would set up a perimeter, like we was instructed, making passage to and from the Langdons' land a matter of permission by the Rangers. The old man huffed and puffed but he retreated with the other men, went back to the house. We took up our positions with me and Scrap behind the house, not that far from here, down a ravine and through a little valley."

Josiah knew the spot Miguel spoke of. The Langdons used the shallow valley as pastureland when they had animals to graze.

"It wasn't long," Miguel continued, "before a rider came upon us at racing speed. We tried to stop 'im, but he kept comin'. He pulled a pistol and shot Scrap on his way past. I don't know who the man was, whether his intention was just to shoot a Ranger, or if he was up to somethin' else. All I know is that I grabbed up Scrap and headed straight here."

McNelly stepped away from the hospital tent and Dobson stubbed out his cigarette on the raised sole of his boot. A brief cascade of sparks showered to the ground.

The captain sidled up to Miguel. The boy trembled with regret.

"That's the first man I ever saw shot," Miguel said. "Might be hard to believe. But I'm only a farm boy. There ain't no battles there except between roosters and maybe dogs when they's a bitch in heat, somethin'

226

to fight for, you know? One is stronger than the other. Seein' a man battlin' with death is fearsome. I'm not sure I'm cut out to be a Ranger, Captain."

"Maybe you're not." There was no sympathy in McNelly's voice. "You did the right thing, though, bringing him straight here. If anybody can save Elliot's life, Doc Tinker can. You didn't do anything wrong from the sound of it."

Josiah exhaled and looked away. He felt sorry for Miguel, for the boy, who was becoming a man whether he liked it or not. The Rangers weren't for everyone. Some men came and went depending on the way the wind blew in their lives. Here one day, gone the next, like Josiah. One day it was too much for him, too, and he packed up and left. He felt for Miguel, he really did. Maybe the boy was right. Maybe Ranger life wasn't for him. If so, this was the time to find out — while he was still walking and breathing.

Miguel was about to say something else but the flap on the dog tent fluttered open and Doc Tinker walked out.

Tinker looked to Dobson, and said, "You wouldn't have an extra pinch of that Bull Durham, do you? I could use a smoke." He wore a bloodstained surgery apron and a grim, tired look on his weathered face. The top of his boots was splattered, too, but instead of drying red, the blood looked black; shiny like a mirror reflecting the dim light from the fires.

"Sure thing," Dobson said. He reached into his back pocket, pulled out his tobacco pouch, and handed it to Tinker. "Paper's inside."

"Thanks." Tinker took the tobacco and started to roll a cigarette.

"How's Elliot doing?" McNelly said, casting a glance at the tent.

"He's a strong boy and that will help." Tinker talked while he finished rolling the cigarette, sealing it closed by sliding it across his lips. "A lucky boy, too. The bullet lodged above his heart. Didn't damage anything major from what I can see, no broken bones, no severed blood vessels that won't heal. If Miguel wouldn't have got him here when he did, though, he'd be dead. The blood would have drained out of him quick as a rain-filled river lookin' for a place to flood. I had to burn the wound shut, then I gave him a dose of morphine. He'll sleep through the night and be real sore for a few days. Good thing he's right-handed." Tinker paused, struck a match, then took a drag on the cigarette. "That was good thinking, Miguel. You saved Elliot's life is what you did."

Miguel relaxed. His looked like a thousand pounds of bricks had been lifted off his shoulders. A slight smile flickered across his face.

"I'll keep an eye on him through the night," Tinker said. "You all can go on with whatever you were doing. I'll holler if I need anything from you."

Josiah was tempted to ask Tinker if he could see Scrap, but one more look at the bloody apron warned him off. There would be time for a reunion later when Scrap was awake. He started to walk off, but McNelly stopped him.

"You got any idea who the shooter was, and what that was all about, Wolfe?" the captain said.

"Hard to say, there's a lot of Langdons. But by my thinking, it was a message to you, to the Rangers, that they weren't going to abide by your orders."

"It's a damn shame there's not a jail around to put 'em all in," Dobson said.

"We might have to clean up the old marshal's office," McNelly mused. "We might have to lock up all of the principals before the judge arrives. That's a battle I really don't want to fight, but I will if I have to."

Josiah had his own thoughts on the matter

but kept his mouth shut. This wasn't his feud to settle. He wasn't a sergeant anymore, and besides, when it came right down to it, he was still in Ranger custody himself. "I think I'll be turning in now that I know Elliot's going to be all right," he said, then started to walk away.

"Wolfe," McNelly called out, demanding that Josiah stop without having to say it.

Josiah obliged, and faced the captain. "Yes?"

"I might need you to ride with us. A man of your skills can't be overlooked and you know the lay of the land. With Elliot out, I'm already a man down. Something tells me there's more of that to come, either with injuries or with men choosing not to fight this fight. The first sight of blood sends a few of the young ones running back to their momma's teat," McNelly said, staring at Miguel.

"According to the sheriff, I'm under arrest, in your custody until the judge arrives," Josiah said.

"You let me worry about Busser. He can count to ten and walk at the same time, but I'm not sure he knows how our world works. Nothing says that I can't have a man ride with me that is under suspicion of a crime by the sheriff, anyway. You need your day in court is all. Unless, of course, you're not telling me everything."

"I told you my side of that story, Captain, and I'm sticking to it. I didn't kill anyone or fire a shot."

"Good. Go on, turn in, but think about what I said. I hated to see you leave us in Austin."

"Thank you, sir," Josiah said.

He stood, wanting to tell McNelly that there was no way in hell that he was going to ride with the Rangers again. It was too soon to even consider. And then there was Ofelia and Lyle to worry about. Stumbling into a gun battle between the Langdons and Halversons was one thing, but choosing sides, going against both families, all the while living on the land between them, was another thing all its own. But the look on the captain's face warned him off saying no, of turning down the request. Leander McNelly was not a man accustomed to being rejected — he got everything he asked for. Still, Josiah couldn't take the risk, or find the desire to put himself in the line of fire this close to home.

CHAPTER 25

Josiah woke just before dawn. He eased out of the barn, doing his best not to cause Ofelia or Lyle to stir. The October night air was cool and starting to drip with moisture. A quick glance upward told him that the clear sky of the evening was covered over by a blanket of clouds. The wind had picked up and the branches on the trees waved, ready to break into a full dance if the gusts grew any stronger. Woodsmoke pushed south, draping the camp in a thin veil of fog. All of the fires had died down to glowing coals or were burned out altogether.

A herd of horses stood inside the fence, an unusual sight, with Clipper mixed in with the rest. The appaloosa knew a lot of the horses, like Josiah knew a lot of the Rangers. That didn't make it any less an odd sight. One of the horses nickered, sending the sound echoing into the dismal sky. It was Scrap's horse, Missy.

He stopped short of the fence and looked around. No one else was awake. He was secure in the thought that there were men on the perimeter, wide awake, on the look-out for any kind of trouble, but they were a good distance away. Comforted, he continued on to a place well behind the barn and relieved himself.

Afterward, he made his way back to the fence, and stared across the field, at the camp, at the change of his land since he'd arrived. It was a lot to take in. There had been little time to be melancholy about the loss of the cabin, of the life lived there, or even to pay his respects to Lily and the girls. The fact that he hadn't visited the small family cemetery since he'd arrived home was not lost on him. No matter that there had been a lot going on, he had avoided the sacred ground and he knew it.

He shivered as he looked past the paddock and into the small thick of woods where the graves lay. He had come home to be close to them, so Lyle would know that his mother and sisters had existed. Along with that, he had come home for a fresh start, and it had been anything but that. He was in the middle of a battle one more time. War and fighting followed him around like a bee after an ever-blooming flower. One of these days he was going to get stung real good, and he knew it.

The sun was starting to peek over the horizon. A shimmering red line pierced the grayness of the sky, promising to burn away whatever it touched. But the wind was strong, and the threat of rain even stronger. It was a weak promise. Josiah figured the light of the sun would disappear soon, overtaken by disagreeable weather, losing a fight the light couldn't win. Gray looked like it would win the day, bringing with it some rain and cooler air from the north.

One more look around told Josiah that he was alone. There seemed no better time than that moment to visit the cemetery, to pay his respects in private. With the aid of dim light, Josiah walked toward the copse of oak trees that housed the cemetery, fortified by need, but more afraid to confront reality than he wanted to admit. The soil had yet to settle on Lily's grave when he had left.

A black wrought-iron fence surrounded the graves. It was in bad repair; pickets were twirled with browning vines and the gate stood ajar, off the hinges. There were stretches of the fence where the pickets were missing, like someone had come along and decided to use the rods for some unknown purpose. Dead leaves covered the ground and Josiah's father's tombstone had started to tilt to the left. His mother's stood firm, but the white stone was starting to weather, turning gray and green with moss and mold at the same time.

Josiah stood over his parents' graves and sighed with ten years' worth of grief. It was difficult to face the loss in his life, the hole in him that still existed, even now, long after their deaths. He had loved both of them.

He knew he couldn't linger there. The chirp of a bird, announcing it was awake and ready to sing to the world, spurred him away from his lonely thoughts about his parents. Each step deeper into the little cemetery he took felt like it was weighted down by a ton of lead. He came to the girls' graves first. Elizabeth, then Clara, then Maddie. Maddie was the hardest. She'd never really had a chance to enjoy life, never knew anything other than being a baby. A tear formed in Josiah's eye, escaped his eyelid, and trailed down his cheek. He didn't try to stop it. It was past time for him to shed a tear for his family.

Lily's grave lay at the head of the girls. By the time he got there his knees were trembling, his entire body felt numb. He had to kneel to keep himself from falling. Her tombstone was still white with a little moss and mold at the base. He wiped the leaves from the top of the grave.

"I'm sorry," he whispered. His words caught on a push of wind that wrapped around him and rustled up a little spin of dead oak leaves. The brittle leaves clicked together, and for a second, Josiah thought he could hear distant voices in the noise. He looked to the camp, but didn't see any movement, didn't hear anything else. The air smelled of rain and tears, and the morning light, as depressed and feckless as it was, was starting to reach inside the cemetery.

"I'll come back another time," he said. "I'll find some flowers and clean up everything. We'll have a good talk then. I'll tell you everything." He stood up and started to gather himself, readying to leave, but he stopped. "Lyle. He's a good boy. He looks like you, like your family. I'll bring him up here when I think he's ready." With that, he turned to leave. It was then that he saw movement out of the corner of his eye.

His vision was murky, glazed over with tears, so the world around him looked wavy, shimmering out of focus, but he was certain he saw a figure moving off through the woods. He could hear footsteps hurrying away, landing on the brittle leaves like tiny hammers shattering shards of glass.

He didn't think. He gave chase, wiping his eyes clear, catching his breath, and pushing away his grief. Twenty feet into the run he realized that he didn't have his revolver with him. He was dressed in his pants and shirt, and had no weapons on his person at all. But that didn't stop him.

The dawn light gave him enough sight to run with confidence after the figure, allowing him to see more than a silhouette as he ran. It was a woman. But more than that, Josiah was certain that the fleeing figure was Eva Langdon. The realization propelled him to run faster, ignoring any discomfort he might have felt. By the time he was close enough to call out to her, he knew that he couldn't.

Eva looked back, saw him gaining on her, then climbed over the fence that separated Wolfe land from Langdon land, and broke into a full-out run.

Josiah stopped at the fence, out of breath, and said, "Eva, come back. I won't hurt you."

But she didn't hear him. She was gone, vanished over a hill. The scent of her washed by him on a strong gust of wind; vanilla mixed with the scent of a woman. Rain had nothing on that, couldn't overpower the remnant of her presence. It took everything Josiah had not to follow after her, but he knew better than to trespass on Langdon land unarmed, chasing after Ethan's only daughter.

Josiah stood outside of Doc Tinker's tent waiting to see if Scrap Elliot could tolerate a visitor. The camp was alive with movement and purpose all around him. Horses were being saddled and watered, men were finishing up their breakfast, and there was an air of certainty that could not be mistaken. A battle, of some kind, was on the horizon.

Gray rain clouds persisted, dropping a drizzle to the ground. It was a cold rain, made even colder by the touch of the north wind. Slickers were already being worn, or shaken out of their pouches. The weather didn't look like it was going to get better anytime soon. The sky looked like it might shed tears forever.

None of the activity worried Josiah. He wasn't going on any missions with the Rangers. He was staying close to home, out of the fray. He'd been shot at enough over the last couple of days.

"You still out there, Wolfe?" Doc Tinker said from inside the tent.

"Sure am."

"Well, come on in then."

Josiah hesitated. He didn't know what to expect even though he'd been in hospital tents before. The last time he'd seen Scrap Elliot was the day he left Austin. He'd watched Scrap ride off to rejoin the Ranger company as he prepared to drive the wagon home. It had been a hard goodbye. Scrap had disagreed with Josiah's decision to leave the Rangers.

He pushed inside the tent and saw Scrap sitting on the edge of a cot, his pants on, his shirt off, with Tinker wrapping a bandage around his chest.

"Well, there you are, Wolfe," Scrap said, feigning as much of a smile as he could muster.

Scrap Elliot winced as the doc pulled the bandage tight.

"Too, tight?" Tinker said, snipping the wrap off with a pair of scissors.

"Nah, I'll be all right."

The inside of the tent was well-lit with two hurricane lanterns burning, and was well-organized. One side housed a couple of cots for sleeping and resting, made up military-style, while the other side served as Tinker's office and surgery room. All of the metal utensils in sight looked shiny and clean, laid out from the smallest to the largest.

"Good to see you up and about, Scrap," Josiah said.

Scrap was shorter than Josiah, and skinnier, too. Months of riding with the Rangers had made him rib-thin and his chest was as white as a bleached sheet. In contrast, his face and arms were browned from the sun and wind; his hair was black as good soil and in need of a good shearing. He wore no mustache or beard. His facial skin looked too smooth to grow any hair at all. Josiah forgot how young Scrap was sometimes.

"I figured you'd cause trouble once you returned home," Scrap said, "but I didn't expect it to take a whole company to get you out of the straits."

"It wasn't meant to be like this."

Tinker finished up with the dressing, then stood back to take a look at his work. "I got more morphine if you need it," he said. His glasses slipped down to the end of his nose and he pushed them back up out of habit.

Scrap turned up his lip. "I don't want no more of that stuff. Made me have some wicked dreams. I didn't know what was real and what was not. Thought I was surrounded by the Comanche all over again. My gun was gone, and I was all alone. Woke up in a pool of sweat, I did, and a foul taste in my mouth. I'll take the pain over that kinda medicine."

Josiah knew the story that haunted Scrap. His mother and father had been killed in an Indian raid, while him and his sister, Myra Lynn, survived by hiding in a tunnel burrowed under the house. Scrap had been a youngster, no more than ten, when he became an orphan. There was a part of his senses that seemed to be missing, and Josiah figured seeing your parents killed by Indians could do some serious harm to a boy. He lacked manners, was quick-tempered, had an opinion about everything, and was as loyal a friend as any man could ask for.

"No need to prove how tough you are," Tinker said. "That wound isn't anything to monkey around with. You're gonna be sore for a while to come."

Scrap extended his right hand and pretended to shoot a gun. "At least it ain't my shootin' hand. I got an appointment with that fella that blindsided me. Hey, Wolfe," he said, turning his attention to Josiah, "do you know if Miguel brought Missy back to camp?"

"She's been tended to. In the pasture, lazing around out there with the other horses."

"Boy, howdy, I'd been fixed with a bucket

241

of spite if anything would have happened to that horse."

Tinker picked up a shirt and handed it to Scrap. "You need help with that?"

"Lordy, Doc, it ain't like this was the first time I been shot. I can darn well take care of myself."

"All right, then, suit yourself."

Josiah stood back and watched Scrap struggle with the shirt for a minute, knowing better than to offer to help. The tent flap opened up and he turned to see Dobson push inside.

"There you are, Wolfe," the sergeant said. "I figured I'd find you in here."

"Is something the matter?"

"The captain wants to see you. Wants you to ride with us today. He wants to pay the Langdons a visit and let them know that shootin' one of our men won't be tolerated."

"Why's he want me to go?"

"We're down a man. And he wants to show 'em you're in custody, under our watch. Make an example out of you."

"That won't work," Josiah said.

"You gonna tell that to McNelly?"

Scrap and Tinker stayed out of the conversation. Both men looked away as if they were trying to find something on the other side of the tent.

"I'm not telling the captain anything," Josiah said.

"That'd be wise. He wants to put an end to this feud as quick as possible, and don't think that you're gonna get out of any of the dirty work. The way the captain sees it, you're right in the thick of it. 'Cause we're camped on your land don't mean he's taken your side of the story to be as true as you think he has."

CHAPTER 26

Josiah stood silent in front of Captain McNelly, doing his best not to resist the order he'd been given.

"Are we clear on this, Wolfe?" McNelly said. Dobson stood next to him inside the command tent. Like Doc Tinker, the captain also slept in his tent. It was as neat as one would expect it to be belonging to a man of high rank. Organization and pride were a McNelly hallmark; the promise of a strict man was not to be doubted on any occasion.

"There is no acceptable answer except for yes, sir." Josiah didn't quiver. He commanded his entire body to freeze and not show a wisp of uncertainty. Never show fear to an angry dog.

"I don't hear conviction, Wolfe."

Noise from outside filtered into the tent. Men moving about, rolling up their bedding, packing for a day's ride. Horses being saddled. Rifles loaded. All done with minimal voices; there was no excitement in the air. Every man knew the potential of battle before they mounted their horses. This day could be their last. It was the life of a Ranger, of a man who chose to set the wrongs of the world right. If they had not settled themselves to the precariousness of their endeavors, then they were ignoring the fact that death was waiting right around the corner for them.

Josiah stared at McNelly, unwavering. "It's not that I have no conviction, Captain. It's the risk, is all. Since coming back home, I've about lost all that's dear to me. My son went missing. Ofelia was almost hanged. My cabin was burned down, I've been shot at, accused of a murder I had nothing to do with, and found myself at the butt end of a rifle. I still have my pains, sir. So, I can't say I'm happy to ride up to Ethan Langdon's front door, even if I am in the company of twenty Rangers. That show of power will do nothing but rile Ethan more, not intimidate him."

"Intimidation is not my aim, Wolfe. Since you are no longer a sergeant, or a Ranger for that matter, you have not been privy to all of my plan. It is my intention to take Ethan Langdon into custody. Sheriff Busser and the rest of the company will be doing the same with Leland Halverson. The jail in Seerville has been prepared for their temporary incarceration. I've received word that Judge Hooper will arrive tomorrow morning. Trials will begin in the afternoon. Once the two men, Langdon and Halverson, are in custody, a gallows will be built on the remains of the town square — whether it is needed or not."

Josiah almost whistled out loud. "You're about to set this county ablaze, sir. You realize that, don't you?"

"No, I'm not. I am ending this feud in a matter of days instead of allowing it to fester and cost more lives than it already has. We can't afford to lose one more man, Wolfe. Enough blood has been spilled. The violence has to end, and it has to end now. I will ask you one more time. Are you prepared to ride with us, or do I need to remind you that you still remain in custody yourself? I would rather you come along of your own free will."

"No, sir. I understand. I won't stay behind."

"Good, I'm glad of that."

Josiah knew he had no choice in the matter. Like the rest of the Rangers, he was aware how fragile everyday life was. If he was ever to hope to have a normal life in Seerville, the feud had to end, and both men who were the cause of it had to be shown that they did not have the power to continue to wreak havoc on the world for their own purposes. While the captain's plan was clear, and made sense, the successful execution of it was yet to be seen. Taking Leland Halverson and Ethan Langdon into custody was going to be like grabbing ahold of a greased pig, while staring down the barrels of a well-fortified and motivated army.

Josiah slid the Winchester into the scabbard, then turned back to Ofelia and Lyle, who stood watching him from inside the barn door. Ofelia wore a worried expression on her face, along with a fresh high-collared dress that hid the rope burns around her neck. She held Lyle's hand. He was still as a mouse who had seen a hawk's shadow.

A steady rain fell from the sky, the wind was moody, gusting one second, then dying down to a gentle breeze the next. Josiah wore his slicker and water drained off his black hard-top Stetson. Clipper, saddled and ready to ride, didn't seem to be bothered by the weather.

A quick glance to the front of the property told Josiah that the men were gathering in their ranks, readying to go. "I hope to be back before dark," he said, as he walked toward Lyle, but was speaking to Ofelia.

"*Estoy preocupado,*" she said. "I am worried for your safety, and ours."

At the same time Josiah heard footsteps behind him, he saw a wide smile burst across Lyle's face.

"Scrap!" the boy called, then ran out into the rain, past Josiah. He almost knocked Scrap off his feet, hitting him hard in a wide embrace at the knees.

Scrap wore a slicker with one arm poking out, and the other, the injured one, hidden inside. His hat drained water like Josiah's when he leaned down. "Well, hey, Lyle." He hugged the boy. "We best get inside before both of us melt."

"No chance of that," Josiah said as Scrap and Lyle hurried past him.

"*Vas a atrapar tu muerte,*" Ofelia said.

Scrap looked at her, annoyed. He didn't speak Mexican and he disapproved of Josiah's relationship with Ofelia. They avoided each other like a person would avoid a rattlesnake, but Scrap had come to terms with Ofelia's presence. Josiah couldn't ride without her help watching over Lyle. There was no one else.

"You're going to catch your death," Ofelia

repeated in English.

"I'll be fine, ma'am." Scrap hurried inside, past Ofelia, dragging a giggling Lyle with him. "Well, that ain't a real toad-soaker, but I'm wet to the gills." He wiped Lyle's head, pushing a sheet of water to the ground, then pulled off the slicker and tossed it over the rail of the closest stall.

"I figured you'd be taking a rest," Josiah said.

Scrap settled himself, tightening the sling on his left arm. He was bandaged down to the wrist. "I aim to, but I thought the boy here could use some company while you was away."

Josiah eyed the holster on Scrap's hip and knew the meaning of the visit was more than a social call. "Well, I appreciate that."

"You're welcome, Wolfe. Seems the least I can do." Scrap turned his attention to Lyle. "Now, once you get dried off, me and you are gonna play us some hide and seek. You up for that, boy?"

"Here? In the barn?" Lyle said.

A horse whinnied behind Josiah, drawing his attention back to the gathering company. The company was formed, standing in wait for Captain McNelly to arrive and lead them out of camp. Sergeant Dobson stood holding McNelly's steed. The rain was falling straight down in small, cold drops. The sky was hazy. It looked like a cloud had eased down from the sky and settled over the camp for a long stay.

Josiah shivered, then said, "I have to go."

Lyle stopped jumping up and down. "Come back, Papa."

"I will. I promise," Josiah said, then turned and walked toward Clipper, wishing more than anything that he was still in Austin, working at some mind-numbing job, like taking tickets at the train station.

CHAPTER 27

To Josiah's surprise, and relief, the Langdons let the company of Rangers onto their property without engaging in a shooting match. Maybe it was the reputation of the Rangers preceding them, or something else, like a trick, an ambush of some kind. It was possible, given the Langdons' previous battles, that they had set a trap. If that was the case, then Captain McNelly had ridden straight into their snare. But strategy was as much McNelly's most valued skill as was his dedication to his perseverance. Only ten men had ridden up to Ethan Langdon's house. The rest of the men had scattered on a picket that surrounded the property. They had been given orders to come running at the sound of a gunshot.

Ethan stood on his front porch, holding a long gun that looked like it had been in his family since the time of settlement. The weapon was a ball and powder outfit, no doubt loaded and ready to fire, but was no more of a threat to the ten Rangers than a king's scepter. He wore his Sunday suit, a threadbare black jacket over a white linen shirt, with trousers to match. There was no shine on his shoes or in his eyes. His face was tight with a steady rage and his thin white hair was slicked back with a fresh dab of pomade. He had prepared for the visit, almost as if he had had an invitation in advance.

Eva stood next to Ethan, offset to his left, close enough to the front door to disappear inside if the need arose. Morris stood to his father's right. He was bigger boned than Ethan, and a head taller. He wore an armed gun belt, two Colts, and a Bowie knife, and held a Winchester across his chest. He looked ready to go to war while Ethan looked ready to surrender.

Josiah didn't like the look of it. There were no other men in sight.

"So," Ethan said, "I am graced by the presence of Captain Leander McNelly."

McNelly held his mount steady in front of the house, fifteen feet away from Ethan. They could speak at a normal volume and see each other's intentions as clear as the horizon. Dobson and the rest of the company fell in behind the captain.

"And you, sir, are Ethan Langdon, I presume," McNelly said.

"Your presumption is correct. I am that man, and you, sir, are on my land uninvited. But you know that. State your business, though I already know what it is."

"How would that be, Mr. Langdon?"

No other man dared to speak or cough as the two men faced each other down.

"I am no fool. I have ears all over this county," Ethan said. "It was only a matter of time before you showed here to cart me away. If there's any consolation, I know that bastard Leland Halverson faces the same destiny. I could fight you, and so could he, but it is my choice not to unless you give me reason."

Eva stiffened, and said, "Father, that language is unacceptable." She carried no visible weapons and stood rigid as a show of support. Her jaw was set as firm as Ethan's in anger, or discomfort, it was hard to tell which. She had searched out Josiah in the crowd of men, let her gaze linger with his longer than she should have, then looked away.

Josiah flashed on the memory of her running away from the cemetery in the dim morning light. A specter herself, ethereal, barefoot in a shift, spying on him for an unknown reason. He couldn't help wondering what she had been up to.

"Spare me the admonishment, daughter. These men are overextending their rights and they know it." Ethan turned his attention back to McNelly. "Do you have proof of my crime, sir?"

"We have witnesses, Mr. Langdon."

"Lopsided witnesses. If I fired a weapon, it was in self-defense. The Halversons fired first."

"It will be the judge's duty to parse the truth," McNelly said. "I am only here to bring peace to the county. Now, I will ask you to accompany us into town without incident, sir. Enough blood has been spilled in this feud."

"Enough *Langdon* blood."

Ethan started to step off the porch, but Morris grabbed his shoulder and pulled him back. "I still don't think you ought to do this, Pa," he said.

"Unhand me, boy. If there's one thing I agree with this man about, it's that there's been too much blood spilled. Losin' Gordy was the end of it. He had his whole life ahead of 'im. It was a shame to see a light snuffed out too soon for no reason."

Josiah wanted to shout that Gordy Langdon died because he burned down his cabin, and was going to kill Ofelia — and maybe Lyle. But he knew better than to speak a word of protest.

"Revenge is yet to be had." Morris glared at McNelly, then did the same thing as Eva and searched out Josiah so he could deliver a hateful look to him, too.

"There will be no revenge," Ethan said. "That's my word. You hear me, boy?"

Morris took his hand off of his father's shoulder. "If you say so, Pa."

"I say so. Now, fetch my horse. It's time to get on with this before somebody does somethin' stupid."

It didn't matter that Morris disagreed with Ethan, he stalked off the porch and disappeared around the house. Josiah expected a rush of horses and gunfire to follow, but none came. Ethan and McNelly remained facing off with nothing but flies and distaste in between them.

It wasn't long before Morris came walking back with a black horse in tow. He deposited the mount in front of the porch, then stood to the side, waiting.

Ethan eased down the steps like each one was lined with hot coals. It looked painful for him to walk, to move, to breathe. His fingers were twisted in an unnatural way, and they rested that way until the man went to grab the horse's reins. He twisted his finger around the leather and his face drew in, like he was being stung by hornets. Josiah couldn't watch the man climb into the saddle. Age had taken its toll on Ethan Langdon in a spiteful way.

"You stay here and mind the house, Morris. No shootin', you hear. I don't want no trouble. Like we talked over. You understand?"

Morris didn't say anything.

Ethan settled himself into the saddle so he was as comfortable as he could be. "Well, Captain, let's get on with this charade."

McNelly motioned for the company to wait, then followed after him. He moved his horse alongside Ethan's and started a slow lope. When he got next to Josiah, he stopped. "I want you and Darkson to stay here until I send word for you to leave. There's watch all around. You know what to do if trouble comes your way."

Before Josiah could say anything, Ethan Langdon interjected. "I thought this man was in your custody, Captain?"

"He is," McNelly replied. "And he will stay that way under Ranger Darkson's watch."

"I don't want no Halverson camped out on my land."

256

"He's not a Halverson. I have made my decision. He stays here. Is that a deal-breaker, Mr. Langdon?" There was no weakness in McNelly's voice even though the wheeze of consumption was present.

A resigned frown fell over Ethan's haggard face. "Giddy up," he said, urging his horse forward.

McNelly did the same, not giving Josiah a chance to object. Not that he would have anyway. He knew it would have been a waste of breath. There was no way to know why the captain made the decisions that he did. He was a tight-lipped strategist, and the proof of his wisdom had played out over and over again. There was no question that Captain Leander McNelly knew what he was doing — and Josiah wasn't going to question him now. Not with Ethan Langdon in custody without issue. The fact that not one drop of blood had been lost from any of the men was a minor miracle.

Morris Langdon sat on the porch, holding his Winchester, nursing a passel of hurt feelings. It was Morris's presence that convinced Josiah that Ethan wasn't up to anything diabolical. If there was an ambush planned, Morris would have been the ringleader. There was no question about that, at least not in Josiah's mind.

The rain had continued to fall in a constant sheet, soaking every living thing inside and out. There had been no offer from Morris for Josiah and Tom Darkson to come in from the rain. After a while, Eva came out onto the porch, and said, "Why are these two men still standing in the rain, Morris?"

" 'Cause it's rainin' is why."

"Well, it's not a nice thing to leave company standing out in the weather," she said.

"Company? These is Rangers. Well, one is, and one was. It is the one that was that bothers me. He can rot for all I care. Him and that greaser he takes up with. They ain't folks. They're foes."

"You're not being very nice, Morris."

Josiah sat in Clipper's saddle, unmoving, surrounded by a shower of rain. His nose felt cold enough to fall off, and his fingers were the same. He felt a little sympathy for Ethan.

He watched Eva with curiosity, not sure why she cared that he and Darkson were uncomfortable. He still hadn't rectified the idea that she knew about the plot to hang Ofelia. "I'm going to put some coffee on," Eva continued. "Why don't you fellas take your horses to the barn, and then come back here. You can shelter under the porch roof until you leave."

"I don't want them to touch the wood of this house," Morris said.

"I don't care what you want, Morris. We're gonna do the kind thing whether you like it or not. You hear? Pa didn't leave you in charge of me."

"Yes, he did. I'm in charge of you."

"Says you," Eva sneered.

"Says Pa."

"You all are despicable." Eva turned away from Morris, looked Josiah in the eye, and said, "I'll bring you coffee in the barn."

He watched her stalk inside, shrugged his shoulders, then motioned for Tom Darkson to join him in the barn. The least they could do was get out of the rain.

CHAPTER 28

The barn was twice as large as Josiah's. All of the stalls had been mucked, and there wasn't a thing out of place. The tack room, visible through an open door, was well-organized; bridles, reins, and ropes were bundled and strung with perfection. Farriers' tools took up half a wall. Rasps, hoof picks, clinchers, pullers, and cutters looked new, never touched. It was easy to see that Ethan Langdon took pride in his land, managed it down to the details, no matter how crippled his fingers appeared to be. For some reason the sight surprised Josiah. Based on their behavior he had taken the Langdons for heathens, uncaring about anything but causing chaos. He had to reconsider his perceptions. It was possible that he had underestimated all of the Langdons, not the worst of them, Charlie and Morris.

It was good to get out of the rain. Josiah

and Tom Darkson shook the water off themselves at the same time, then tied their horses up to posts inside the barn. Josiah took his slicker off, while Darkson left his on.

"Good to be dry," Josiah said. He rubbed his hands together to generate some warmth, as he looked around the barn. Every inch of him was cold, felt wet to the bone.

"There's a shed on the other side of the house," Darkson said. "How about I take up my position there? That way if anyone comes or goes, we've got 'em in a cross fire."

Josiah looked across the field that bordered the Langdon house, and saw the shed Darkson spoke of. "I'm not your sergeant anymore, Tom."

"Can't help but treat you that way, Wolfe. It was all I knowed you as 'til now. It feels familiar with you in the saddle, is all. I can make up my own mind since Captain McNelly wasn't too specific on our duty."

"I think taking up your own spot's a good idea, Tom."

Darkson smiled wide, reminding Josiah how young the man was. He looked more like a little boy than a Ranger prepared to take on a gun battle if necessary.

Josiah didn't say anything else. He stood

there and watched after Darkson as he made his way across the field. He had eased his hand to the grip of his Peacemaker in case Morris Langdon, or any other Langdon that was holed up in the house, decided to take a potshot at Tom Darkson. He breathed a sigh once the boy arrived at the shed and took up a sitting spot under a wide eave.

With the picket of men surrounding the house, and them covering the back, their presence seemed like a good plan on the captain's part. What still surprised Josiah was the ease that Ethan left with. Josiah had never known a Langdon to quit so easy — unless they were up to something. The gnawing in the pit of his stomach warned him not to get too comfortable.

It wasn't long before Josiah watched Eva Langdon hurry from the house, dodging the raindrops, while carrying a silver tray with a coffee pot on it. She had the grace of a swan; she looked like she was floating instead of walking.

Once Eva made it to the inside of the barn, she set the tray down and took off her rain slicker. She was dressed in black — in mourning for her cousin Gordy — from neck to toe. A cameo necklace adorned her throat, with the silhouette of a woman that

Josiah assumed was her mother. She freed her hair by taking off a bonnet that had kept it from getting too wet. Her black silky hair complemented her outfit, sang in the same sad chorus of the material of death.

"Where's the other one?" Eva said, looking for Tom Darkson.

Josiah cocked his head toward the shed. "Took up his spot over there."

"Well, darn. I'll have to get twice as wet."

"I'll be happy to take the coffee to him."

"That would be nice."

"Morris isn't going to like it if you're out here too long," Josiah said.

Eva ignored him. "Don't you worry about Morris."

"Last time I didn't worry about Morris I took a rifle butt to the face."

Eva picked up the tray and set it on a blanket chest, preparing to pour the coffee. She stopped what she was doing and looked up at Josiah. "He did that to you?" Meaning the bruises that had now taken up residence on his face.

"It was a battle."

"Shouldn't have been, and he shouldn't have been there any more than you should have."

"I was riding by and the shooting started. I had no choice but to take refuge inside the house with Leland and Luke. I didn't know they were there. I knew nothing about any of this. If I had, I might of reconsidered moving back here."

Eva looked at Josiah like she didn't believe him.

Josiah noticed, and felt compelled to explain further. "I have no reason to lie to you any more than I have a reason to lie to Captain McNelly or Sheriff Busser. I have no fight with your family, Eva. If I did, I wouldn't have set myself up right next to your family's land. I thought it had been long enough since the trouble with Charlie had passed. I didn't give it another thought. Then I came back and found myself in the middle of a feud that I had no skin in. No skin in it at all. I want a better life for my family. What's left of it anyway. That's why I'm here. I wanted some peace and quiet."

Eva went back to readying the coffee. The aroma of fresh-brewed Arbuckle's offered a bit of comfort to the gloom of the cold, rainy day. She moved about with continued ease and grace. The disbelief had fallen from her face, replaced by purpose and deep thought. Her eyes were almost purple, a blue so deep they could have been born of the ocean, not the piney woods of east Texas. With one last graceful move she handed a steaming mug of coffee to Josiah.

He took it and wrapped his hands around the ceramic body to warm them. "Thank you. You didn't have to do this."

"I beg to differ," Eva said, pouring herself a mug. She stood in front of Josiah and took a sip for herself.

Josiah didn't take his eyes off her. The world beyond them had vanished. Rain was background noise; an October song that promised nothing but more of the same. Cold had come to stay. The sunny days of spring were too far away to think about. Tom Darkson was the least of Josiah's concern. He was a Ranger, capable of whiling away the time, keeping an eye out for trouble. Even the thought of Morris, or any other of the Langdons who might pose a threat, was lost to his notice. He took a drink of the coffee, looking over the lip of the mug at Eva.

"I don't want you, or anyone else, to think that we lack manners," Eva continued. "You must hate every one of us."

"No, of course not," Josiah said. "I don't know you. I don't know you at all. I've had dealings with some of your brothers over the years. We never mixed well is all. Except Charlie, when he was my deputy in Seerville for that short amount of time. And the war. We all had our time in the war. Some of us marched together. Saved each other's lives. That was a long time ago though, seems like it happened to another person, not me. No, now, don't go thinking I hate anyone. That's not my way of living. At least, it hasn't been."

"I like that," Eva said. She forced a smile, and seemed as focused on him as he was on her.

Silence settled between the two of them. It was uncomfortable, like they were both trying to figure out what to say to each other. For his part, Josiah was blinded by Eva's presence and kindness. He couldn't believe that she was Charlie or Morris's sister, that she was of the same blood as them, even though close up he could see the family resemblance.

"Is that your mother?" he said, motioning toward the cameo.

Eva reached up and touched the jewelry with the tips of her fingers. "It is. I've worn it for so long that I forget it's there most days. Funny, this outline of her face is all I know of her. I try to pick out the parts of my father's face I know when I look in the mirror, then I look for the unknown parts, like my nose, and I assume hers was the same. Over the years, I've put together a picture of her in my mind. That's all I have, but this helps." She let her fingers fall from the cameo, then took another sip of coffee.

"I should have one made for Lyle."

"That would be nice. It would be a nice keepsake for him, something to treasure. He will have the same plight as me, never knowing what his mother looked like."

"It would be something for him to have."

Eva set the coffee down and looked out to the house. A quick veil of concern fell over her face until she turned back to Josiah. "I'm sorry about the other morning," she said. "I wasn't spying on you."

Josiah was surprised by the admission. He wasn't going to mention it. "I thought I was the only one awake, out and about at that time in the morning."

"I rise before dawn every day," Eva said. "I like the quiet before the hustle of boots hits the floor. I have a lot of cooking to prepare for all my brothers, and whoever else stays on our place. I sneak out for some alone time if I can — so I can breathe for a minute or two without someone tellin' me what to do or where to be."

"I 'spect it's hard being the only girl in the house."

"You have no idea."

"No, I don't."

Eva kicked at the floor at something unseen, then said, "I was worried about your boy. What he might have seen or heard. I couldn't stand the thought of him bein' sad or upset after seein' him at the Danskers' store. All of this trouble makes me ill. I beg for it to stop, but no one listens. Well, maybe father, maybe I got through to him. I'm happy to be standing here talking to you, not mopping more blood."

It was then that Josiah had to confront the idea that Eva might have had something to do with the attempt to hang Ofelia. Instead of saying anything, fearing he would seem ungrateful for the coffee, or rude to her, he turned and walked away. He stopped at the barn door and stared across the field to the shed. Tom Darkson waved, and Josiah waved back.

Eva walked over and stopped at his side. "Did I say something wrong?"

"No, it's . . . Well, I'd rather not say to be honest with you."

"I've offended you somehow?"

"No, no. I appreciate your kindness. You brought Lyle home and you've been kind to him every time you've seen him. He's drawn to you, and I trust that."

"But?"

"You're not going to let me out of this,

are you?"

"I expect you to tell me what's on your mind, Josiah Wolfe," Eva said. "I have to deal with closed-mouth men every day, and I was hoping you were different. That you'd at least say hello, or more than that, if we had the chance to speak at all. I don't get much time like this. You have to know that. Every brother of mine scares off any man that so much as looks at me. I'm gonna be an old maid before I get to say hello to anyone." Eva stopped as a distressed expression swept over her face. Her confident eyes held a look of terror in them. "I'm sorry, I didn't mean to imply anything. I should go. Morris will come looking for me any second. I have to go. I'm sorry."

She hurried back to the chest, grabbed up her slicker and bonnet, threw them on, and darted past Josiah, out into the rain, without saying another word.

Stunned, Josiah wanted to reach out to her, to stop her, to tell that he was sorry — even though he didn't know what he was sorry for — but he couldn't bring himself to move, to say anything else. All he could do was watch her disappear back inside the house and hope that she had nothing to do with the hanging.

CHAPTER 29

Night had fallen before Josiah saw a living soul other than Tom Darkson. Sergeant Dobson rode up to the barn, alone, looking no worse for the wear from the day. He dismounted and made his way to Josiah, unconcerned about the continuing rain, or anything else for that matter.

"Captain McNelly sent me out to tell you that you can disembark, Wolfe," Dobson said, tipping his hat, draining the water off it.

"So Ethan Langdon is in jail?" Josiah said.

"Him and Leland Halverson. Neither of the families caused us any trouble."

"That surprises me."

"Why's that?"

"Neither of those men are quitters. They're like snakes. Once they get a bite into something, they don't let go."

"A company of Special Force Rangers can change the tune of the worst man when Leander McNelly is in the lead."

"Well, I hadn't considered the power of the Rangers," Josiah said. "I've seen it, felt it, been part of it, but I never thought that I'd see those two men walk into a jail without being dragged."

"You missed it, because that's what happened."

"I have to tell you that makes me uneasy. I still think they're up to something."

Dobson looked around and caught sight of Tom Darkson standing under the shed. "I take it there's been nothin' of note around here?"

"Quiet. Only Langdon I've seen is the girl, Eva. She brought us coffee hours ago and disappeared. I haven't seen hide nor hair of her since, or any of the Langdon brothers. Not even Morris. I've been expecting an attack any second, but none came. It's been me and the mice here in the barn. That's it."

"All right," Dobson said. "Gather up Darkson and head back to camp. Or your own barn. No sense in you stayin' here for another second. If the Langdons try anything, we still got men on watch."

"I hope you're right about that, Dobson. I sure hope you're right."

■ ■ ■ ■

Josiah and Tom Darkson had an uneventful ride back to his land. Half of the Ranger company had remained in Seerville guarding the jail, along with a handful of Sheriff Busser's men. Dobson had told Josiah that the Rangers were on twelve-hour shifts, with the next rotation coming in the morning. Along with that, the circuit court judge was expected to arrive early the next day, and preside over the first trial at noon. McNelly hadn't included Josiah in the rotation, but he had demanded his presence for the first court date. Dobson had returned to town after the picket around the Langdons' property had been refortified.

To say the Special Forces were strained was an understatement. There were men in town, at the Halversons, the Langdons, and on a perimeter around the camp. While Josiah was relieved that he hadn't been pulled deeper into duty, he wouldn't have groused about it if McNelly had assigned him to watch one place or the other. As it was, he remained in loose custody. No one in their right mind would have thought that Josiah would run off, and they would have been right. He had done nothing wrong, at least in his mind. If anything, he wanted his day in court. A fair-minded judge didn't cause him any fear. He had done nothing criminal, was not responsible for the death of the sheriff. He'd been in the wrong place at the wrong time.

Tom Darkson went off to take care of his own needs and Josiah found his way to the barn, with Ofelia and Scrap waiting for the latest word on what was going on. He filled them in with what he knew, then shed his gear and prepared to eat a bit of Ofelia's *menudo.*

The rain had slowed to a drizzle and the air had grown colder than it had been during the day. The night was dark, gray, and wet, allowing for no easy comfort to be found by anyone.

Once Josiah was dried off and settled with a bowl of stew, Scrap joined him.

"You look worried," Scrap said. "Don't tell me you're not. I've seen your face drawn down and eyes fidget uncertain before."

Lyle slept in a bedroll at the back of the barn. Ofelia toiled about to and fro, doing a little bit of nothing, giving a wide berth to both men. She'd said little since Josiah's return. On a normal day he wouldn't have noticed or thought a thing about her distance, but considering what she'd been through — and being left behind with Scrap for company — gave Josiah cause for concern. He didn't seek her out, though, to ask what was the matter. "This whole thing feels wrong. I think Captain McNelly is being played for a fool."

"You should tell him. Or send a message with Dobson. I know you don't know Sarge, didn't ride with him, but he seems all right. He's a fair type, not mad with power like some hard-soles turn out to be. I wasn't talkin' 'bout you. You was a decent sergeant, too."

"That's a fair assessment of a man from someone who's pretty hard on the upper ranks most of the time."

"The upper what?"

"Never mind." Josiah spooned some beans up and took a slurp of the stew. Even it tasted off. "How'd Dobson come on, anyway? No one's said, and we haven't had much of a chance to talk since you came into camp. The arm still hurt?"

Scrap rubbed his elbow through the sling. "Doc gave me something for the pain. Eased back the dose so's I wouldn't fall dead to sleep. I'll be okay. He said it would take time. I figure I'll be back in the saddle tomorrow."

"You think?" Josiah set the bowl down.

"Dobson came on a few days after you headed out. Him and the captain fought together in the war."

"I thought they seemed comfortable with each other. I 'spect that's a good thing."

"You gonna tell me what's got you unnerved then? I know it ain't all about Dobson," Scrap said.

"Doesn't have nothing to do with him except I don't think he sees things here any more certain than the captain does."

"You should tell 'em what you think."

"I said something to Dobson. He thinks everyone's been tamed by the reputation of the Rangers."

"If it ain't that, then what is it?"

"Don't know. But it sure feels like a ploy to me."

"By both of 'em, those Halversons and Langdons?"

"You know, Scrap, I wouldn't put it past them to get together and partner up to take on the Rangers. I'm not saying that's what's going on. I got a bad feeling is all. They're up to something. I know it as sure as I'm sitting here, I can't figure out what it is. Ethan and Leland walked into jail without one ounce of trouble. That's like a cow jumping over the barn to me. Impossible, unless there's some unseen force behind it."

Scrap stood up and dusted off his trousers with his good hand. "Well, let's me and you go find out if you're right."

Josiah stared up at Scrap, still pale from his injury, arm in a sling, and his eyes glazed a bit from the last shot of morphine Doc gave him. "Sit down. You're not going anywhere."

"What are you gonna do, Wolfe, if it turns out you're right and there's more blood spilt? Maybe the blood of someone you know? I'll tell you what you're gonna do, you're gonna beat yourself up, then disappear into a cave of guilt and not be good for anyone for a long time to come. I've been 'round you too long not to know that. If you think somethin's afoot, then let's take a ride and find out. You and me know how to do that. We was spies in Corpus, then rode out undercover pushin' cattle north, pickin' up trails, and makin' our way on our own — and here we are faced with a situation that needs looked into. It ain't your future that's on the line, it's that boy's over there, too. Why can't we go now?"

"Because you got a bullet hole in your arm is why. You're not yourself."

"I'd say you're not, either. You might not have a bullet hole in you, but you've had the bravery beat out of you. It shows on your face, and I don't mean with those ugly bruises you're a carryin'. No, it's somethin' else. You let those Langdons get to you is what has happened. You're a feared of them. I don't blame you, I don't. I was the one that took the shot that brought Charlie down to earth, at least long enough for 'im to hang. I saw one of them Langdons take a boy hostage and not think a thing about it. They's a scourge. Animals more than men. But this is your land, your life. I know you got a boy to consider, but you can't raise him up to have his tail tucked like some dog, so cowed he can't stand the sight of his own shadow. He sees you do it, he will, too."

Josiah stood up and faced Scrap. "You calling me a coward?"

"No, I'm tellin' you that you're a feared is all, Wolfe. I ain't never seen you like this before. I'm a scad worried 'bout you. And that boy. I'm worried about him, too." Scrap flicked his head to the back of the barn where Lyle was sleeping.

Josiah followed Scrap's intent and motion. He caught sight of Ofelia as he looked. She looked down and away from him as soon as they made eye contact. "You and Ofelia must've had a long talk while I was gone."

277

Scrap looked away, too. "She don't talk much."

"If you say so."

"Unless you ask her questions, I guess."

Ofelia disappeared to the back of the barn, out of sight. Maybe she was embarrassed, or upset, Josiah didn't know. He would talk to her later. He had to. There was no way around it now. He was a little rattled that Scrap could look so deep inside of him. Not many people could do that. Ofelia had helped him, that was for sure, but Scrap had still wanted to know what was going on, and that meant something to Josiah. It sure did.

"So," Josiah said, "you think you're up to sneaking out of camp with me and poking around in the dark to try and figure out what the hell is going on?"

A wide smile crossed Scrap's face. "Be like old times, wouldn't it? Me and you on the trail, flushin' scoundrels out of the bush. If anything'd make me feel better, it'd be that."

"Me, too," Josiah said. "Me, too. Let's go."

CHAPTER 30

As Josiah cinched up Clipper's saddle, he heard someone approach him from behind. He turned to face Ofelia. "I don't think this is a good idea, *señor,*" she said. "I know it is not my place to say so, but I fear for your *la seguridad,* um, your safety." The collar of her dress was still tight around her plump neck, and worry had settled on her brow like it planned to stay for an extended visit.

"Scrap is right," Josiah said. "I can't be afraid to follow my instinct. If something happens and more lives are lost, then I will never forgive myself."

"These are bad, bad men." She looked away, out across the silent camp. The rain had stopped, leaving the air moist and chilly. Ofelia wore a shawl draped across her shoulders. She shivered and pulled it tighter across her chest.

"I'm sorry about what happened to you. I failed you."

"No, they were lying in wait. I killed a man. There are consequences for a woman like me."

"There shouldn't be. You were protecting yourself, Lyle, and the cabin. You had no choice."

"No, I didn't."

"Lying in wait is what they do. That's why I think I need to go find out what I can. I want to make sure you never have to worry about being attacked again. Me and Lyle can't lose you."

A quick tremble replaced Ofelia's shiver. Even in the dim light put off by a low fire, it was easy see her eyes glaze with tears. "I do not like being afraid, either. Perhaps, you are right." She took a breath. "I do not blame you for what happened. I am lucky to be alive. If the Rangers would not have shown up when they did *Yo estaría muerto,* I would be dead. The Langdons have yet to claim their revenge. My luck is thin. The Rangers will not be here forever, and we will continue to live on edge if nothing is done."

"I'll be careful," Josiah said, as he climbed into the saddle.

"I worry that *Señor* Scrap is not up to the task."

"I'd have to tie him up to keep him from going."

A smile flittered across Ofelia's face. "You are right there. Please be cautious. I will not sleep a wink until you both return. These are bad men, *señor.* They want us dead. Remember that."

"I know, Ofelia. I want our worry to end so we can get on with what we set out to do, start over, and get on with our lives." With that, Josiah pressed his boots against Clipper and loped away. He didn't look back, didn't have it in him to glance over his shoulder and see the concern and care he was riding away from. That kind of thing was fragile in any form. If he had learned one thing since leaving home, and then returning, it was that.

Josiah and Scrap had made arrangements to meet up outside of the camp. One sighting of Scrap sneaking off from Doc Tinker, or any of the other Rangers who had stayed back, would have ended their plan before it had a chance to start. As luck would have it, there were few men in camp. The trick was going to be getting past the picket.

Scrap eased his blue roan, Missy, out on the trail beyond the light of the campfire. He edged up alongside Josiah and matched

Clipper's pace.

The two horses were accustomed to each other. Clipper perked up his ears whenever Missy was around, stood a little taller at the withers, if that was possible. Josiah had thought his mount had a horse crush on Missy from the first day they met.

Scrap sat tall in the saddle, with his bad arm hidden by the slicker he wore. It was black and helped conceal his body. "Anybody see you get away?" It was a whisper.

"I didn't bother to care. I rode out like I had someplace to go. Nobody's up and about anyway. It's the guard up the road we need to worry about."

"We got that covered."

It didn't take long to find out. A guard, a Ranger named Jim Baez, confronted them on the trail. "Hey," he said, lighting a torch with a match, "where you goin', Elliot?"

Josiah and Scrap stopped their horses a few feet shy of the guard. Neither of them bothered to go for their revolvers. There was no need.

"They's an ointment at the mercantile Doc wants me to put on as soon as possible," Scrap said.

"Mercantile's closed by now," Ranger Baez said.

"Them folks live there. They're used to

gettin' woke up at all times of the night."

"What are you doin', Wolfe?"

Josiah sat relaxed in the saddle, the reins loose in his hands. "Couldn't let the boy be out here in the dark by himself, now could I?"

"Who you callin' 'boy'?" Scrap said.

"You. Compared to me," Josiah said.

"Well, I guess you are an old man. I'm surprised you can stay awake after dark."

"Only because I have to babysit you."

They ignored Baez with intention. He watched them, studying one to the other. "You two ain't playin' with me, are you?"

"Why would we do that?" Scrap said.

"Don't seem to me that either one of you should be away from camp," Baez said.

"Well," Scrap said, "let's go back and ask Doc Tinker hisself. That'd mean you'd have to leave your post, but if you don't believe me, I 'spect the trouble that might come from that would be worth it. What do you think, Baez? Come on, let's go back and ask Doc." He tightened Missy's reins, and pulled her head back toward camp.

"No, wait," Baez said, jittery. "You ain't never lied to me before, Elliot. I guess you ain't gonna start now."

Scrap stopped, while Josiah sat quiet, watching the guard. He wanted to smile, to applaud Scrap's performance, but that would have to wait.

"Okay, well, I appreciate that, Baez," Scrap said. "The sooner I get that ointment, the better off I'll be. I got me some pain, I'll tell you." He rubbed his shoulder and cocked his jaw to exaggerate the pain.

"You best get goin', then," Baez said.

Neither of them waited for Jim Baez to change his mind. They urged their horses to an easy trot, riding out of the torchlight, into the darkness, proud as hell of themselves for getting past the first hurdle. Now all they had to do was come up with a reason for showing up at the Halversons' front door so late in the evening.

CHAPTER 31

The Rangers weren't the only ones who had a picket set up around their camp. The Halversons had a perimeter of guards set up, too. Josiah had expected them to, and wasn't surprised when he and Scrap were stopped by two riders beyond the entrance to the Halversons' farm.

"Who goes there?" the first man said. There were no stars or moon to give off light to aid in seeing, only adjusted eyesight from being in the dark long enough to adapt to it. The man wore all black clothes and his horse was either chestnut or black, too. It was hard to tell. But what was easy to see was the rifle in his hand.

"Josiah Wolfe. I'm here to see Luke."

Scrap sat next to Josiah, so close their knees almost touched. It was a good thing the two horses tolerated each other well. Neither man had pulled their weapon. No use sparking a fire if it could be avoided.

"You got a lot of nerve riding up here at night with all that's going on, Wolfe. We got orders to shoot first and ask questions later, but Joe here thought that was your horse. Not too many appaloosas around here. Said you was a Halverson, that I should hold off."

Josiah didn't recognize the man. He couldn't see him clear enough to know if he knew him. His voice didn't sound familiar, but that didn't mean anything. Lily had a lot of family. A man couldn't be expected to remember every voice he'd heard three years on. Joe, on the other hand, was a cousin to Luke. Josiah knew that much, so he figured the unknown man was kin, too, not a hired hand set out on the picket. Had to be somebody they trusted.

Josiah decided not to defend himself and claim he wasn't a Halverson. For once, the connection might come in handy. "Who do I have the pleasure of speaking to?" he said.

Neither man moved nor made any effort to make their identities known.

"Joe's brother, Clem. We's cousins to Luke," the man said.

Josiah resettled himself in the saddle. "I remember now. I've been gone awhile."

That didn't seem to matter to Clem, who was in the lead. "What business do you have with Luke at this hour?"

"I need to talk to him. Something I over-heard," Josiah lied.

"What was that?" Clem said.

"I'd rather talk to Luke." Josiah used his best command voice.

Clem leaned over and whispered some-thing to Joe that Josiah couldn't understand. He didn't interfere, just sat there and waited.

"He ain't around," Clem said. "He's over at the Keystone Hall. You know where that's at?"

"That place at the crossroads over toward Bullard?" Josiah said.

"That'd be it."

The Keystone Hall had been a saloon ever since Josiah could remember. One of those establishments that continued to survive whether there was prosperity or depression. The owner, whoever that was, had chosen the right place to offer a watering hole to weary travelers. Tyler was still a bit of a ride, and there were few places to offer a rest and stopping place for the stagecoach lines. Not being a drinking man, or a traveler, Josiah never had much reason to visit the place. He'd passed it a few times. Wandered in out of curiosity, but never stayed around. It had a rough reputation, and was a magnet for men looking for a good time, trouble, or both. They most often came in the same package.

It was a quick ride to the Keystone Hall. The place sat alongside the road, lighting up the darkness with the same intention of a fire set to draw moths. Every window was lit, and the chink of tacky piano keys danced out the open door on the night air. The music reached Josiah's ears long before he saw the light. A line of horses stood in wait at the hitching post, and a few wagons with their teams were scattered off the road. The building itself was long and narrow, one story with a peaked roof, dotted with chimneys. The smell of grilled steak filled the air, along with the charred aroma of a long-burning fire. A couple of small shacks sat behind the building, but those were hidden in the shadow of darkness. There were no other buildings or houses at the crossroads. Beyond the hall was miles of nothingness. Forests and fields. Until the road reached Tyler, and then civilization started to show itself.

Josiah found a spot and hitched Clipper up to the post. Scrap did the same thing, only at the end, farther away from the appaloosa than his horse wanted to be. Missy nickered and complained as he tied her up.

"Hush, girl, you'll be fine," Scrap said.

Josiah stood in wait next to his horse, taking in the sight of the roadhouse. It was an oasis for the weary and the wanton, for the thirsty and the satisfied, for the loveless and the lonely. The lights were bright, the sounds noisy — laughing and yelling mixed with the music — and the smells were delectable. He couldn't remember the last time he'd had a good steak.

Scrap joined him, and Josiah said, "I think maybe you should wait out here."

"What in tarnation for, Wolfe. I got a little pain comin' on in the shoulder and a taste of whiskey could tame the beast."

"And let another one out."

"What're you sayin'? That I can't handle my drink?"

"I think that's what I said." Josiah could see Scrap clear enough from the light emitting from the Keystone Hall to know he'd touched a sore spot, but he didn't care. "The last thing you need is to get riled up and throw a punch or two. You're a one-armed man. It wouldn't take much of a man to knock you down."

Scrap looked to his hurt arm, then to the saloon. "Ain't a man in there I can't whoop with one arm tied behind my back."

"Says you."

"Yeah, says me."

"That's not why we're here, is it?" Josiah said as calm as he could.

Scrap looked at Josiah with rage building in his eyes, but after a second, thought better of letting the anger grow into a fury. "I 'spect not."

"Good. The last thing we need is trouble. All we're here to do is talk to Luke and see if we can find out what they're up to."

"Yeah, yeah, I know."

"I'm serious, Scrap."

"Okay. I'll be a good boy."

"Sure you will."

The inside of the Keystone Hall gave the place its name. It was nothing but one long room — a hall — ample enough to hold two full-length bars, and a healthy collection of sitting tables. There were some game tables at the back of the room, along with a piano player, set up on a dais. A picture of a naked lady stretched out on a sofa hung over the piano. The painting left nothing to the imagination. Every inch of her flesh was exposed. The piano player was a Negro man, the only black face in a sea of white. There were at least twenty men in the saloon, standing at the bar, sitting at the tables having idle chats, or playing poker or faro. A few dolled-up girls made their way around the room, servicing the customers' beers, or bringing them food. They were dressed in revealing blouses, low slung so a majority of their breasts showed, along with tight-fitting dresses that hugged the curves of their bodies. The smell of steak outside found its way inside, mixed with the yeasty beer, and the smoke of cigars and cigarettes.

It didn't take Josiah long to find Luke Halverson. He was sitting at the bar alone — which came as a relief to Josiah. It would be easier to talk to him.

Scrap followed Josiah to the bar, quiet, checking the place out — and like Josiah, looking for an alternative way out. They had gotten the attention of a strapping lad who stood at the end of the bar. He was a chucker with broad biceps, a square jaw, and wore a pair of pearl-handled Colts on his hips. There had to be another armed man or two scattered throughout the hall, waiting for trouble to break out. Authority rested in the chucker's eyes like it had been born there, and he eyed both Scrap and Josiah with suspicion.

"I thought I'd find you here," Josiah said to Luke as he eased up beside him. Scrap stood back, watching the three chuckers starting to circle, like vultures about to descend on a kill.

Josiah's presence startled Luke. "What the hell are you doin' here, Wolfe?"

"Wondering why you left me on my own, first off."

"You know why."

Both men elevated their voices, fighting to be heard over the crowd, over the music. "To tell your father that the Rangers had arrived?"

Luke wore a day-old beard and his clothes were stained with dirt. He looked weary, out of sorts, as he picked up the beer mug in front of him and took a long drink. "They took him in, but 'spect you already know that since you're tight with them fellas."

"I rode with this company. Sheer luck that they were the ones to show up."

"Bad luck, you ask me."

"You had to figure something was coming once Sheriff Cliburn was killed," Josiah said.

"We didn't have nothin' to do with that, and you know it. The shots that took that man down came from behind, from where the Langdons were staked out. You know that's true as much as I do."

Josiah had been paying full attention to Luke, and had lost sight of Scrap, but a loud voice caught his attention.

"I asked you your business here, stranger?"

It was the muscle-bound chucker standing in front of Scrap, tense, intent on winning the confrontation.

"I'm thirsty," Scrap said.

"I don't see no drink."

Josiah turned around, about to ask what the problem was, but Scrap puffed himself up and said, "I don't like your attitude."

The chucker reached out to grab Scrap's good arm, but he dodged the reach.

"I think you need to leave," the chucker said.

"Is there a problem here?" Josiah said.

It didn't matter. Scrap said yes, there was a problem, then jumped forward and took a swing at the chucker with his good fist. The swing landed upside the man's cheek and sent him sprawling backward. He toppled over one table, scattering food and drink, rolling on the floor, and knocked over another. The punch ignited a swarm of fists and yells that stung as fast and furious as hornets, and both Josiah and Scrap found themselves in the middle of a fight with at least ten men.

CHAPTER 32

The bloodied chucker dove at Scrap, sending him sprawling backward onto the floor. Scrap took out a plump woman wearing a green satin dress and a fake diamond tiara. She screamed and dumped the trays she'd been carrying, dropping a plateful of steak and potatoes on a thin, slicked-back black-haired man wearing a large dark brown checked suit. That man came up swinging and yelling, his suit dotted with butter and grease from the piece of meat, hitting the first face within reach. The slap of flesh echoed upward, knuckle to nose, boots to shins. The fight was in full force and the piano player played on, adding to the noise and urgency of the melee. No matter where Josiah looked someone was fighting someone else.

He dodged his way over to Scrap, grabbed the boy by the collar, and pulled him to his feet. "We need to get the hell out of here," he said, ducking a punch from the plump woman.

"I spied a door at the end of the bar," Scrap said.

"We got to get Luke," Josiah answered. They both looked to the bar, but Luke was already in the midst of fighting off two men. One of the men looked to be another chucker, and he was working on wearing Luke down, battering him with a flurry of punches.

"Looks like he needs our help," Scrap said, then dodged more fists and punches, while he made his way to Luke. He grabbed the chucker by the collar, spun him around, and punched him in the nose. Blood exploded outward, spraying forward like a hose had been busted.

Josiah was close behind, but stopped short of jumping into the fight. A sudden gunshot silenced the crowd, but it didn't end the fighting. Fists still jammed through the air, including Scrap's. He took care of the other man attacking Luke, with Luke's help.

Josiah yelled to Luke and Scrap, "Come on, let's get out of here." Then he headed down the bar, zigzagging between punches, looking over his shoulder, trying to see who had fired off the gunshot, making sure he wasn't a target. Scrap and Luke followed, pushing through the fighting as they went.

Scrap had been right about the door next to the bar. It led to the back of a hall where all of the beer barrels were stored. Josiah pushed through until he found another door that led outside. He was free of the tangle and danger of flying fists, and took a deep breath of fresh air. He waited until Scrap and Luke joined him, then broke into a run toward Clipper. All three of them were on their horses in a matter of seconds, riding into the darkness, away from the Keystone Hall.

Another gunshot fired off inside, echoing into the night, assuring Josiah that he'd made the right decision to run.

The trio stopped about a mile down the road to gather themselves. Once he'd calmed himself, and realized that he was safe, Josiah came to the quick conclusion that the fight in the hall had all been Scrap's fault. Now that he wasn't afraid of being shot, he could be angry. "You about got us killed, Scrap," he said, resettling himself in the saddle.

"What're you talkin' about?" Scrap said. His incredulousness shined through in the dark of night.

"I told you that we weren't there to fight,

and what did you go and do? Start a fight."

Luke turned his horse and eased to the other side of Josiah. "Let the boy alone. It would have happened no matter what. The minute the Ranger walked in he had a target on his head. They's men there with enough drink in 'em that will look for a fight to prove their worth to any onlookers, or for the fun of it, for that matter."

"See, Wolfe, get off your high horse," Scrap said.

Josiah ignored Scrap and took what Luke said into consideration. "We went there to talk to you."

"I figured as much. I didn't 'spect you showing up was happenstance."

"I figured you'd be camped outside the jail, to be honest with you," Josiah said.

"What for? Pa's locked up. Nothin' I can do 'bout that. There's Rangers and sheriff's deputies swarmed all over the place. It ain't like we could bust him out."

Scrap sat back, able to pass off any discomfort. Josiah hoped he would keep his mouth shut and let him do all of the talking.

"That wouldn't be a good idea," Josiah said.

"Never our plan, anyways," Luke said. "I gotta tell ya, none of this was. Sheriff Cliburn getting kilt changed everything. I kept tellin' Pa there was trouble comin' after that, but he wouldn't believe me. I told him we should make peace with the Langdons, but he wouldn't hear of it. Stubborn old mule. He said he wouldn't stop fightin' 'til he was six feet under, which by the way I see it, won't be long. If the judge don't send him to the gallows, the Langdons'll get to him. It's only a matter of time."

"That why he surrendered so easy?"

Luke cast Josiah a sideways glance. "You're family, but you're not, you know that, don't you?"

"What's that got to do with anything?"

"I can't tell you everything, is all. That's what I mean. Here you are ridin' with a Ranger yourself. Far as I know you could be back in their good graces. Sheriff said you was under arrest, but McNelly vouched for you, and, well, here you are. Once a Ranger, always a Ranger."

"So, your pa gave himself up for a reason?" Josiah said, ignoring the comment.

"You don't quit, do you?"

"Curious is all."

"Sure, you are." Luke looked down the road, back toward the Keystone Hall. They could still smell the smoke, hear the noise, though it was muted by the distance and trees. "Look, I gotta get movin', but I'll tell you this, Josiah. This feud ain't over. Pa won't let it go and I won't neither. Not now. He didn't kill the sheriff and he don't belong in jail. He's an old man."

"Ethan Langdon's in jail, too."

"And he damn well should be. You know that shot came from where the Langdons was holdin' back. If he didn't fire it, he ordered the shootin' to start. Same thing, you ask me. He tried to end this feud that day and his plan backfired." Luke was working himself up into a rage. His face glistened with sweat in the darkness and his breathing had accelerated. "Ethan took something from me, from us, all of us, by bringin' the Rangers here, and puttin' Pa in jail, so we ain't got no choice but to retaliate. He took somethin' of ours, so we're gonna take somethin' of his. Somethin' real valuable to 'im."

"What are you talking about?" Josiah said.

Luke didn't answer him. He sat stiff in his saddle, glared at Josiah for a long second, then turned his horse and rode off like lightning was chasing after him.

Josiah was speechless, trying to figure out what had happened, what Luke meant by what he'd said.

"Well, that sure wasn't worth a lick of salt.

Whatcha gonna do now, Wolfe?" Scrap said.

"I don't know. Wait for a minute, I guess."

"Wait for what?"

"Let this settle is all, so I can figure out what to do next."

"You still sore about me startin' that fight?"

"No, I figure Luke was right about that. All you had to do was show up and them fellas would have lined up to take a shot at knocking you down. Doesn't matter that you're one-handed. You made it more attractive to them is what that did."

"Yeah, they figured they had a chance at whoopin' me, but they was wrong is what they were."

"They were." Josiah stared off down the trail after Luke. He couldn't see a thing. A line of pine trees towered over the road and the sky was covered with clouds. There was only natural light to see by. "He's up to something," Josiah said.

"Figured that, regardless. But what's he think he can take from this Langdon fella that's so valuable? They been fightin' over land and braggin' rights the way I see it, and that ain't worked out too well for either of 'em. Seems to me both families are at a draw. They ain't got nothin' left with both head men in jail. They lost their freedom now. I know a thing or two about that, about bein' tossed in jail when I didn't deserve to be there. Lucky I had you to prove I was innocent. Maybe Luke's up to the same thing?"

Josiah still stared after Luke, half-listening to Scrap, half-remembering what Luke had said. "No, I don't think that's what he's up to at all," he said.

"What then?"

"I think I know what Luke's up to."

"You know what he's gonna take?"

"It's not what, it's who."

"And who's that, then?"

"Eva. They're going after Eva. She's the most valuable thing Ethan's got left."

CHAPTER 33

There was still a chill in the air, left over from the recent rain, being pushed along on a steady breeze. The camp was quiet; what Rangers remained on the rotating shift were catching as much rest as possible. No one moved about, satisfied with the security provided by the picket. Most of the fires had burned down to the coals. Only a few bore any flames. Short shadows flickered on the sides of the white dog tents. There was no insect or bird noise to taint the peaceful night. It felt like returning home to Josiah as he rode in with Scrap. Not the home where the cabin sat, or the graves where his loved ones laid in their eternal rest, or the land he had known since he was a boy. Not that home. But the home he'd had with the Rangers. Camp life, riding with Scrap, having a purpose, a sense of belonging to something larger than himself. He hadn't realized how much he liked — and missed

— being a Ranger, until the company showed up in Seerville. It was almost like old times. Almost. But things had changed. Josiah was no longer a Ranger, but under the protection and in the custody of Captain Leander McNelly. He had been accused of murder. It was a cloud that hung over his head no matter where he went, or how much he wanted to forget that it had happened to him.

Josiah headed for the barn, dismounted, and hurried inside to check on Ofelia and Lyle. He found them asleep in the back stall, comfortable, safe, covered in a thin layer of colorful Mexican blankets. Ofelia stirred at his presence, raised, and looked to him. Josiah put his fingers to his lips, mouthed the words "Go back to sleep," then backed out of the stall.

Scrap was waiting for him outside the barn. "What're you gonna do, Wolfe?"

"See if the captain's here and tell him what I think. If he's not here, then Dobson will be in his place, and I'll do the same. I figure I'm going to need some help, at least let them know what I'm up to."

"And what's that? Somethin' me and you can do?"

"I'm going to bring Eva here where she's safe. No offense, Scrap, but I think I need a

303

man with two hands for this job."

"You get hit upside the head a little too hard at that dance hall? I held my own, thank you very much. Both of us got out of there alive."

"With a few new bruises and scrapes." Josiah exhaled and looked out over the camp. "It's not going to be easy getting to Eva. The Langdons are expecting something from the Halversons. They might be a little relaxed since the Rangers are here, too. Think they have an eye on the Halversons, which is true. But they're as riled that Ethan's in jail as Luke was that Leland's there, too. Morris is in charge, but still taking orders from Ethan, even though he's in jail. Morris won't let his guard down. You're not yourself, Scrap. You still have morphine in your blood and you used yourself up back there in a way you shouldn't have."

"You're going tonight?"

"As soon as I talk to the captain or Dobson."

"You're gonna sneak over to the Langdons and snatch up that girl, then waltz your way back to camp. That's your plan?"

"Something like that."

"I hope the captain has a better idea," Scrap said. " 'Cause that sounds like a surefire way of winding up in that cemetery over there."

"You got any better ideas?"

"Yup. Let those fellas fight it out between themselves, and whatever falls will fall. That girl don't mean nothin' to you. Seems like a foolhardy plan to me. You can't save everyone, Wolfe. Lord knows I've seen you try."

Josiah didn't say anything else. He knew Scrap was mad because he didn't want him to go with him. Plain and simple. His sour attitude was nothing more than that.

"Where you goin', Wolfe?" Scrap said, as Josiah walked away.

"I done told you," he said over his shoulder. "I'm going to go talk to the captain."

McNelly was in town. Dobson was in charge of the camp. It took him a minute to answer when Josiah called out his name at the door of his tent. The sergeant roused and answered Josiah. "What?"

"It's Wolfe, Dobson, I need to talk to you."

Dobson peered out of the tent. He had his nightshirt on. "What time is it?"

"Late, sir. I'm sorry to bother you. But I've found out some information and I think we need to act."

Dobson's face went from half-asleep to angry. A burst of red pushed up his neck and didn't stop until it reached the tips of his ears. "What'd you say?"

"Can I come in? It would be easier to explain."

Dobson threw open the tent door and cocked his head with a hard turn, motioning Josiah inside.

The dog tent was smaller than McNelly's, but larger than the rest of the company's. There was room for a sleeping cot, a desk, and a chair. It was as tidy as a West Point dormitory. Nothing out of place. The next day's clothes hung at the foot of the bed over a pair of polished boots. Dobson was neat, ordered, and had ambition. It was easy to see him as a Ranger captain someday.

"How'd you come across this information?" Dobson said, walking to the back of the tent, going after a pair of trousers.

"Me and Scrap took a ride over to the Halversons. Luke wasn't there, but we found out he was over near Bullard at the Keystone Hall. We found him there."

Dobson pulled his trousers on, not taking his eyes off of Josiah. "Oh, you and Elliot up and decided to leave camp without letting anyone know. The same Elliot who took a bullet to the shoulder and was dazed on morphine the last time I saw him." Dobson was furious. He looked like a trapped mountain lion. "Let me guess, you got yourself in a bit of a scrape? Exchanged fisticuffs with more than one of those men at this dance hall? Then came running back here for protection."

"We didn't need protection. How'd you know?"

"You got a few new bruises. I pay attention, Wolfe. Did you think I wouldn't notice?"

"I'm not hiding anything."

"Keep it that way."

"Okay, I will. Things didn't go as I'd planned, but Luke rode off with us and I got him to talking. I think the Halversons are going to go after the Langdon girl. I think they're going to ambush her on the way to the jail tomorrow. They're going to try and take her — or worse, kill her."

"And what's that got to do with anything?"

"You don't understand, Dobson. There will be no peace if that happens. If anything happens to Eva Langdon, this feud will go on for generations. It won't matter if the Rangers build a fort here. That war will last forever and countless lives will be lost. Innocent lives."

"And you think if you what? If you intervene, you can stop this war?"

"I think we should bring her here. Protect her. There's no other choice."

"Bring her here? To the camp? How do you expect us to do that? Ride over to the Langdons' farm and offer to guard their sister? Don't you think it was a considerable risk for the captain to ride over there and take Ethan Langdon into custody? And now, you think we should do it again? How do you think that will go over, Wolfe? You know the Langdons better than any of us."

Josiah stiffened as Dobson stopped in front of him, intent on dressing him down further. "I didn't say that was my plan. I can make my way to the house through the back of my property, get her attention, and bring her here."

"So, you're going to get past their perimeter and go up to their house without alerting anyone, and convince this woman to join you here?"

"Yes, well, that's what I'm thinking."

"That's a ridiculous plan. You won't get ten feet on the Langdon property without getting your head blown clean off, Wolfe. Then what happens to that boy of yours? Seems to me you're intent on makin' him an orphan." Dobson had raised his voice. Josiah was sure every man in camp could hear their conversation, had been awakened by the thunder of the sergeant's discontent. "I forbid you to do such a thing, Wolfe. It's as bad a plan as I've ever heard."

"I'm not a Ranger."

"You're in our custody."

Disappointed, Josiah walked to the door. "I'd like to speak to Captain McNelly."

"You know that's not possible. Not this late. It's too dangerous to ride into town. Besides, he would side with me. I've made my decision, and it's final."

Josiah exhaled and opened the tent flap to exit.

Dobson stopped him. "I'm serious, Wolfe. If you disobey my order there will be consequences for your actions. Consequences you will not like. Do you understand?"

"Yes, Sergeant Dobson. I understand," he said, as he pushed outside, already thinking about a different plan.

CHAPTER 34

Josiah roused before dawn started to break. Darkness still covered the camp, and the first bird had yet to practice its first note. Silence reigned over his small parcel of the world — which was the way he wanted it. Ofelia and Lyle slept in their stall, and Scrap had taken up a spot close by, rolling out his bedroll, making himself at home under Josiah's roof. Scrap's presence was more of a comfort than an annoyance.

The air was moist and cool, urging Josiah to stay under the blanket for as long as he could. It took him a minute to wake up, to clear his eyes and let them adjust enough to know the time of day. Once he was awake, he eased to his feet, shivered, then grabbed up his gun belt. Once outside, he stopped shy of the corral and checked his revolvers.

As much as he hated the idea, Josiah's plan relied on a matter of luck. But that didn't stop him. After he buckled his belt on, he edged toward the cemetery staying as deep in the shadows as he could. The risk he was taking was not lost on him. Dobson's warning had been clear, but there was no turning back, no dissuading him that Eva was not worth saving.

He passed by the gravestones without offering a hello. He ignored them the best he could, easing along with care, avoiding the snap of a fallen branch, or the crunch of dead leaves. He'd had plenty of practice at his stealth skills as a Ranger and a soldier, and needed to employ every practice of silent travel he could use. For all he knew, Dobson had a watch on him.

It wasn't long before he was at the fence that separated his land from the Langdons'. He stopped and looked out over the field, across the rising hill, then to the gray sky. A robin stirred not far from him, drawing his attention by flittering from one ash tree branch to another, then onward to the top, where it stopped and jutted out its breast to sing in the new day. There was hope in the song, but that was the only place Josiah could find it. There was no sign of Eva. He had gambled on her taking some quiet time again, coming to the fence to look out over his land to find some peace and comfort in the presence of the Rangers, or something more.

There was nothing else awake for as far as the eye could see. A thin layer of fog hovered over the hill, stationary wisps hanging in the air like daggers. The wind had died to nothing. Stopped. A row of tall pine trees stood over the horizon, the detail of branches and color lost to the gray morning. There was little sun shining through the clouds overhead. The robin continued to sing, but its notes were sullen, marked by long stretches of silence. Any exuberance the bird held had been used up in the spring.

The choice was clear: Cross the fence or go back to the barn.

He'd come this far. There was no turning back. With that, Josiah hoisted his foot up on the first rail of the fence. But a rustling behind him caused him to freeze, almost in midair. He glanced over his shoulder expecting to see Dobson, or one of the Rangers. Instead he made eye contact with an animal. It was no ordinary animal. It was a wolf, and it was as still as Josiah was, staring at him, judging the risk, eyeing him like it was deciding whether or not to attack.

There was no question that the beast was a wolf and not a coyote. It looked to weigh about sixty pounds, a healthy weight for a female. The tips of its ears were red, while most of the other fur was gray, with some red mixed in. The thing that confounded Josiah was that it didn't look afraid of him. Anytime he had ever seen a wolf it was on the run, or a fleeing shadow. Men he knew used them for target practice. The only good wolf was a dead wolf. The same thing Luke had said about the Langdons. And that thinking was right, at least about the wolves. He had heard tell of settler stories of a wolf carrying off a baby, or a pack circling a sick calf, bringing it down with ease. Cattlemen loathed the wolves and swore to obliterate their existence. They were Indians in fur. Men feared their wildness, hated their heathen ways. They had to be dominated, or destroyed, so the white man could thrive.

The wolf was a frightful creature. Standing before him, silent and intelligent. If wild horses could be tamed, why not a wolf? He had also heard of wolves mixing with farmers' dogs, mating to ensure their bloodline continued. Maybe that was what this one was. A half-breed, part tame, part wild. Josiah wondered if it belonged to the Langdons. They would be the type to try and own a creature like this one.

The wolf growled, bared its teeth, and stepped closer to Josiah. He moved his right hand to the grip of his Peacemaker. Sweat broke out across his lip, and whether he liked it or not, his heart raced a little faster. He wondered if the wolf could smell fear.

The wolf stopped. Its hackles were up — angry, in a rage, threatening to attack. There was no reason that Josiah could see for its attitude, other than it was wild. Men had their reasons to hate and fear.

The robin had stopped singing, ushering in more silence. Like a breath held. Waiting. Not even the wind had stirred back up. The fog lingered, moving on a slow, unseen — or felt — current of cool October air.

Josiah lifted his revolver out of the holster, aimed the barrel at the wolf, and pulled the hammer back with his thumb. The animal didn't back down. It continued to growl. The whites of its teeth glowed bright in the dim morning light. They were fierce — long, pointed, meant for tearing apart flesh.

He wrapped his finger around the trigger and hesitated before he applied any more pressure.

"Josiah, stop."

It was a female voice. Eva's voice.

He flinched, but didn't break eye contact with the wolf. He feared looking away from it. He didn't want to give it a chance to attack.

Footsteps approached him from behind. Gentle, nonthreatening, footsteps. "Go on," Eva continued, not missing a beat. "Get out of here. Go back to your home. You're not welcome here."

The wolf's ears twitched, then it broke eye contact with Josiah, and looked past him, to Eva, to the voice from the fog. It looked at her with suspicion, then backed up, turned around, and disappeared into the brush.

Josiah didn't take his eyes off the place where the wolf had disappeared. It was then that he saw the pups. Three of them. First years, born in the spring, weaned, and learning how to live in the world from their mother. They bounded after her, unconcerned with Josiah or Eva.

A slight tremble rippled up Josiah's arm as he lowered the Peacemaker. He had almost taken the mother from the pups. They would have been orphans. What would he have done then? He holstered his gun and turned to face Eva. "I was hoping I would find you here." He tried to hide the rattle in his voice, but he heard it and so did she.

"You were going to kill her." Eva was dressed in a shift, barefoot, with a white shawl wrapped around her shoulders. Fog spiraled at her feet. Her black hair glistened like it had been soaked in early morning dew and her eyes were wide open, full of judgment and diminishing anger.

"Only if I had to. Is she yours?"

"That one doesn't belong to anyone. Wild as her ancestors," Eva said. "I see her around. Leave her bones when I have them. Some things can't be tamed." She looked at the spot where the wolf disappeared with a forlorn expression on her face. "Why are you here?"

"To find you. There's trouble coming," Josiah said.

"The Halversons want to take me away."

"You know?"

"Morris knows. He would tan my hide if he knew I was out here. If I was giving them a chance to take me."

Josiah extended his hand across the fence. "Come back to the camp with me. We can protect you. No harm will come to you as long as you're with the Rangers."

"Oh, Josiah, if only that were true. The Rangers can't stop this. Nothing can. This fight will go on until we're all dead. Even me. I wish it wasn't so. I wish I could have a day of happiness, of freedom like that wolf, but I can't. I'll never know such a thing."

"She has her worries," Josiah said.

"She can vanish into the woods. Not see a human being for days. Imagine what her life would have been like if the railroad *had* come through here. She would have lost her home, had to have moved on. If death is not my fate, losing my home is. We are the same, the wolf and me. Creatures unwelcome in the place of our birth. Isn't that sad?"

"Don't talk like that."

"There is no hope, Josiah. Not even in your presence, in your little boy's eyes. You will move on. You will leave, too. Nothing can flourish here."

Josiah wanted nothing more than to climb the fence and wrap Eva in his arms, promise that he would take care of her, that he would make her happy. The thought shocked him, almost knocked him off his feet. He couldn't believe what he felt, what he thought.

There had been a time in Austin with Pearl Fikes, the captain's daughter, that he thought he could feel something for another woman, leave Lily's life in the past, but that relationship hadn't worked out. Pearl had been too complicated for him. A city girl with city girl tastes. Josiah was a simple man. He didn't know how to afford the fineries that a woman of her stature required. He could have never made her happy. The loss of that relationship was one of the reasons why he had left Austin, why he had left the Rangers and come home. He wanted to get as far away from Pearl Fikes as he could.

With the wolf gone, the robin started to sing again. The trill of the song got both of their attentions. They were focused on the top of the tree, on the music of the world, as another robin answered back. Then another and another joined in as sunlight cut through the clouds and sliced away the gray as if it were a sharp knife.

"You can't give up, Eva. You can't. I'll do anything to protect you. I promise."

Her face was blank, unreadable, but her eyes were locked on his. She took a step toward him without making any effort, almost like she didn't know she had moved. Unlike the wolf, she didn't bare her teeth. Desire had found its way to her eyes, to her face. She wanted to believe Josiah. But she stopped and looked over her shoulder, toward the house, invisible over the hill. Out of sight, but not out of her mind.

"I have to go home," she said. "I have to go."

"Eva, wait." Josiah hoisted himself up on

the rail of the fence, but it was too late. She had broken into a full run.

She vanished from sight, like the last time. Josiah jumped over the fence and ran after her.

CHAPTER 35

Eva stopped once she realized that Josiah was coming for her. She was halfway up the hill, standing in the middle of a cloud of low-lying fog. Tiny droplets of water danced around her, shining like diamonds as the sun poked holes through the clouds. A woodpecker knocked on a distant tree, while the sparrows, finches, and cardinals joined in with the robins, adding luster and depth to the morning chorus. The air smelled fresh and new with a little early autumn decay underneath.

Josiah caught up to Eva, but resisted taking her into his arms. He had to convince her that he could be trusted, that he meant what he said, that he could protect her from whatever harm was heading her way. "I'm not giving up," he said.

"Morris will kill you if he finds you on our land. You know that, don't you?" Her breath smelled as sweet as a garden of flowers. She was breathing heavy from the run.

"I'm not worried about Morris or any other of your brothers. I'm only worried about you."

"You mean that, don't you?"

"I do."

"Why? I'm a Langdon. There's no escaping that."

"I know that." Josiah thought for a long second, trying to form what he wanted to come out of his mouth next. He had a question that needed put to rest, but he didn't know if this was the right time to ask it or not. "Do you trust me?"

"As much as I can trust any man."

"I hope I'm not like other men."

"Maybe you're not. I don't know. I have my suspicions."

"I want to trust you," Josiah said. "Can I ask you something?"

The sun continued to increase in brightness, burning off the fog. The ethereal wisps disappeared, taking the floating sparkles with it. Another woodpecker answered the first one back; a casual conversation of hammers separated by a hundred yards. The season of love was past; maybe the long-billed knocks were nothing more than frustration.

"Yes, you can ask me anything you want."

Eva looked to the sky, then back to Josiah. "But you best hurry. Morris rises with the sun. He'll come looking for me. Or send one of the boys after me. He doesn't approve of my need for alone time in the morning. But then he wouldn't, growing up in a house filled with men. I think silence scares him."

Josiah sucked in a deep breath and forced his question up his throat. "Were you there when they tried to hang Ofelia?"

Eva didn't answer the question right away. She stared at him as if she was parsing his words, trying to understand any hidden meaning in them. "I had nothing to do with that. Once I left you at the mercantile, Morris sent me home. I drove the buggy from town and left him there. I didn't ask questions. I knew better. Trust me, I learned at a young age when to keep my mouth shut. I only heard what happened once they returned to the house, after they outran the Rangers who stopped them. I yelled at Morris, but it didn't do any good. He said Gordy's death needed avenging and that was that. I have no say in such things. He went after Ofelia whether I agreed with it or not. You ought to know that."

"I do, I think. That's what the law's for, to decide if Ofelia deserved to be hanged or not. That's the problem with all of this. They take the law into their own hands."

Eva looked away from Josiah, toward the house. "My family isn't the only one who does that."

"I didn't say they were. That's not what I mean to do, get on your bad side about this. I wanted to know is all. I couldn't imagine you standing there watching them hang another woman. She was protecting Lyle and herself. They burned down my cabin. They meant her harm. Ofelia had no choice."

"I should go. Please don't follow me." She started to walk away but Josiah reached out and pulled her back, spinning her around so they were standing toe to toe.

He couldn't restrain himself any longer. He pulled Eva to him and kissed her like he knew her, like he had been away for a long time and was returning from a tragedy in need of welcoming arms.

To his relief, Eva responded in kind, kissing him back like she had missed him as much as he had missed her. Only it wasn't that. It couldn't be. They really didn't know each other. Each of them hungered for a touch, a moment of kindness, a season of love of their own, even though winter stood at the gate, along with their family's hatred of each other warning them off, warning them that their desire was impossible, wrong, and unwelcome. Their feelings had no possibilities, but that didn't matter. All they wanted was each other.

Josiah pulled away first. "I'm sorry," he whispered.

Eva put her fingers to his lips and shushed him with a sweetness he hadn't heard since he had courted Lily. Her face was flushed and the moist diamonds that had been floating around her congregated in her eyes. They twinkled like a hundred stars had fallen into them. She looked over her shoulder until she was satisfied that she was safe, that no one had seen the kiss. "I've been waiting for that."

"I'm glad to hear that." Josiah took her hand into his, but he could tell it made her nervous. He was reluctant to let go of her, but he did. "Please come back to the camp with me. Let us keep you safe."

"I can't. Morris would come after me. You know he would. I couldn't stand the thought of any blood being shed over me, over a choice I made. I have to be with them. I'm a Langdon. That's where I belong."

"But the Halversons . . . ."

"Your family, you mean."

"They're not my blood."

"Marriage binds the soul of more than one."

"I don't believe that. My heart belongs to what's right. I don't take sides blindfolded."

Eva stepped back and turned toward the house again. "I have to go. Don't worry about me. My brothers'll keep me safe."

Josiah followed her gaze, angry that he couldn't stop her, that Morris and the rest of the Langdons had such a heavy pull on her that she would put her life at risk for them. He had failed to convince her that she was in danger, that Luke Halverson was serious about getting even. "I can't stop you?"

A smile flickered across Eva's face, then she rushed in and kissed him hard on the lips. She parted from him with one foot in a run. He could have reached out for her, but he knew better. The last thing he wanted to do was force her to be with him, to force her to stay if she felt she couldn't.

It was like watching a deer bound away. Her feet confident as much in the air as on the ground. Eva was graceful and determined to get away without being stopped by anything. The light glistened off her black hair, shining like a mirror as the sun broke away from the clouds. He had never seen anything that beautiful in a lot of years, since Lily.

A strong ray of light touched Josiah's face, warming him, blinding him for a brief second. When he regained his sight, Eva was gone. Vanished over the hill, safe on the Langdon compound, carrying a newborn secret, doing her best to hide any desire and thrill she might have felt.

Her vanilla scent lingered and he was hesitant to leave, to go back to camp, but he had no choice.

He stood on the side of the hill, an open target for anyone, Langdon or Halverson. His list of enemies was long and reasons to be concerned about his own safety were growing by the second.

Morris wouldn't like Josiah kissing his sister, and neither would any of the Halversons. Holding feelings for Eva was a bad idea, simple as that. A sure recipe for trouble. But he hadn't been able to help himself. Not from the second he saw her walking across the paddock, holding Lyle's hand, a woman with a soft touch and a full heart, born of the woods and nothing more. The feeling for her surprised him. He knew falling for a Langdon girl was the worst thing he could do, but none of that mattered to him. All that mattered was keeping Eva alive and safe so he could steal away

with her again. If that would ever be possible.

CHAPTER 36

Ofelia and Scrap were awake when Josiah
returned to the barn. They both looked at
him in unison as he walked up. It was Scrap
who spoke first. "You went after her, didn't
you?"

Josiah didn't answer. "I had no choice.
She wouldn't come back with me, though. I
should have stayed in bed. Dobson was
right. I should have stayed out of it."

Ofelia went back to straightening a pile of
blankets, folding them over and over again,
making them as neat as she could. She acted
like she wasn't listening but Josiah could
tell that she was. Lyle was in the stall, wide-
eyed, still in his sleep shirt. The little boy
didn't seem to understand what was going
on, and that was okay with Josiah.

A tame fire burned outside the barn door.
Woodsmoke and the smell of coffee mixed
together, offering comfort and desire at the

same time. "That coffee about ready, Ofelia?"

"En un minuto."

Josiah didn't need Lyle to interpret what she said for him. He knew he'd have to wait for the coffee, so he turned his attention back to Scrap. "You look suited up and ready to go."

"We're all goin' into town with ya, Wolfe."

"All of you?"

"I 'spect so. You'll be facin' the judge today, and then there's whatever else happens with those two men who kept this feud burnin'. All the Rangers'll be there. No one here to look out for any trouble. Don't you think it's best everybody goes?"

"I guess so. I didn't realize that McNelly wanted the entire company in town."

"Dobson came up and told me a little while ago."

"Oh."

"He asked where you was."

"I figured he might have. What'd you tell him?"

"That you was up at the cemetery payin' your respects. I know it was a lie, but that's all I could think of. I figured if you brung that girl back here, the explainin' was up to you. But since that didn't happen there ain't nothin' to worry about, now, is there?"

"You didn't have to lie for me," Josiah said. "I don't think Dobson likes me too much."

"I'm surprised you care."

"I do. I was disappointed when he wouldn't help go after Eva and bring her back here. I'm still worried about her."

"I can see that."

"Why do you say that?"

"Ain't none of my business, is it?"

"It's not something I was expecting, let me tell you that."

"Well," Scrap said, "you tend to find a way to complicate things, Wolfe. You have ever since I knowed you. As far as that girl goes, well, that ain't my business, but it seems to me that you're askin' for more trouble than it's worth if that glint in your eye means what I think it does. I don't know how this day is gonna work out for you, but I sure do hope your trial is fair."

"Me, too." Josiah looked past Scrap, out into the camp, ignoring the commentary about Eva.

A few men bustled to and fro, readying to depart. Fires died down. Smoke wandered. A horse nickered as someone put a saddle on it. And a restrained energy vibrated through the camp as the sun pushed away the last of the clouds, promising a clear day ahead. That didn't mean it would be un-eventful. But at least the weather wasn't threatening. Josiah had had enough of the cold rain. If he were anywhere else but on the land of his birth, with a burned-down cabin in the distance, and a heavy-hearted cemetery out of sight, Josiah would have been happy for the prospect of the coming day, riding with the Rangers. That was, of course, if he didn't have to face a judge with McNelly, his family and friends, and the entire company looking on.

"Coffee is ready," Ofelia said. She was by the fire, offering him a mug.

"I should get ready to ride, too," he said as he walked to Ofelia. "No use putting off what can't be stopped." He took the mug and took a long sip.

Scrap joined them and Ofelia poured him a mug. He took the coffee, but didn't say thank you. Still, it was an acknowledgment, and Josiah was glad to see that the two of them seemed to have come to an under-standing of some kind, a truce laid to the bare ground. Now, if the rest of the world could follow suit, life would be a lot easier for them all.

The buckboard stood ready to roll. Ofelia was in the driver's seat with Lyle sitting next to her. Josiah sat on Clipper on the right and Scrap restrained Missy on the left. The rest of the Rangers had started to form a troop behind them. Everyone was waiting on Dobson to gather formally. His horse, a fresh sorrel, waited ahead of the buckboard with an empty saddle.

Scrap looked to the wall tent with disgust. "If it was one of us holdin' up the show, he'd have his boot up our behinds faster than you can say 'move along.'" He had turned his attention back to Lyle, aware of his language, controlling it only because the boy listened to everything Scrap said — and then would parrot it back, whether the words were appropriate or not.

Josiah ignored Scrap's impatience. He was in no hurry to ride into town. Facing an unknown judge against a charge he was innocent of didn't sit well with him. But what really concerned him was Eva out of his sight. Knowing she was at home, or on her way into Seerville herself, gave him reason for more concern. His stomach burned like he'd eaten a plate full of hot coals.

"You look nervous," Ofelia said to Josiah.

"I'm okay. Ready to get on with it is all."

Lyle fidgeted in the seat, signaling he felt the same as Josiah. "What we waitin' on?"

"The sergeant," Josiah said.

"Oh."

"Calm down, we go soon," Ofelia said.

Lyle looked up at her, pouting. She ignored him. "Everyone will be in town," Ofelia said.

Clipper danced to the right of the wagon, as impatient as the boy. Josiah reined him back. "Your family?"

"I have not seen them since I have arrived. There has been no time."

"I'm sorry about that," Josiah said.

"No worry. It is not your fault. I know they have heard I am returned. They could come see me here as easy as I go to them. Family is *complicado.*"

"I had forgotten."

Ofelia was about to say something else, but stopped. Dobson exited his tent and headed for the buckboard. He was dressed in fresh blue trousers with creases sharp enough to cut a feather, a beige linen shirt with a blue handkerchief at the neck, and a black Stetson that matched his riding boots. He looked like an officer in charge even though he was only a sergeant. Even his gun belt, a light tan leather, looked like it had been scrubbed with soap.

Dobson stopped short of Clipper's head. The horse exhaled and looked away, like the man's presence was not welcome. "I see you've joined us, Wolfe."

"Why wouldn't I, Dobson?" It was tempting to call the man 'sir,' the way he carried himself, but Josiah restrained himself. Even if a sergeant did demand a certain amount of respect, Josiah remained a civilian, not given to protocol like the rest of the men. He didn't like the tone in Dobson's voice and the hard look in his eyes.

"You were nowhere to be found when I came looking for you," Dobson said.

"Elliot told you where I was."

"I took a look to see for myself."

"So you did."

"Couldn't find you anywhere. Not a sign of you at the cemetery. Not a sign of you anywhere I looked."

"Well," Josiah said. "I'm here now. That's what matters, isn't it?"

"I warned you against interfering with that Langdon girl."

"So you did. I'm sure she is at her home where she belongs."

"That's a swift change of tune."

Josiah glanced over to Scrap, who was doing his best not to get pulled into the conversation. Unlike Josiah, Scrap was under Dobson's direct command.

"Remember," Dobson said, puffing out his chest, "that you're in the custody of the

Texas Rangers until the judge says other-wise."

"How could I forget."

Dobson glared at Josiah, his eyes burning holes in him.

"Sergeant," Josiah added because he had to.

"Let's ride." Dobson spun around, stalked to his horse, mounted, and called the troop to formation.

Horses rustled behind the wagon, snort-ing, pushing into place, while their riders got settled in their saddles. All told, there were nine men, including Scrap and Josiah, behind the sergeant.

Dobson waved his hand forward and the company started to move.

Josiah didn't look back at the camp, the barn, or the burned-out cabin. He couldn't bring himself to believe that it would be the last time he would see his land. He knew he was innocent. All he could do was ride forward, unsure of what awaited him around the next bend, in town, and after the trial, knowing full well that he didn't fire the shot that killed Sheriff Cliburn. He had been in the wrong place at the wrong time is all.

CHAPTER 37

The ride into Seerville was quieter than Josiah had expected it to be. He'd watched for an ambush around every bend. Even when none came, it was hard for him to relax. He still didn't trust that they were safe as more buildings came into view. For a town that was near death there sure were a lot of people around.

A crowd had swelled outside of the hotel and it seemed to Josiah that there must have been at least fifty men, women, and children milling around. They were dressed in their Sunday best. Women wore their nicest dresses, covered with shawls to ward off the cool October air, even though the sun beat down from a cloudless sky. Men wore suits — funeral suits — all black, fit enough to be buried in. And the children were dolled up the same. Someone had festooned a red, white, and blue bunting over the entrance to the mercantile and there was a smell of food in the air. It felt like the circus had come to town, offering entertainment to the weary masses. But the gathering was not anything to celebrate. The crowd stood in the shadow of the recently built gallows. One rope dangled from the top beam with a single noose swaying in the slight breeze. Everyone gave the frame a wide berth. Most of the people waited in front of the hotel, far away from the gallows.

Still in the lead, Dobson cut through the crowd with ease. Everyone made way, backing to one side of the street or the other. He sat stiff in his saddle, his shoulders ceremonial square, aware that he was leading the parade, that he was the object of everyone's attention. The position suited him; the uninitiated would have mistaken him for Captain McNelly.

While the sergeant was soaking up his short-lived fame, Josiah was watching the roofs of the vacant buildings for any sign of the Langdons. So far, he hadn't seen anything out of place. But that didn't relieve his worry. The fact that Morris Langdon hadn't pulled something only made Josiah more uncomfortable. He couldn't imagine that Morris would let his father stand trial. Even if Ethan Langdon had shot Sheriff Cliburn at point blank range, the family would have found justification for it one way or another. The law was only useful to the Langdons if it benefited them.

Josiah edged Clipper along the wagon as close as he could. He wanted to stay near Lyle and Ofelia, in case trouble of any kind broke out. Some people in the crowd pointed and whispered as he passed by them. It was difficult to ignore, or understand, until he saw some newspaper handouts. A rendering of his face was plastered across the front page. The sight almost toppled him from his saddle. Once Captain McNelly had assumed custody of him it had felt like he was still free, that the acting sheriff's arrest order had had no real meaning. Busser had backed off, shooed away like a fly by McNelly. But the arrest did have meaning. All that was left now was to face the judge. Maybe he should have taken Sheriff Busser more seriously, prepared more for the trial. It was too late for that. There was no hiding from the crowd, or the reality he had ridden into.

He glanced over at Scrap, hoping to settle himself, knowing he had at least one friend he could count on, but Scrap was taken with the crowd, not paying attention to anything but the pretty girls he was waving at, smiling like they had assembled for only him.

That left Josiah to face his own thoughts and fears.

He hadn't considered what would happen to him if the judge found him guilty. All it took to throw his stomach into turmoil was a quick glance at the hanging rope. That noose could be for him.

Scrap looked over at him, and said, "What's the matter with you, Wolfe? You're as pale as a fresh-bleached diaper."

"Nothing," Josiah said, angling Clipper away from the crowd.

"If you say so."

"I do."

They were talking across the wagon, drawing Lyle's attention. When each man spoke, the boy turned to see what they were going to say. Josiah wished that Lyle was at home, far away from the crowd and the impending proceedings. His presence made him even more nervous. He wondered if Morris Langdon would kill a father in front of his young son.

The feeling of dread deepened as Dobson steered his mount to the front of the hotel, and came to a stop. He raised his right hand, motioning for everyone behind to do the same.

Ofelia let out a gentle *whoa,* and eased the buckboard close to the boardwalk. "You wait," she said to Lyle. He had a habit of jumping off the wagon as soon as it stopped, but he complied with a nod.

The crowd was silent, watching the Rangers, but more so Josiah, with curiosity and judgment. It didn't take long for someone to yell out, "Killer! You should be hanged!"

Josiah flinched, and ignored the commentary as he dismounted.

People nodded their heads in agreement, but no one said anything else. It was like they were waiting for Josiah to defend himself. He wasn't about to. All that mattered to him was getting Lyle and Ofelia inside as quick as possible before the crowd turned into a mob. He could feel the hate. It was almost as bad as what he had expected: A confrontation with the Langdons — which had not happened.

Josiah lifted Lyle out of the wagon and eased the boy, feet-first, to the ground. Ofelia must have felt the same way. She hurried off the driver's bench and was at Lyle's side before Josiah could stand up. "Go inside," he said. "I don't guess we can sit together."

Ofelia agreed, took Lyle's hand, and pushed forward, parting the crowd as she made her way to the front door of the hotel.

Josiah wondered if they had cleaned up Billy Pike's blood from the day before. The lobby had been a mess. He couldn't imagine it being a temporary courthouse, but it was the largest building in town. He thought they'd had no choice but to hold the trial there. At the thought of Billy, he scanned the crowd, looking for the Pikes. He didn't see any of them. Hadn't expected to since they tended to keep to themselves. But what he did see was a familiar face. Once his eyes locked with Eva Langdon's, he quit searching for anything else.

The sight of her surprised him. For a second he thought she was alone, standing by the door, waiting on someone. But as he looked closer, he saw Morris standing in the shadow of the roof, his head down, a lit cigarillo dangling from his mouth, and his sharp-crowned black hat tilted downward, like he was trying to keep the sun out of his eyes, or hiding. Josiah figured it was the latter. Morris was trying not to be seen. He had to wonder why.

Eva didn't look away from him. She looked stricken. An urge shown on her face, but the rest of her body ignored it, wouldn't allow her to run to him even though that was what she wanted.

This was not the time or place to declare his feelings for Eva — if that's what they were. He wasn't sure what he felt, but now was not the time to show fondness or familiarity to anyone.

Eva looked away as Josiah approached but her presence still hindered his walk. Lyle had spotted her, was getting excited, pulling on Ofelia's hand. "Not today," Josiah said.

Lyle ignored him, pulled out of Ofelia's hand, and darted toward Eva. She tried not to smile, tried to fend off the coming hug, but she was too late. Lyle wrapped himself around her leg, looking up at her like she was the rising sun. "Hello, Miss Eva."

Before she could say a word, Morris stepped out of the shadows. "This boy needs to mind his manners."

"Leave it alone, Morris."

Lyle ignored Morris and everything else. His focus on Eva was unwavering.

Josiah reached the steps in a bound, standing face to face with Morris.

"You need to teach your boy how to obey, Wolfe." Morris crossed his arms and a smug look settled on his face.

The crowd had increased, and Josiah felt fifty pair of eyes staring at the back of his head. The last thing he needed was trouble before he went inside to face the judge. "Lyle, tell Miss Eva goodbye. We have to go inside." He reached around Morris to grab Lyle's arm, half expecting Morris to stop him, but he didn't. He stood there like a cigar-store Indian, wooden and unmoving.

"I don't want to leave her," Lyle said. She was dressed in black like the men, in her funeral clothes, mourning her cousin, Gordy.

Eva didn't say anything. She stared at Josiah with eyes longing to say more.

Lyle planted his feet, defying Josiah with all of his strength. It was not enough. Before the little boy could let out a holler, Josiah had yanked him up off his feet, spun him around, and raised him into an embrace. He could feel Ofelia at his side, could sense that she was there to help, but he wasn't about to let go of Lyle. He pushed past Morris and Eva and hurried inside the hotel, ready to face whatever waited, and leave the Langdons — and Eva — in his wake. She made his heart skip a beat, caused his throat to go dry, and no matter the circumstance, made him feel like a bumbling schoolboy. He couldn't remember the last time he was so unsteady on his feet around a woman.

CHAPTER 38

The inside of the hotel was as crowded as it was outside. The lobby was open all the way to the second-floor ceiling, with a grand staircase clinging to both sides of the cavernous room. People stood four deep on each step, looking down to the center of the room. The mezzanine was as packed with people leaning over to see, and hear, what was going on below. A low murmur buzzed through the crowd; muted voices, scuffling feet, and heavy anticipation.

The first thing Josiah noticed was how much warmer it was inside the hotel than it was outside. His heart was still beating faster than normal and sweat had beaded on his lip. He held onto Lyle as tight as he could until he found a spot beyond the door where he could wait for Ofelia.

It only took her a second to squeeze in the door and find him. No one paid any attention to them. There were too many people inside the hotel to care about one more person pushing inside. The place was beyond its capacity as it was.

Anger was foreign to Ofelia's face, but her jaw was set as she looked to Lyle. A scolding was on the tip of her tongue but she kept her feelings to herself. The hotel was full of Anglos. Josiah knew she was aware that no one would take to a Mexican woman giving a white boy a swat, or a balling out. Besides, as far as Josiah was concerned, Lyle was reacting to the crowd. Scared by it. The boy'd been on edge since the cabin had been set on fire, since he'd had to run into the woods and hide from the Langdons. He hadn't connected Eva to the bad people.

"He's fine," Josiah said to Ofelia. They stood in a six-inch circle, pressed against the wall as more people made their way inside the hotel. Scrap. Sergeant Dobson. A few unknown faces. There was no sign of Eva or Morris. Josiah wondered if the lobby was too full for them. He didn't want Eva to witness his trial.

"I will take him," Ofelia said, motioning for Josiah to give the boy up.

Lyle buried his face in his father's shoulder. "I want Miss Eva," he whispered.

"Not today," Josiah said. "We have to do this."

"Tomorrow?"

The voices around him were loud and growing louder by the second. The man next to Josiah jabbed him in the ribs with his elbow, by accident. Josiah gasped but tried not to react. He saw that the move wasn't intended to mean anything.

"Maybe," he said to Lyle as he handed the boy to Ofelia. She took Lyle by the waist, then put him on his feet.

"You stay." The anger remained on Ofelia's face and in her voice. Lyle looked away from her, sheepish and unsure.

Josiah was a little concerned, but he knew that Ofelia was as nervous and unsettled as he was inside the crowded hotel. "I have to find McNelly."

The man who had jabbed him heard what Josiah said. "He's up front with the judge. Bad for anyone who has to face that man today. He had to have a tooth pulled on the way here. Heard he's in pain, cranky, and not in the mood for any of this."

Josiah wanted to ask the man how he knew that, but on days like these, news traveled through a crowd as fast as a grassfire spread over a dry field after a lightning strike. "Good to know," he said. With that, he started making his way to the front of the lobby, excusing himself, easing through

346

the crowd. He had expected to know people from Seerville, but the truth was, he didn't know anyone at all. They were strangers. He wondered where they were from.

It didn't take Josiah long to find Captain McNelly. He stood at the front of the room with his hands clasped behind his back, feet apart, wearing a stoic look on his face as he gazed over the crowd. There was no mistaking the parade rest stance, but only a fool would have mistaken the captain as relaxed. Concern about the mood of the crowd was plastered all over his face.

Dobson had found his way to McNelly's side, along with four or five of the other Rangers that Josiah had seen around the camp. There was no sign of the judge. An empty desk sat in front of the clerk's stand, not far from where Billy Pike had taken his last breath. A circle of onlookers, including Sheriff Busser, and a few other men who looked to be his deputies, waited with impatience showing on their faces. There were men three rows deep, all dressed for the trial in suits made for business and government, not mourning. The reality of the situation Josiah found himself in felt like he was carrying a load of bricks on his back and on his feet. He glanced up to the mezzanine, knowing that was where the women would be. There was no sign of Eva.

"There you are, Wolfe," McNelly said. He was dressed in his best clothes, too, though there was little of the uniform look Dobson wore. If a man didn't know who either of the men were, he would assume that the sergeant was in charge, not McNelly. But that was not the case. Every man, woman, and child who made their way to the hotel in Seerville knew who Leander McNelly was.

Josiah took his hat off, and said, "You weren't worried that I wouldn't show up, were you?"

"You would have dug yourself a deep hole."

"I'd like to find my way out of the one I'm in." The air was thick. It smelled of stale cigar smoke, toilet water, and fresh pomade.

"I appreciate that," McNelly said. "I've put my trust and faith in your word." He cast a look over to Sheriff Busser, who was studying the two men like they were thieves in cahoots together. "If I'd had one suspicion that you were lying, or a runner, I would have tied you up and held you like an ungrateful desperado. You've always been a man of honor, Wolfe, but I have to tell you that the judge had no interest in hearing my petition for leniency when it came to your situation."

Something deep inside Josiah wasn't surprised. His fate had a history of being precarious in a court of law. It was a world he didn't understand, and like most things that were mysterious, he distrusted the law and those who were in charge of it.

"I appreciate your confidence, Captain." Josiah squared his shoulders and took in a breath to steady his nerves. "Do you know the judge?"

"Personally?"

"Or by reputation?"

"Both. I believe you do, too."

The captain's words made Josiah uncomfortable. He didn't know any judges that he could recall.

"He hails from Austin," McNelly continued. "Judge Evan Dooley. He presided over that charade of a trial that Ranger Elliot got himself tangled up in."

Josiah's mouth went dry. He remembered Judge Dooley. It hadn't been that long ago that Scrap had been arrested and charged for a murder he didn't commit. With some luck and help along the way, Josiah had no trouble proving Scrap's innocence. There had been a gallows built for the trial, like there had been in Seerville. The takeaway for Josiah was that Evan Dooley was a strict old man with little bend in his back. He didn't suffer fools with any more patience than McNelly did. And to make things worse, Dooley was a relative of Pete Feders, the previous captain, who had taken over for Hiram Fikes, and betrayed the Rangers. Josiah had a hand in the man's downfall and demise. He sure hoped the judge didn't hold a grudge.

Before Josiah could say anything to McNelly, Judge Dooley entered the lobby from somewhere inside the hotel. He was tall as a cornstalk and as thin. A long white beard jutted down from his angular face. His bespectacled eyes were beady, black, and unemotional. As black as the robe he was dressed in. A thin shock of white hair topped his head and a fresh dusting of dander coated his shoulders. His right cheek was larger than the other, and he held his mouth funny, like breathing hurt him more than he wanted to let on. Dentistry of any kind seemed like barbaric torture to Josiah.

The judge's entrance signaled every man, woman, and child in the room to shut up and hope for invisibility. Feet shuffled, throats cleared, then silence fell upon the lobby like an executioner was coming for them.

Sheriff Busser stepped forward, acting as

a bailiff, and said, "All rise for the Honorable E. Dooley."

No one was sitting down. No one moved.

Judge Dooley made his way to the desk and sat down with a groan of discomfort. He had a handful of papers and set about organizing them, without paying any attention to anything else.

Josiah stared at the man for a second, then looked over his shoulder, searching for Ofelia and Lyle. When he couldn't find them, he continued looking through the crowd, hoping to catch sight of Eva. But she wasn't anywhere to be seen. Neither were any of the Langdons. He didn't see one of them inside the hotel lobby. He reasoned that the crowd was thick, and they were in the room somewhere. There was no way they were going to miss this trial. It meant too much to them. As he was about to turn back to the judge and face the charges against him, he heard the main door of the hotel slam shut.

The bang caused everyone to jump. Everyone but the judge. He was oblivious to everything but the papers in front of him.

Josiah strained to see who had entered or who had left, but the crowd was too thick. It had to be a frustrated resident hoping to see the trial, unable to find a way inside.

The room was packed to the rafters. It was almost like everyone from outside had made their way inside. You would think it was the trial of the century. In reality, it was the biggest event to have occurred in Seerville in a long time. Nobody was going to miss it, if they could help it. Nobody, it seemed, but the Langdons.

CHAPTER 39

"How do you plead?" the judge asked.

"I didn't fire any shots, Your Honor," Josiah answered.

A scowl crossed Judge Dooley's face and found a home there. "That was not the question. Guilty or not guilty."

Josiah didn't hesitate. "Not guilty."

A wave of low voices pushed through the crowd. Disbelief hung in the air like a bad smell. The newspapers had already found Josiah guilty of killing Sheriff Cliburn. It didn't matter that Ethan Langdon and Leland Halverson were on trial, too. Or that those two men had started and engaged in the feud that had brought the sheriff and his men to Seerville in the first place. The court of public opinion had fallen on the ugly side of Josiah's fate because he had gone away. Some folks never forgive you for leaving.

"Not guilty?" the judge said.

"Yes, sir."

"And you're claiming self-defense?" There was a tone of disbelief in Judge Dooley's voice, but that didn't surprise Josiah. The grudge had been obvious as soon as the judge had walked into the room and they made eye contact.

"No, sir," Josiah repeated. "I'm claiming I'm not guilty of anything other than being in the wrong place at the wrong time."

Judge Dooley sat back in his chair, took off his glasses, and rubbed the swollen side of his face. He stared out at the crowd. "I have read the reports, and as much as it pains me to say so, I have to agree with what I have read. There is no conclusive evidence to show that you shot Sheriff Cliburn. Or shot a gun at all."

Josiah could feel the tension drain from his shoulders to his toes. But he held his breath, fearful of celebrating, of showing any emotion.

"It is, however, not beyond my scope of experience with you, Wolfe, not to consider your past history, and brushes against the law. This is not the first time you have appeared in my courtroom."

The lobby was sweltering with body heat. Overhead fans stood still, dry as the day they were made, the maintenance of water

354

long forgotten. The doors and windows were closed tight and every man stood overlapping the next one. Along with the judge's hot air, the natural event of so many humans packed in one small space was taking its toll. The autumn air was cool outside. It would have been unbearable if the trial had taken place in the height of summer. July heat could kill a cow on a hill. Hard telling how many people would have succumbed to the heat inside the hotel if that had been the case.

Josiah didn't interrupt the judge, even though he was tempted to.

Dooley leaned forward, grabbed up the gavel, and said, "Much to my own personal distaste, case dismissed." He banged the gavel and followed up with a roar, so he would be heard over the disbelieving crowd, "Next case!"

The voices were deafening for a minute afterward. Josiah felt the swell of people push forward from behind him. He was afraid for his life, sure that he was going to be dragged outside and tarred and feathered — or worse, given the noose by vigilantes seeking justice. But the fear didn't last. McNelly and the other Rangers surrounded Josiah, protecting him with a shield of muscle and reputation. No one was going to take on so many Rangers in one place.

It only took Josiah a second to realize he was safe. Or at least as safe as he could be. The judge, in the meantime, banged the gavel, calling out, "Order in the court! Order in the court!"

Chaos seemed to break out every time Josiah was in Judge Dooley's presence. He didn't know if it was him, the judge, or the nature of the law. It didn't matter. He didn't like it.

The crowd calmed down, allowing the judge to continue on.

"Bring on the next case," he said to his acting bailiff, Sheriff Busser.

Busser grabbed up a piece of paper off the judge's desk, and said, "The state of Texas versus Ethan Langdon. The charge is murder in the first degree. Please step forward, Mr. Langdon."

Silence settled over the lobby and everyone turned their attention to the back of the room. Josiah had not seen Ethan, or Leland, for that matter, since he had arrived. There was no where for him to move to. As much as he would have liked to have left the building, he was trapped inside, forced to witness the proceedings until they were over. He could leave McNelly and the rest of the Rangers now that he was a free man. It was a nice thought while it lasted. He didn't feel free.

There was no movement from the back, though several men had parted and tried to make a path for Ethan to come forward and face the judge.

After a long minute, Judge Dooley called Busser over to him. He tried to talk in a low voice but there was no whispering in a room packed with people. "Is he here?" he asked the sheriff.

Busser shrugged his shoulders and looked out over the crowd again. "Ethan Langdon come to the front of the lobby to face the judge."

Silence again.

The judge called Busser over to him again. "He was in custody, was he not?"

"Yes, of course. I saw him in the jail right before I came inside."

McNelly backed up and asked Dobson what he knew. There were Rangers and deputies in charge of guarding both men. Dobson shrugged his shoulders like Busser had.

"I rode in with Wolfe. I assumed you had everything in check here, sir," Dobson said to McNelly.

The judge banged his gavel again. "Bailiff bring the next case forward." It was an angry order, full of impatience and embarrassment.

"It doesn't look like he's here."

"Well, go find out what's going on." The judge dropped the gavel and rubbed his cheek again, annoyed by the pain left behind from the extraction of the bad tooth.

"Yes, Your Honor," Busser said, then hurried into the crowd, navigating the path the men had opened for Ethan.

"I don't like this," McNelly said. "Go with him, Dobson. See what you can find out." Then he turned his attention to Josiah. "You know both of these men. What do you think is going on?"

Josiah didn't answer right away. He stared down the open path, then upward to the mezzanine, then to the crowd again. "I don't know them that well. A lot has changed in the three years since I've been gone. I don't trust either man if I'm being honest. But it's the Langdons that concern me the most. I have only seen two since arriving here. The eldest, Morris, was trying to hide himself at the door when I entered, and the daughter, Eva. I assumed Morris was her chaperone, in charge of looking out for her, so I didn't think much of it. But there's not a single Langdon to be seen inside this room."

"Any Halversons?" McNelly said.

"Not a one."

"And you don't find that odd that neither family is inside?"

"I find it curious and troubling," Josiah said. He was about to say something else, but he stopped and took a deep breath. He smelled the first hint of something burning. He smelled smoke.

CHAPTER 40

The sight of fire followed the detection of smoke. Flames jumped in front of a window like a red-hot curtain pulled up instead of dropped. Panic vibrated through the lobby as men at the back of the room, opposite Josiah and McNelly, tried to open the front doors. But they couldn't. A lock, or a blockade, had been set up. People pushed forward, squeezing into a mass of arms and legs, willing to do anything to get out. It didn't take long for them to realize that they were trapped.

Every window was blocked by impassable flames. Smoke was visible, snaking into every nook and cranny it could find. Fire spread quickly on the outside walls because they were so thin and dry and served as nothing more than kindling.

"This is the Langdons' doing," Josiah said to McNelly. He searched the crowd for Ofelia and Lyle. He had his own fear and panic, but he could see no way to penetrate the wall of men pushing to the door. He looked up then, to the mezzanine, and saw Ofelia struggling against the throng of women trying to get to the stairs. She clutched Lyle to her and had the sense not to rush to the door like everyone else. Josiah wasn't sure she and the boy were safe, but they were out of harm's way. But there was no sign of Scrap. The last time Josiah had seen him, he was at the door. Josiah had lost sight of him once the judge's proceedings had begun.

The captain was already considering his options. The perpetrators didn't seem to be his concern. He ordered the closest Ranger to take protection of Judge Dooley, then barked orders to Sergeant Dobson. "Go to every door and window and find a way to get out of here."

Dobson acknowledged and took a few Rangers with him. They had plenty of room, going away from the crowd like Ofelia had.

Someone yelled. Then came a scream, followed by another and another, as the realization that they were all trapped became clear. The pounding on the doors sounded like a hundred blacksmiths hitting their anvils with all of the strength they could find. Smoke grew thicker, and the heat started to rise.

It was only McNelly and Josiah now. The judge had been scurried to the back of the building, out of sight.

"What'd you mean, it's the Langdons' doing?" the captain said, his eyes darting about, trying to figure a way out.

Josiah couldn't focus on his thoughts, caught up in the panic and fear for Ofelia and Lyle. Time was running out for all of them — unless Dobson found a way out. "It was their plan all along. It's why Ethan surrendered without a fight. They knew the whole town would be here. Once we were inside, they could get rid of us all. Me, you, everyone."

"But," McNelly said, almost in a yell, "Langdon and Halverson are in custody."

"I don't think they are now. At least Ethan. I figure his boys busted him out, took control of the crowd outside somehow, then set the fire. With all of us dead, they can continue their land grab. It's easy pickings now. They'll control all of Seerville without worry." Josiah coughed, then pulled out a handkerchief and covered his mouth. He looked like a bandit with irritated eyes.

McNelly followed suit and protected his face. "They have to know an action like this will bring in the army. It won't work."

"If there are no survivors, they'll call it an

accident. If they aren't believed, they'll fight to the death. Trust me on that."

"I do," McNelly said. "I do."

A shot rang out from the back of the building, followed by another.

"That's Dobson," Josiah said.

"They got the doors covered. Pinned us all in." Fear resonated in McNelly's voice. It was the first time Josiah had heard anything but confidence issue from the captain's mouth.

Josiah looked up to the mezzanine. He made eye contact with Ofelia. She pointed upward. "We need to get to the roof," he said.

McNelly started to disagree, then looked to the front of the lobby. The wall was smoldering from the outside and flames were starting to poke through. It wouldn't be long before the front of the hotel was engulfed in flames, inside and out.

The main part of the crowd remained, fighting to get out the front door, beating, screaming, pleading. There was no one willing to help.

Josiah didn't wait for the captain to decide what to do next. He headed to the set of stairs that led up to the mezzanine on the opposite side of the room. "Come on, this way," he said to McNelly.

They both hurried up the stairs. The entire room was filled with smoke, and the higher they climbed the thicker it got. It didn't take long for Josiah to reunite with Ofelia and Lyle. The boy was afraid, and said nothing. He didn't have to. He jumped straight into Josiah's arms. There was nothing else he could do but catch the boy. He wouldn't want it any other way.

It took Josiah a second to get his bearings as Lyle buried his face in his shoulder. By the time he was settled to where he was at, McNelly was leading the way down a hall, searching for a set of stairs that would lead to the roof. It was Josiah's turn to follow. And he did, without question, pulling Ofelia along with him.

"Have you seen Scrap?" Josiah asked Ofelia.

She shook her head. They both looked down to the crowd but there was no sign of Scrap. *I hope you're all right.*

A few other people realized they were heading for the roof and followed. Three or four women, and one man that Josiah didn't know. Like most of the men in the lobby, this man was armed. Which was a good thing. They might need him.

McNelly stopped halfway down the hall. "Once we find a way out, we'll get everyone to come up on the roof."

It was getting hard to breathe. Josiah's lungs burned like they had been soaked in kerosene. Sweat poured from his pores, and his heart raced with fear, dread, and anticipation. He couldn't let anything happen to Lyle or Ofelia. He didn't want them all to die. Not like this.

McNelly was frantic, opening every door he came to, looking for a staircase that led to the roof. Josiah followed close behind with Lyle glued to him. Ofelia was right behind him, along with a growing line of searchers from downstairs.

The captain found the right door, but his knees buckled, stopping him cold. Josiah ran to his side. "Are you all right?"

McNelly was breathing like a fish out of water. "The smoke. I overexerted myself." Each word took a great amount of effort to say.

Josiah understood. The consumption, mixed with the fire, had weakened the captain's body, but not his spirit. His illness was known by everyone, but hidden as much as possible. McNelly worked hard at not letting the consumption define him, get in his way, make him look weak. Whether or not he had overexerted himself was a question for another time.

"Go on, get up there," McNelly gasped. He was bent over and looked to be half the man that Josiah had known.

"No, not without you."

Everyone had stopped. Yells and screams echoed upward. Another round of distant gunshots followed. There was no way to know what was happening, but the captain was right. The Langdons were taking shots at anyone who tried to escape.

Josiah looked up the stairs, then to McNelly. The captain was in no shape to lead, to give one more order. It was up to him to see everyone to the roof. Whether or not that was to safety, was an unanswered question. The fire would reach them soon and then there would be no getting away from it. Still, it was a better plan than waiting to burn up in the lobby, or get shot trying to escape.

It took Josiah only a second to decide what to do next. "You wait here," he said to McNelly, then turned to Ofelia and handed Lyle off to her. The little boy started to scream, to panic. There was no time to comfort him. Josiah turned away, pulled his Peacemaker from its holster, and made his way up the stairs.

CHAPTER 41

Thick smoke wrapped around Josiah's ankles like a ship's ropes holding a boat at the docks. His lungs still burned and his eyes felt as if they had been touched by the tip of a red-hot poker. The discomfort didn't stop his ascent. He had no choice.

The stairway turned a few more steps up, forcing him to face the unknown one more time. Battling tearing eyes and reduced vision, trying to see what lay ahead. Fresh air was coming in from somewhere, doing its best to push the smoke inside. It was a losing battle. There was an open door at the top of the stairs. Josiah was sure of it.

He stopped at the corner and considered his options. He hadn't heard any evidence that anyone was up there waiting for him, but he wasn't going to risk that there wasn't. The Langdons seemed to have every exit of the hotel covered. There was no way that they'd overlooked the roof. The trick would have been getting a man to stand on top of a burning building to cut off that escape route unless there was a way down, a way to flee the flames. That gave him hope. No one was going to sacrifice themselves to a fire. There had to be a way down to the ground.

He poked his head around the corner with the Peacemaker raised. Like he had suspected, the door was cracked open, and the way to the roof was clear. He didn't rush upward. Instead, Josiah looked behind him, down the staircase, before turning the corner. He caught sight of McNelly still gasping for breath and he could hear Lyle screaming in fear. There was nothing he could do for either of them except climb the rest of the way up and find a way off the roof.

He reached the door without any trouble.

Fresh air pushed inside and Josiah stood for a minute, allowing his eyes to clear and his lungs to gather as much strength as possible. He coughed as he took off the handkerchief. There was relief for him as his breathing cleared, but he knew that Captain McNelly struggled every second of every day with consumption, trying to breathe, trying to live a normal life. McNelly had to be in a stew of misery, caught in the smoke like he was.

The gunshots were louder now. He was closer to them. Crackling sounds from the fire had turned into a roar. The screams from inside the hotel rode upward on the smoke, reaching the heavens and unsympathetic ears in the town of Seerville.

He peered outside and saw nothing. There was no stopping him. He had to find a safe place for his family and the strangers below. He led with his gun, poking it outside, clearing the way as he went. As soon as he stepped outside, a gunshot rang out — close by. The wood of the doorframe next to his head shattered as a bullet exploded into it. He looked to see a man jump back behind a chimney about thirty feet in front of him. There was no time for recognition. Josiah fired off a round, then backed into the stairwell to cover himself. He was as trapped as the men downstairs.

He kept an eye on the chimney, watching the roof for movement of a shadow. When he saw it, he fired off another shot. He knew there was no way he was going to hit the man, not unless he showed himself, but he wanted the shooter to know he was serious.

There was no response, no shot back. At least not right away. But Josiah heard footsteps easing up the staircase behind him. Now he was in a quandary. He had nowhere to go and didn't know if the person who approached was friend or foe. They would have had to have gotten by McNelly, and there would have been a scuffle. He could still hear Lyle crying, so that had not changed.

A quick look over his shoulder told Josiah that it was the man who had joined them in the hall. He was portly, looked a little sloppy and afraid, but he carried a Colt, and looked ready to use it. Two guns would be better than one. Maybe they could flush the shooter.

"You had me worried there for a second," Josiah said.

"Couldn't stay down there, especially when I figured there was a man on the roof keepin' you pinned in." The man extended his skillet-sized hand. "Name's Earl McCann."

"Josiah Wolfe." He shook the man's hand, then turned back to the door.

"Everybody knows who you are, Wolfe."

Josiah didn't acknowledge McCann's words. It didn't matter. "How much ammunition you got?"

"A belt full."

"Good. Me, too. I figure I'll start shooting at one side of the chimney, and you take the other. I can move closer with you covering me. My intent isn't to kill the man, but flush him and see if he runs."

"Ah, you want him to show you the escape route."

A smile flicked across Josiah's face. "That's right."

"Good plan. Let's do it."

Josiah reloaded, and McCann readied his Colt. Once they were both ready, Josiah motioned for McCann to go to the door and shoot first. The hefty man didn't need to be told twice. He leveled the barrel of the revolver out the door and fired off a shot. Josiah eased opposite him, fired, crouched, and headed to the closest air stack that jutted up from the roof.

The shots chipped away at the brick, holding the shooter back — for a second. He fired back before the debris could scatter across the roof, taking an unplanned potshot at the door, like before. He fired again and again, using all of his cartridges.

Josiah fired again, could see the shooter's shadow a little clearer. He motioned for McCann to shoot again, then planned his next move, which was to zigzag to another chimney that stood about ten feet from the other.

McCann did as he was instructed and

fired off three quick shots, holding the shooter back. Josiah hurried to the other chimney, hugging it close. He could see the man's side but couldn't tell who he was. There was a clear shot at the man; he was reloading his gun. But Josiah restrained himself from taking the man out.

Gunshots echoed from downstairs and outside of the hotel as the Rangers tried to shoot their way out, trying to rescue those trapped inside. The screams continued and the fire was a rage. If they didn't get out soon, this was going to be a disaster for the ages. The Langdons had planned the attack with precision and were holding their own. There had to be a lot of them on the outside to hold everyone inside. Time was running out.

Once the shooter had his revolver loaded, he hugged the chimney, then looked out to the door and fired again.

Josiah was ready. He shot at the man's feet, missing them by inches, then working his way up the chimney. McCann fired off one shot after the other, too, trapping the man. Then they let the shooting stop — the man would figure he had a chance to run because the two men would need to reload — and he would be right. That was the plan. Josiah wanted him to make a run for it.

That is what the shooter did. He tore away from the chimney, firing as he went, with the bullets flying in the air, not aimed, only used to intimidate. The roof was vacant in the direction he ran, except for a six-foot wall that was the false front of the hotel where the sign was.

Josiah watched the man scurry, was as interested in his face as he was the direction he was heading. He knew the man, or at least recognized him, had seen him over the years. He was a cousin. Not to the Langdons, but to the Halversons. His name was Cleve. Cleve Halverson. It was almost worth taking a shot at the man, to wound him and find out what the hell was going on, but again, Josiah restrained himself.

Cleve Halverson hit the wall running, then stopped, opened a hidden door, and disappeared into it.

Josiah hadn't seen the door until then, had not considered that one would be there. It could only lead to a ledge and nothing more. That would be enough room to escape, though, if there was a way down to the next floor, or a ladder set for that reason. Every move had been well thought out. But the point of it was lost on Josiah now. Even though he claimed not to be part of the Halverson family, he felt betrayed and angry. Angry enough to follow Cleve Halverson, to do his best to get off the roof alive, and put an end to the madness once and for all.

CHAPTER 42

Once Josiah was sure the roof was clear — it looked like Cleve Halverson was the only man assigned to defend it — he motioned for Captain McNelly and Ofelia to come on up the stairs. He wanted them as far away from the hungry flames as possible. There was no escaping the smoke, or the potential threat that might pop up around the corner at any second.

McNelly's face was red from the struggle up the stairs and it was obvious that his breathing was becoming more and more difficult for him. Ofelia and Lyle looked relieved to be outside of the building, though they both seemed to understand that they were not out of danger yet. Lyle hung onto Ofelia like he feared falling off the tall building.

"One of the Halversons was in charge of the roof." Josiah still could not believe what he saw, what he had to report to the captain.

He felt a rage growing that he was not sure he could contain.

"That's not what I was expecting you to say," McNelly said.

"Not what I was expecting to see, either."

"So, it's not only the Langdons."

"I can't imagine they've joined forces, but I expect anything is possible when you're faced with a judge who is prone to hanging a man instead of setting him free. That, and a company of Rangers who have set up stakes on land they had intended to take."

"We're not going anywhere until we have this feud under control."

"Your presence could have been the spark, Captain, that lit this fire." Josiah looked back to the door as more smoke roiled out from it. "We need to get off this roof."

"You go on. Take that fella with you," McNelly said, nodding toward Earl Mc-Cann. "I'll keep the women and children as safe as I can." There was a tough mettle in the captain's voice that warned Josiah not to argue. He understood the command even though he didn't agree with it. McNelly was having trouble breathing the way it was. Staying on the roof could have dire consequences for him. How could he protect the women and children if he couldn't stand?

"We're running out of time," Josiah said.

"Go," McNelly answered.

There was no choice but to go after Cleve Halverson and leave Ofelia and Lyle behind one more time. It pained Josiah, but he turned and headed toward the hidden door without so much as saying goodbye. He knew Lyle would cling to him like a lamb on a ewe's teat.

Neither Josiah nor Earl McCann burst out the door or gave direct chase to Cleve Halverson. Josiah opened the door and peered outside through the false front of the building.

Noise from the fight below worked its way upward — a mix of gunshots and roaring fire. Smoke reached to the sky, making it difficult to see, but it looked like the hotel was the only building on fire. The street was clear of people, though there were horses and wagons scattered about, far enough away from the hotel to be safe. There was no sign of the Halverson cousin.

"I want you to start shooting as soon as I make a run for it," Josiah said.

"Shoot at what?"

"Anything that moves."

"Where are you going?"

"Looks like there's a ladder that leads down to the next floor. My guess is there are ladders that lead down to the ground."

"You'll be an easy target," McCann said.

"Not if you keep your eyes open and cover me."

"You should let me go. You've got a young son."

"Captain said I should go."

"McNelly said we should both go." McCann pushed his sizable girth in front of Josiah. "Now, move and cover me."

"You're sure?"

"As sure as the sky is blue beyond this smoke. I don't know what this fight is about, but if I'm going to die today, I'd rather it be in the service of doin' something about it instead of standin' around waitin' to burn to death. My feet are startin' to sweat and it ain't from over exertin' myself, I can tell you that."

Josiah looked over his shoulder to see Lyle hugging Ofelia's long skirt. Even in the dim light, the boy's forehead glistened. "All right, go on." He aimed the barrel of his Peacemaker to the ground, to the front of the mercantile across the street, and fired off a round. McCann took that as his cue to creep out onto the ledge.

"Good thing I'm not afraid of heights," he said as he fired off a round, too.

A puff of gun smoke answered back. Like Josiah expected, there was a man stationed behind a barrel in front of the mercantile. More gunshots exploded, but they weren't engaging him or McCann. It was a gunfight between the Rangers and the organizers of the attack.

Josiah still couldn't bring himself to blame the Halversons with entirety. His hunch held firm that they had joined up with the Langdons, that they had somehow brokered a peace deal with their own interest at the heart of the deal: their survival over everything else. It was the only thing that could explain the situation, how they had managed to remove the onlookers and set fire to the hotel, then hold everyone inside it. There had to be more men to give them a fighting chance against the company of Rangers.

Josiah fired again. This time his aim was better and he hit the shooter behind the barrel. It wasn't a kill shot, but he wounded the man, hurt him enough to elicit a scream, followed by a roll to the ground. "Hurry," he said to McCann.

Earl McCann had seen the shot and hustled over to the ladder. Bad thing was he had to turn his back to the street to climb down.

Shooting increased down below and a trio of Rangers broke out of the hotel, firing toward the mercantile. They had their Winchesters loaded, creating a screen of lead as they pushed toward the building, doing their best to end the gunfight.

The street was littered with dead bodies. Five that Josiah could see. He fired downward again, helping the Rangers and giving cover to McCann at the same time.

Shots were returned, but they were scattered, missing the Rangers.

Josiah focused on covering Earl McCann as he climbed down the ladder.

The big man made it halfway down before he took the first shot. It hit at the base of his neck, thrusting him forward, face into the wall. Another shot hit him a few inches down before he had the chance to bounce back. He was dead before he slid down the ladder. He hit the ledge and tumbled to the ground, falling two stories. Josiah heard the thud over all of the other noise, and cringed with regret.

More gunfire erupted below, drawing Josiah's attention to the trio of Rangers. They had backup and had managed to flush two shooters from the side of the mercantile. There was no surrender, only quick shots that put an end to both men's lives. There was no way to tell if they were Langdons or Halversons.

It looked like the Rangers were taking the upper hand in the gunfight, but while they were occupied with the shootout, the hotel continued to burn.

Movement in the distance distracted Josiah for a second. He was about to make his way to the ladder — with the hope that he would not meet the same fate as Earl McCann — but he stopped, not certain what he was seeing.

A group of fifteen men on horses were running at breakneck speed toward town. There was no mistaking Scrap on Missy, in the lead. Behind him were a few men that Josiah recognized, even from a distance. They were Pikes. River people sworn to stay out of trouble in town. Josiah had lost sight of Scrap in the lobby of the hotel, during the trial. He must have slipped off, gotten away somehow when the fire started, and gone for help.

It didn't take long for the Rangers in the street, or the shooters on the other side, to realize that Scrap had brought reinforcements. The fight wasn't over, but it looked like there might be a chance for it to be won. All was not lost.

CHAPTER 43

An all-out fight was taking place on the street with the burning hotel as the center-piece. Josiah stayed put at the door of the false front, shooting when he had a target. In the meantime, Captain McNelly was leading people out of the stairwell to safety — as safe as they could be on top of a burning building. Men and women alike gasped for breath, weakened by their time inside the hotel. Ofelia offered help to the women if they needed it, with Lyle by her side. McNelly commanded the men in between bouts of coughing. He came over and joined Josiah. There were at least twenty refugees on the rooftop.

"Shooting's picked up," McNelly said.

Josiah took his attention away from the gunfight below. "Scrap arrived with the Pikes." Josiah looked to the mercantile. He could see a host of men, six or seven, mounting their horses in the back. They took off in a shot, scattering as they went. "They're on the run."

McNelly peered out the door, saw what Josiah saw, then looked back to the stairwell. Josiah followed his gaze. Smoke rolled out the doorway, thicker and blacker than before. He could only assume that the flames were getting closer. "We're going to have to get down soon, or there'll be no escaping our fate."

"Agreed," McNelly said. "But it's not safe yet."

Three more Langdons rode off. Scrap saw them this time and sent three men after the trio. Shots were exchanged on the run. In a matter of seconds, the three runners were on the ground, either dead or injured. No one checked to see which. The pursuers returned to the battle and took up arms against the remaining shooters.

"I can't stay here," Josiah said. "They need my help."

Before McNelly could say anything, Josiah watched another man exit the rear of the mercantile. It was Morris Langdon. He mounted his black horse and rode off alone. There was no sign of Eva.

Men scattered and the battle turned toward a Ranger and Pike victory. Chase was given, while the rest gathered themselves and looked to save whoever they could inside the burning hotel.

"I have to go," Josiah said to McNelly. "I'll trust you to get my family to safety, Captain."

"It will be my first priority."

By the time Josiah scurried down the first ladder, Morris was out of sight. He had escaped. There were riders on his tail who would not give up until he was caught. Josiah was sure that Morris had a plan that would ensure his survival. The man was a roach who could live through anything. Or he believed he could, which was the seed of his power.

The hotel fire hadn't gone to plan, though. There would be survivors. A lot of them. Thanks to Scrap, the Rangers, and the Pikes. Morris obviously hadn't counted on them showing up. His plan had a hole in it. All Josiah could hope for was that Morris's escape was as uncertain.

By the time Josiah reached the ground, the shooting was over. Now, everyone was focused on rescuing those that were trapped inside the hotel. People stumbled out coughing, holding their mouths, covered in soot, as the smoke still roiled upward.

A crowd emerged from what once was the

livery. There were some recognizable faces that Josiah had seen before he'd entered the hotel. He had wondered what had happened to the onlookers once the doors were blockaded. It looked like they had been rounded up and held captive inside the livery. Whoever had kept them at bay was either dead or on the run.

A line of humans formed from the river to the hotel, passing buckets of water back and forth. Trying to save the hotel was a valiant effort, but the building was lost. Flames were visible everywhere — except the roof. Which Josiah had his eye on as one person after another descended the ladders. He couldn't breathe until Ofelia and Lyle climbed down safely. McNelly was the last man down.

Relieved, Josiah found Scrap, who was throwing water on the fire. "You did good," Josiah said.

Scrap had lost his hat somewhere. His thick black hair was plastered to his head and his face was dotted with soot. His clothes were wet, mixed with sweat and water, but none of it mattered to him. He was determined to beat the fire, like he had been determined to run the Langdons and Halversons out of Seerville.

"Did what I had to," Scrap said, swinging

385

a bucket.

"How'd you know to go to the Pikes?"

Scrap stopped with a bucket dangling in his hand. "Funny thing is, they met me halfway. They was comin' in as I was goin' for 'em. Good thing Darkson knew where they lived on that river. He figured they might hold a grudge against the Langdons and jump into the fight. Turns out he was right, don't it? Old Man Pike was coming to hold Morris to account for Billy's death. He didn't figure no judge would see fit to do it, so he was gonna do it hisself." Scrap shrugged. "I was happy they was comin' to help."

"Where's Leland and Ethan, do you know?"

"Beats me. Last I knowed they was still held in the jail. But with no Rangers on 'em, they might be on the run, too."

"I saw Morris take off on his own."

"Coward. He shoulda stayed and fought. He started all of this."

"What makes you say that?"

"Old Man Pike. He said it was Morris that shot the sheriff. Billy talked with Luke some, so word got back to them about what had happened."

Josiah lowered his head and tried to remember back to the incident. All he could remember was taking the butt end of Morris's rifle to the face. He couldn't prove or disprove Old Man Pike's claim any more than he could have sprouted wings and flew off the top of the hotel. But he knew who could. All he had to do was find Ethan Langdon.

Chapter 44

No one stood guard at the jail. Every available hand, Ranger, deputy, or otherwise, had been called to action by the fire and gunfight. The door to the jail stood open, but both cells were locked and occupied. Leland Halverson sat in the cell on the right and Ethan Langdon paced in the cell on the left like a trapped bobcat. Both men looked up when Josiah walked inside. The office looked familiar to him even though it was more rundown than he remembered. Everything was dusty, untouched since the position of marshal had been abolished. A desk in the middle of the room, gun cabinets empty, yellowed wanted posters on the wall. It smelled like a mouse had died somewhere close. More like a family of them once Josiah took another breath. He had spent a lot of time in the office when he had been the marshal of Seerville. Then the war came and he left it, never giving the position

388

another thought. Once the railroad had not passed by the town there was no need for a marshal. Or there didn't seem to be, or a way to pay a man a decent salary for taking on the charge. That hole had left the Langdons, and Josiah had to acknowledge, the Halversons, too, to take on whatever kind of trouble they wanted to get into.

"I can't say that I'm unhappy to see that you're both still locked up," Josiah said.

Leland took no notice of Josiah. Ethan, on the other hand, quit pacing, walked to the front of his cell, and grabbed ahold of the iron bars. "You should be in here, not me."

"I was cleared of all charges," Josiah said.

"You ain't never gonna be cleared as far as I'm concerned. Charlie's dead because of you."

Leland rustled, looked toward Josiah, and said, "Good god, Ethan, let it be. Wolfe didn't have a damn thing to do with Charlie's death and you know it. The state hanged him and that's that. The grudge your aholdin' is about as thin as ice on a Mexican pond."

"Ain't no ice on ponds in Mexico," Ethan said.

"That's my point."

Josiah stood watching the two men. He

had never seen them interact with each other before. Not that a pairing of the two was expected; they hated each other like dogs hate cats. Still, they had a rapport, something between them; they'd known each other their whole lives. They had been enemies since they were little boys.

"What are you starin' at?" Ethan said.

"Nothing," Josiah answered. "It's that I saw one of the Halverson cousins taking shots at the Rangers, and it struck me as odd. I figured maybe you two made a deal, came to terms to team up against the Rangers. Once they were dead and gone, all burned up in the fire, then Seerville would be yours to split up. No one to stop you from doing whatever it is that you want to do."

"That's some kind of dreamin'," Ethan said. "I ain't never made a deal with a Halverson that I didn't get took on. There's no way I'd do such a thing now. You're as wrong as a man who dances on Sundays."

Leland stood up and walked to the front of his cell. "I hate to say that I agree with the old coot, but he's right. We didn't make no deal. There ain't room in this town for the both of us. You ought to know that. The best thing that could have happened is all of them Langdons could have burned up, too."

"Halversons," Ethan snipped.

"They've been a thorn to everyone in these parts," Leland continued, ignoring Ethan, "since I can remember. Laws never meant nothin' to 'em. You know that, Wolfe. Charlie took Lyle hostage, used him as a shield. Who does that? A Langdon, that's who."

"Here's what I know," Josiah said. "The hotel is burning to the ground. Somebody set fire to it and barricaded the doors so nobody could get out. When they tried to flee, they were shot at. The streets are littered with dead men trying to escape the fire. All this is going on while you two are in here safe and unharmed. Oh, and word has it, Morris was the one that shot Sheriff Cliburn, which is what started this whole thing. Without that there'd be no judge, no Rangers in town, nothing. Life as normal. You two feuding over property that ain't worth an ounce of salt on a pickle. Maybe that was your intention from the get-go. Bring everybody in place, including me, so you'd have the upper hand around here."

"There you go, making stuff up again," Leland said.

But Ethan stood quiet, his eyes to the floor

as Josiah talked.

"Me and Luke would've never agreed to such a thing," Leland continued. "Luke'd rather die than go into business with them Langdons. There wasn't no deal. I swear to you. And there never will be."

"I wouldn't be so sure of that," Ethan said. It was as if all of the air had been sucked out of the office. Leland's face turned red and Ethan walked to the back of the cell and started pacing again. Josiah was left to assume that he'd been wrong. Maybe there was no grand deal between Ethan and Leland. But maybe there had been a deal between Luke and . . . "Morris," Josiah said aloud. "It was Luke and Morris who concocted this entire scheme. Why would Luke do such a thing, Leland? I rode with him. Trusted him as much as I could trust any man I hadn't spent a lot of time around. Why would he risk everything?"

"Everything?" Leland said. "Luke ain't got squat. He lives under my roof, under my rules. You go figure why a man with no prospects would join with a no-good scoundrel like Morris Langdon and get a little power in a town that treated him like he was good enough to spit on."

"Watch yourself there," Ethan said. "That's my boy."

"All your boys are scoundrels," Leland said.

"Your boy, too," Ethan fired back. "Luke's stood in your shadow forever. That boy can't tie his shoe without askin' you if it's okay to do it. You're so gall-darn blind to what everybody else sees, that you'd never take the blame for your boy turnin' tail and runnin' with Morris."

"Maybe you're right," Leland said. "Maybe Luke's tired of me and my ways. Maybe this whole thing is my fault, Josiah. I raised 'im wrong if this is all true."

"My guess is," Josiah said, "after they had the hotel under control and were sure their plan had worked, they were going to do the same to you that they did to those innocent folks in the hotel: Burn you alive. Then they'd be in charge of everything. The both of them. Except I don't think Morris would have stood for that. He would have killed Luke, if he hasn't already."

Recognition paled Leland's face. "You don't know where Luke's at?"

"Haven't seen him," Josiah said. "I saw Morris run off, but I haven't seen Luke since this thing started. You got any ideas where Morris might be running to, Ethan?"

"Why would I tell you if I knew?" Ethan said.

"Like I haven't seen Luke, I haven't seen Eva, either." It was a risk and Josiah knew it, but with all the talk about Luke and Morris joining up, he realized he knew something that Ethan didn't know.

Ethan's rage boiled over. He jumped at the bars. "Nothin' better happen to that girl. I swear I'll eat my way through this iron if a hair on her head is harmed. Eva don't have nothin' to do with any of this, you hear?"

Josiah struggled to remain calm. But he was worried about Eva, too. "Luke's not as dim-witted as you think he is, Ethan. You, either, Leland. Luke told me he had plans to go after that girl to get even. Now, if you ask me, he's figured out how to do that. He needs some insurance in case Morris thinks he can kill him and take over everything for himself."

"That's a fair amount of thinkin', Wolfe," Leland said.

"Well, Leland, whether you like it or not, I care about that girl. Lyle does, too. Ever since she brought him home, he's been over the moon about her every time he sees her."

"What in the heck are you sayin', Wolfe?" Leland said.

Josiah didn't hesitate. "If things were different, if I had come home and was allowed to get settled and found I felt the same way about Eva, and Lyle, too, I'd march right up to Ethan Langdon and ask his permission to court her. That's what I'm saying. Except I can't do that, because things didn't work out that way. I don't even know if that girl is dead or alive." He stared at Ethan Langdon, unwavering, doing his best to convince the man he wasn't backing down from his feelings or his thinking that Eva was in trouble.

Ethan didn't break Josiah's gaze. "Over my dead body," he said.

"Have it your way," Josiah said. He turned to walk out the door.

"Mine, too," Leland offered.

Josiah kept walking. "Both of their deaths are on your shoulders. Luke's and Eva's. You going to live with that?"

He was about to close the door when Ethan said, "There's a barn behind the Keystone Hall. Old Man Higgins hid his children from the Comanche there. Morris uses it as a place to keep out of sight until trouble calms down."

Josiah stopped. "You sure that's the only place he'd be?"

"Yes."

Josiah turned to Leland. "What about Luke?"

"If he ain't there, check the root cellar at

that house we got shot up in. He runs there like Morris runs to the inn. If they's still alive, he'd be there or with Morris."

"All right, I'll do my best to bring Morris back alive. He needs to stand in front of the judge for killing the sheriff and the trouble this fire has caused. But if it means him or Eva, then there's no choice, you understand? I don't want to face a grudge from you for the rest of my life. You, either, Leland. No matter what happens, you hear," he said, offering Ethan's words of warning right back to him.

CHAPTER 45

Josiah found Captain McNelly at the head of the water line. The fire reached up the whole front of the hotel. It was easy to see that there was no saving the building — or anyone that was left inside. There were no more screams, no pleas for help, only the roar of the flames and an occasional cough caused by the thick smoke. Every available man, woman, and child was engaged in trying to put out the fire.

Josiah filled McNelly in on what the two men in the jail had told him.

"You're sure that it was Morris Langdon you saw fleeing?" McNelly said with a troubled look on his soot-stained face.

"As sure as I'm standing before you."

"All right. Go find Dobson and Elliot. Take them with you. If there's more of a need, send Elliot back on that horse of his and I'll send what men I can spare."

"Yes, Captain," Josiah said. He had never

felt more like a Ranger than he did at that moment.

"I don't like this, Wolfe. I don't like it at all. But I want my men here if there's more to their plan than we think there is."

"I understand. The three of us can handle this, I'm sure of it." Josiah didn't wait for a response from McNelly. He went off to find Dobson and Scrap. Every second mattered more than it had when he'd been on the roof. It was Eva's life he was concerned about now, not his own. Or Ofelia's or Lyle's.

He caught sight of Scrap and Dobson standing in front of the mercantile, helping with the water line. Ofelia was calming down an old woman who was on the verge of hysterics. Her gray hair was singed, and her face and clothes were covered with black soot.

Lyle stood at Ofelia's side. He waved at Josiah and Josiah waved back, fighting off the urge to go pick the boy up and run home. But there was no way to know if that was a safe place. At least McNelly and his men were here.

Scrap looked up when Josiah approached. "There you are, Wolfe," he said, taking a bucket and passing it on to Dobson.

"We need to ride," Josiah said.

"Ride? There's a fire to put out."

"Captain's orders. Dobson, too. We need to bring in Morris Langdon. He's behind all of this."

"Tried to kill you all," Scrap said.

"He did, but he failed."

"I'm up for that. I've had a Langdon in my sights before and I'll sure as hell take another shot. That man's left more blood in the street than his brother."

"There's a Halverson, too. I think they've taken Eva as insurance."

"Cowards. Using a woman as a shield is about as low as you can get, ain't it?"

Josiah didn't answer, he was already moving on to grab Dobson and go.

Scrap and Sergeant Dobson rode hard next to Josiah. The fresh air felt good against his face, and it wasn't long before the smoke cleared from his lungs. He didn't look back, only forward, urging Clipper to run faster. All three wore the same focus on their faces. They knew they were about to face a battle. Morris and Luke would not go down without a fight, walk into jail without a whimper like their fathers did.

Each man was outfitted with an extra gun belt, carried two Peacemakers, and two Winchester rifles. Dobson wore a long

Bowie knife and Josiah knew that Scrap carried a smaller blade in his boot. McNelly had seen that they had everything they needed. All Josiah could hope was that Ethan Langdon had told him the truth, that Morris was hiding in the barn behind the Keystone Inn, and not setting them up. The thought had crossed Josiah's mind. He had considered that they were riding straight into a firing squad. If that were the case, then both of the old men, Ethan and Leland, had been in on the plan all along. He couldn't stand the thought of Lily's father being on the wrong side of the law.

The weather didn't hamper their ride. The sky was clear, the air crisp, and there was no sign of any bad weather on the horizon. They had that — and daylight — going for them.

It wasn't long before they were close enough to the inn to slow down, to be leery of a perimeter setup. But that was counting on Morris and Luke having men willing to protect them.

Dobson had led the way on a big brown gelding, while Scrap and Josiah held back a bit, knowing full well that Dobson was in charge. It didn't matter that Josiah wasn't an official Ranger; there was no difference in the three of them, other than rank. Josiah was quick to acquiesce, happy to not be in charge, even though he had his doubts about Dobson's battle prowess. The man led every action with his cock-of-the-walk attitude and Josiah had been in enough skirmishes, between his time in the Rangers and the war, to know how dangerous that was — not only for Dobson, but for him and Scrap, too.

Dobson rushed out ahead, then signaled them to stop. He reined the brown gelding around, and eased in between Josiah and Scrap. "You're certain that Langdon's here?"

"No," Josiah said. "Ethan said this was one of Morris's places that he holes up in when there's trouble. He could be anywhere. But my guess is he'll lay low, and this place is as possible as any. The settlers dug tunnels before they built cabins. Some of them were pretty complex with storerooms, cellars that they used to store food, that kind of thing, along with escape routes. There's still a lot of them around, even though the Comanche threat has not been around for a few years. We're going to have to go down and flush him out if that's the case."

"Only him," Dobson said.

"Luke Halverson's with him, and his

sister, too. My guess is she won't be a threat. But those two will be. It'll be like trapping a badger in a corner. They'll claw their way out if they have to."

"All right," Dobson said. "Let's go find this tunnel. Maybe we ought to smoke them out. Give 'em a taste of their own medicine."

"I'd be all right with that idea if Eva wasn't with them."

"You don't know that for sure."

Scrap sat silent, listening for as long as he could. He jumped in and said, "I think the sergeant's idea is a wise one. Langdon might have a series of traps down there. I'm not one for dark, tight spaces myself. I say we smoke them out. If the sister's among 'em, then she'll break out, too. It ain't like dirt's gonna catch fire and eat her up. Besides, Wolfe, how in the hell can you know for sure that she's not in on this anyways?"

"Because I know her, that's how," Josiah said. "She's not the type to hurt anything that breathes, more or less innocent women and children. She had nothing to do with the hotel fire and the plan to kill everyone. I'm sure of it."

"I hope you're right," Scrap said.

"I am," Josiah answered. "I'll guarantee it."

■ ■ ■ ■

A man called Tibor Johnson was tending bar at the Keystone Inn. He looked up when the trio walked inside. Unlike the night before, the place was empty. It was midday. All of the chairs sat on the tables, upside down, and the tall drapes on the windows were pulled closed.

Johnson was a boulder-sized man with a walrus mustache, bald head, a hard-set jaw, and suspicious eyes. He stopped drying glasses with a bright white towel, and said, "What can I do for you fellas?"

Their gun belts signaled an intention that wasn't lost on the barkeep. All three men had business on their minds that didn't involve drinking or carousing. Not that there was anything to carouse.

Dobson led the way to the bar. "We're lookin' for Morris Langdon."

"What makes you think he's here?" Johnson said. He threw the towel over his shoulder and glared at Dobson.

"Let's say we got reason to believe he's hiding out on the property."

"I don't know nothin' about that. Who in the hell are you, anyway?"

"Paul Dobson. I'm a sergeant in the Texas

403

Rangers."

"That so?" Johnson was not impressed.

"It is. I got reason to believe that Morris and Luke Halverson set fire to the hotel, the Seer House, in Seerville."

Tibor Johnson let out a laugh so deep that it sounded like a foghorn. His whole body jostled in humorous disbelief. "Good Lord, man, what in the hell have you been drinkin'? Ain't no way a Halverson and a Langdon is gonna do anythin' together, much less go around settin' fires for the fun of it. Those two families hate the air the other breathes. You ain't from around here, are you?"

"Doesn't matter," Dobson said.

"You are, though, aren't you?" Johnson said to Josiah. "You was in here last night when the place got busted up."

Josiah looked around. There wasn't any hint of the fight that took place. Everything was clean and mended, ready for another night of business. "I've been away for a while. I don't know what's going on."

Johnson leaned forward on the bar. "Seems to me none of you do. Like I said, Morris ain't around here."

"You didn't say no such thing," Scrap said.

"I imagine you're a Ranger, too." Johnson had moved. He looked like he was about to launch over the bar.

"I am," Scrap said.

"I guess I should be trembling in my boots."

Dobson shot Scrap a look that said "shut up" without saying it. "We're not lookin' for trouble. We're lookin' for Morris Langdon and Luke Halverson."

"I told you. I ain't seen them."

"Then you don't mind if we have a look around for ourselves, do you?" Dobson said.

"Doesn't bother me. Suit yourself. Be careful. I hear there's a nest of rattlesnakes in the barn."

"Thanks for the warning." Dobson turned to Scrap then, and said, "You stay here. Keep an eye on him and make sure he doesn't set off an alarm of some kind. Me and Wolfe'll look around. If we need you, you'll know it."

Scrap cocked his jaw, ready to protest, but decided not to after taking a long look at Tibor Johnson. "Whatever you say, Sarge."

Dobson didn't wait for Johnson to back off, or Scrap to get over being ordered around. He spun on his heels, and headed toward the door. Josiah followed, hoping like hell that the man knew what he was getting himself into.

CHAPTER 46

"We need to find the tunnel exit," Dobson said. "Then we need to collect enough grass to set fire to so we can flush Morris and Luke out."

"If they're in there." Josiah stood at the entrance to the barn behind the inn, hoping to see a sign of the men or Eva. He hadn't seen anything that suggested anyone was around. It was possible that the barkeep, Johnson, was telling the truth, that he hadn't seen the men. If that was the case, then they were wasting time, allowing for jeopardy to find its way to Eva. Dobson wouldn't hear of leaving now, he was a hound on a scent. An admirable quality, unless the rabbit turned out to be a skunk.

"Well, I ain't gonna holler down no tunnel and offer a fine hello." Dobson's face twisted into something Josiah couldn't read, then he set off, studying the ground, careful not to stomp and let anyone below ground know that he was there.

It was difficult keeping his mouth shut, not offering another way to go about the search, but Josiah knew his place. He was less than a Ranger, not part of the company, even though McNelly himself had ordered him to participate. The rationale was easy to understand. McNelly was short on men, time was ticking away, and Josiah had the experience of more missions than he could count on two hands. Still, it was difficult for him to follow instead of lead.

Josiah took the opposite side of Dobson, walked out about twenty yards, then slowed, looking for any sign of the tunnel exit. He had never been inside one of the escape tunnels, though he had heard plenty of tales about them. Cynthia Ann Parker and her brother had been snatched by the Comanche south of Seerville before Josiah had been born. Every man in the state swore that wouldn't happen to his children, and the tunnels were one way to help prevent that. They were dug before a cabin was built. At the least the escape routes provided peace of mind and a place to hide. But the Comanche were smart. They caught on to the tunnels, knew how to find them better than anyone thought — which shouldn't have been a surprise since the Indians knew the land better than the white man. When the Indians found a family, they smoked them out and took their revenge on them when they fled. It was the same strategy they were going to use against Morris. That was the part that worried Josiah. Eva. He wouldn't be able to live with himself if any harm came to her. He didn't have the conscience, or rage of a Comanche, to rely on, to see past that kind of pain. The thought of her stuck in a smoky tunnel made him want to call the whole thing off.

The buffalo grass that surrounded the barn was already starting to turn brown at the stem, but was green enough to smoke and not sizzle to a crisp once it was touched by a flame. The shoots looked weak and tired, drooping, waiting for a good wind to topple them over. There was no disturbance on the ground that Josiah could see — until he made his way to the back of the barn, still twenty yards out, and found a patch of tramped-down grass. It didn't take long to find the lid.

He whistled to get Dobson's attention.

It took two calls before the sergeant realized the sound was Josiah and not a bird.

Josiah kneeled and pulled the lid up, exposing the tunnel exit to light. The round hole was wide enough for a decent-sized man to fit through. A bulky fella like the barkeep at the Keystone Inn would have to struggle to get inside. It was possible that he might even get stuck. Luke and Morris were not small men. Josiah was starting to doubt the plan even more, starting to doubt what Ethan had told him. Maybe the hiding spots were a setup, too, like everything else had been. There was no trusting a Langdon, no matter the cause or reason.

Dobson showed up with a load of grass. He piled it up on the edge of the hole, then motioned for Josiah to fetch some more. They both set about finding the driest grasses they could. It didn't take long before there was a bundle waiting to be set on fire.

"You're sure about this?" Josiah whispered to Dobson.

"You got a better plan?"

Josiah pulled out a Lucifer, lit it, then set the grass afire.

He waited until the flame was starting to rage, then he beat it out with another load of grass. Once the pile was smoldering, he knocked it down the hole, then added more fodder. Smoke roiled upward out of the tunnel and Dobson took off for the barn. It was there that they expected Luke and Morris to emerge if they were hiding in the tunnel.

Josiah stood and watched Dobson, then realized he was standing out in the open. There was nothing to cover him except for the pillar of smoke that was billowing out of the ground. He crouched down, already accustomed to the smell and sting to his eyes from the smoke. Though this was different from the hotel fire; the grass burned in the dirt, ejecting a singed earthy smell that reminded Josiah of a grass fire spreading across the plains after a lightning strike. He covered his face with a soiled bandanna, then pulled his Peacemaker from the holster and cocked it; he was ready for whatever came next.

Dobson edged his way to the barn and stopped at the open door. A thin stream of smoke was starting to exit into the barn, solidifying their theory that the tunnel entrance was hidden inside.

Josiah watched, listened, and waited, doing his best to stay hidden and avoid the smoke. His throat and eyes burned, but not so bad that he couldn't see or swallow. He took a deep breath when the sergeant disappeared into the barn.

There was no sound other than the crackle of the fire. Josiah fed more grass down the hole to keep the smoke steady. Behind him, the Keystone Inn stood without patrons, a lone building on a silent road. That would change once darkness fell. The roadhouse drew drinkers and gamblers to it like it was the only oasis in the state of Texas.

Left on his own, Josiah was starting to wonder, again, if Morris and Luke were hiding somewhere else. On their ranch, like Ethan had said. But he didn't have to wonder too long. A gunshot caused him to almost jump out of his boots.

The shot had come from inside the barn. It was followed by two more shots. Both sounded like Colts, so it was hard to tell who was shooting. Regardless, Dobson needed help, backup. Josiah was counting on Scrap to hear the gunfire and come running, too.

He made his way to the barn, keeping low to the ground, while pulling out the other revolver from the holster. Cocked and loaded, Josiah stopped at the door, and peered inside, ready for a gunfight, hoping Eva was somewhere else.

Dobson had taken cover behind a slatted stall with his back to the door. Josiah was tempted to run inside and join him, but he didn't know where the shots were coming from, and didn't want to make himself an easy target.

It didn't take long for another shot to ring

out. Josiah couldn't tell if it was Morris or Luke. The shot came from the back of the barn, the darkest point. All he saw was an orange burst of light, followed by a puff of gun smoke. If there were two men — they both had to be armed — and he needed to take that into account.

Smoke snaking across the floor of the barn helped. It was starting to build to knee-high, which would allow Josiah to crawl over to Dobson. As long as it lasted. Without anyone to feed the fire it was going to die soon.

It was now or never.

Josiah took his chance and crawled to Dobson. Gunfire volleyed back and forth. Bullets whizzed over his head and Josiah still wasn't sure if the sergeant knew that he was coming to join him. He would have hollered out, but he didn't want to give himself away.

He was able to find his way to Dobson.

"We were right," Dobson said. "There's two of 'em."

"The gunfire ought to bring Scrap running," Josiah answered, peering through the slat of the stall, looking for movement of some kind. He saw the shadow of a man, then a burst of orange again. The shot splintered wood six inches from his head.

He shot back, then lost sight of the man again. He couldn't tell if it was Luke or Morris. But it didn't matter. It was one or the other.

Another shot came, and Josiah and Dobson answered back, firing off three shots each, one right after the other. The smoke grew thicker and a man hollered out in pain. A familiar sound followed. The thud of a body falling to the ground. But that didn't stop the two from continuing to shoot. They emptied their weapons.

It took a second for Josiah to gather himself and realize he had to reload. He expected shots to be returned, but none were.

Dobson went about reloading, too. Both men were preoccupied, but kept an eye out toward the shooters. There was nothing to see but smoke.

No sounds came from beyond their range of vision — which was declining by the second. "We can't stay here much longer," Josiah said, restraining a cough.

"Agreed," Dobson said. "There's only one way they're gonna get out. Let's make a break for the door before it's too late."

Josiah checked through the slats again. He thought he saw a flame inside the smoke. A prolonged flicker of light that showed him

413

nothing. If a man had fallen to the ground, shot, he was impossible to see. Certain that there was no point in staying inside the barn — he'd been close enough to one fire — he backed out, eyes darting, searching for any movement, doing his best to breathe. Smoke wrapped around him like a thin burial linen, intent on suffocating him. His feet responded and he had no choice but to look away to gauge his journey to the door, to clear air and freedom.

Dobson led, was a few feet in front of Josiah with his back to him. Every second that passed in silence was a surprise. Tension rested on the trigger of his Peacemaker, ready to respond. But no shots came. Josiah was beginning to wonder if both men had been hit. He was almost outside before his questions were answered. He heard a call for help from inside the barn. It was Eva's voice, panicked and afraid.

CHAPTER 47

Josiah and Dobson stopped. "Don't be . . ." Josiah said, intending to warn Dobson not to be fooled. He was wary of Morris's tricks. But it was too late.

"Is that you, Miss Langdon?" Dobson called out.

It was enough for whoever was shooting to figure out where they were. Voices carried through deep smoke. Gave away positions. Josiah had seen it more than once in the war.

A shot rang out before Josiah could react, before he could pull Dobson to the ground so he would be harder to hit. The bullet took no mercy on the sergeant. It was a lucky shot that nailed the man square in the forehead. He gasped, had enough time to realize that he'd been shot, then tumbled backwards, propelled by the force of lead. Warm blood splattered on Josiah's face and he knew in a second that there was nothing he could do for the man.

Eva screamed. Only this time it was loud and sounded painful. Followed by a murmur, like someone had put their hand over her mouth.

Rage erupted inside of Josiah. "Let her go, Morris. I know it's you that's got her. Luke would have already killed her if he had the chance."

More murmurs. A struggle. Josiah's skin felt like it was being pricked by hot pins, and his lungs were full of smoke. But he wasn't going to run outside and leave Eva behind.

No one answered.

"What do you want, Morris?" Josiah said.

Finally, an answer came. "Your life for hers."

The small flicker that Josiah had seen was starting to grow. A flame jumped upward from the ground and caught on one of the beams, allowing enough light to see the silhouette of a man standing behind a woman, holding her with one arm, while another covered her mouth. There wasn't a clear shot to be had, or Josiah would have taken it. "Sure," he said. "Let her go, and it'll be you and me."

Josiah sensed movement behind him, then felt someone ease up next to him. A side glance told him that Scrap had joined him. "I ain't lettin' her go. I'm comin' out with her. Then we'll see who's in charge," Morris said.

"What about Luke?" Josiah asked.

"How do you know it was Luke?"

Scrap said nothing, readied himself with two revolvers, one in each hand. He watched Josiah for a signal of what to do.

"Where's Luke?" Josiah said.

More murmurs escaped from Eva's lips as she struggled to free herself.

"Knock it off, sister." Morris coughed, then he looked over his shoulder to see the fire growing behind him.

A flame jumped up the hay-bound floor to ceiling beam, traveling on the dry wood like it was a train track built for a fire-eating locomotive. It was difficult to see Morris and Eva through the ferocity of the smoke, hard to make out the detail of their faces, but it didn't take much to see — or know — that they both feared for their lives. In different ways.

Scrap motioned to Josiah to keep them talking, then tipped the end of the barrel of his revolver up. Josiah knew what that meant. Scrap had taken out Charlie Langdon and saved Lyle. That had been the spark that set off this fire. Charlie Langdon captured by the law, then hanged with the permission of due process and a fair trial. That should have been that. But Josiah had failed to see the consequences of a long-held grudge. Now he had to face that, and it had nothing to do with Scrap. If anyone was going to put an end to Morris Langdon, and save Eva, it was going to be him.

"Drop your guns and I'll bring her out," Morris said.

Scrap eyed Josiah and waited.

Josiah remained focused on the images he saw through the smoke. "Doesn't look to me like you've got a choice, Morris. You stay, you'll burn up. You come out, you have to face what you've done."

"And what is it you think I've done?"

Josiah was betting that Morris wouldn't choose to burn alive, or in the end, let any harm come to Eva. It might have been a fool's bet. His only alternative was to start shooting, and he couldn't get a good bead on Morris. His eyes stung and the smoke was too thick, or moving too much.

"Doesn't matter what I think," Josiah said.

Eva struggled, protesting as loud as she could. Then Josiah heard a stomp, then a yell of pain from Morris. The smoke swirled and the fire danced to the roof. Eva ran out of the smoke, straight to Josiah. He had no choice but to lower his arms and welcome her into them.

Morris recovered and chased after her. As soon as he was clear of the smoke, he started shooting.

Josiah spun Eva around behind him, hugged her tight against his back, and covered her while he raised his Colt and fired. Scrap joined in. Both of their bullets hit Morris, first in the chest, then in his arm, sending his pistol flying. Death settled in his eyes like darkness stealing in after a long day, just waiting to take over. It took Josiah a long second to believe that Morris Langdon was really dead.

It was less than a joyous reunion in Seerville. By the time Josiah, Scrap, and Eva rode into town the hotel was a smoldering ruin. None of the other buildings had caught fire, but that seemed less than a blessing as they stood vacant with a less than glorious past, and an even more uncertain future. Dobson's body was slung over the back of the brown gelding he rode, and Morris's horse was not far behind, with his body, too, ready for delivery to the undertaker.

Captain McNelly stood waiting as the trio arrived. A crowd still lingered, folks still catching their breath, recovering from the fire, waiting for the sad recovery of those who remained inside the hotel.

"I see we lost Dobson," McNelly said, his face ashen and gray.

"Nobly, sir," Josiah said as he dismounted from Clipper. Eva had ridden with him and remained on the appaloosa. Scrap sat with a solemn look on his face as he surveyed what remained of the hotel.

"And the elder Langdon, too?"

"Not so nobly. He tried to use his sister as a shield, a cowardly move one more time. He was where his father said he would be, which I would think should bode well for his future."

"Father?" Eva said, stiffening.

"He is fine, ma'am," McNelly said. "Still in the jail, though it is only a matter of time and formality before he is released. There have been several men who have reinforced the story that Morris is the man responsible for Sheriff Cliburn's death. Now with news that Ethan Langdon aided in the capture of Morris, the judge should see fit to let him go. He has kin to bury."

Relief crossed Eva's face.

"The Halversons, too," Josiah said. "Dobson shot Luke, but we could not retrieve the body. The barn was set ablaze. I fear there is nothing left of him."

McNelly said, "That would validate the thinking that Morris and Luke had joined together to set the hotel on fire and continue the feud on their own terms instead of their fathers'. I hope those two men will see fit to lay down arms against each other, see that enough has been lost, and nothing gained. No property, or grudge, is worth the loss of human life as we've seen here."

"You're right, sir. I hope the feud is over," Josiah said. "Maybe life can get back to normal." He looked up to Eva, who it seemed was starting to grasp the reality of her brother's actions. "Or as normal as possible."

"Papa!" a boy's voice rang out.

Josiah knew it well. He turned to see Lyle running toward him, with Ofelia not far behind. Whatever anyone else said was lost to him. He leaned down on one knee and welcomed his son's embrace. He had never been happier to see Lyle.

CHAPTER 48

There were four Langdon brothers left. Two of them had died on the street, shot and killed by the Texas Rangers. Ethan Langdon had charged them all to rebuild Josiah's cabin. By the time a month had passed after the Seerville fire, Josiah, Ofelia, and Lyle had moved out of the barn and into the new cabin. Ofelia had done what she could to make the house a home, in a short time, but she knew that it was not her place to make it too comfortable. Josiah had been true to his word, and asked Ethan Langdon if he could court Eva. The old man had agreed with expected reluctance. To prevent trouble down the road, Josiah told Leland of his intentions, too. After some grumbling, Leland promised there'd be no trouble from him. Lyle needed a mother, he'd said, and the pickings in and around Seerville were few — even though he thought Josiah could do better than to spend time with a Langdon woman. Both men had been freed by Judge Dooley in a matter of days, after a formal trial could be held, and proper witnesses could be examined. In the end, it was determined that Morris Langdon had indeed killed Sheriff Cliburn. With that, the Rangers had gone on to more adventures, putting an end to the Seerville feud, offering one more example of the need and power of the Texas Ranger organization.

It was a pleasant November day that found Josiah outside the cabin, chopping wood to add to the winter stack when a rider approached. He stopped, wiped his brow, and shaded his eyes to see if he recognized the rider.

Ofelia and Eva sat on the front porch tatting new doilies for the house, while Lyle played at their feet. A rapport had been established between the two women, both seeing the need for the other in Josiah and Lyle's lives. What one couldn't do, the other could. The four of them were finding their place in the new cabin — though Eva returned each night before sundown on Josiah's arm. Ofelia acted as a chaperone, even though none were needed.

Lyle recognized the rider before anyone else did. "Scrap!" he called out, and ran off the porch.

Josiah sat the axe down and wondered what Scrap Elliot was doing in this part of East Texas. He hadn't heard from him since the Ranger company had pulled out of the paddock.

Scrap jumped off Missy and picked up Lyle like he was a long-lost nephew that he hadn't seen in a hundred years. "Why look at you, boy, you've done growed a foot since the last time I saw you." He sat Lyle down, smiled, then doffed his hat to the women.

Eva smiled, while Ofelia sat stone-faced. Scrap's sudden appearances were not reasons to celebrate.

Josiah walked over to Scrap and shook his hand. "Wasn't expecting to see you on this fine day," he said.

"Wasn't expectin' to see you anytime soon, Wolfe." Scrap looked over to Ofelia and Eva. "Captain sent me," he said in a low voice. "Think we ought to go up to the barn?"

"Sounds like a good idea." Josiah looked down at Lyle, and said, "You stay here with Ofelia and Eva."

"Don't want to. Want to come with Scrap."

"You do what I said." There was a serious tone in Josiah's voice that Lyle seemed to recognize right away.

"Yes, sir."

Josiah and Scrap walked toward the barn, leaving Lyle behind. "I take it this is no social call," Josiah said.

"Wish it was," Scrap answered. "McNelly is taking some time off. Gone back to his ranch for a spell. His lungs took a bad turn after we left you in October. I'm ridin' with Company D again."

"That's Jones's outfit."

"It is," Scrap said as they walked to the barn. He fished a tobacco pouch out of his pocket, and started the process of rolling a cigarette.

"What's that got to do with me?" Josiah said.

"Jones could use you. Sent me out here to see if you'd ride with us. He's got a sergeant, but he knows of your skills, heard all about how you helped put an end to the Seerville feud. There's trouble over in Mason County and there's some Comanche still raidin' in the north. He needs a man like you is the truth of it."

Josiah stopped and looked back at the cabin, at Lyle, Eva, and Ofelia. "I'm starting to get my feet under me here. Besides, I have a boy to look after. That's against the rules as far as I know."

"Jones figured that would come up. It was overlooked by Captain Fikes, and he's willing to do the same. He said he could pay you sixty dollars a month and give you extra time off to come back and spend time with the boy."

"There's more than that," Josiah said.

"I figured as much when I saw that Langdon woman on your porch."

"I've got a chance at a new life here. This is my home."

"Ain't no reason for it to be anything else, Wolfe. I'm only the messenger."

"Jones sent you for a reason."

"He knows we rode together."

"I know he does."

Scrap finished rolling the cigarette, put it to his mouth, and lit it. "I ain't here to bend your arm," he said with an exhale. "But you said it to me more than once that you liked bein' a Ranger more than a farmer. Maybe you can do both. Ride a bit, then come home for a bit, rebuild your new life while keeping a boot in your old one."

"I don't know, Scrap. I'm starting to like the life I've got. It's been a long time since I've been able to say that."

The afternoon sun fell toward the horizon quicker than usual, given the season, and before he knew it, it was time for Josiah to walk Eva home. Scrap was staying the night,

426

riding out in the morning, after a bit of dinner, and a night's rest.

Josiah and Eva walked the well-worn path through the woods to her home. The sky had burned white, and night was coming on fast. A dog barked in the distance, bringing them to a stop. Both of them knew it wasn't a dog. It was a wolf. The same one Josiah had seen with the pups, out making a living, trying to survive like him.

"I knew this day would come," Eva said. They stood under a tall oak, shy of the fence line that separated Wolfe land from Langdon land.

"What day is that?"

"The day when Scrap Elliot came riding in with a cause of duty in his pocket, urging you to ride off with him."

"How did you know that would happen?"

"Because, Josiah Wolfe, I know what kind of man you are. You're a restless spirit. You think you can be happy here, but you've been tempted off this land by adventure and duty before. The war called you off, then the Rangers. You've got trail dust under your skin, and you're happiest when you're riding."

Josiah looked away from Eva because he couldn't offer up an argument that would match her words. "I'd say I'm sorry . . ."

"You can't help bein' the man you are, Josiah, I know that."

"It doesn't make it easy."

Eva smiled, then let it flitter away. "I've never known easy, and I don't expect to anytime soon. I'm happy to stay here, help Ofelia with Lyle, and wait for you to come home when you can. I've got a hope now that I've never had before. So all I ask is that you promise that you'll come back in one piece. Not do anything to get yourself killed. You got people here that love you."

Josiah leaned in and kissed Eva as deep as he could. She made him warm, feel more like a man than he'd felt in a long time.

When he pulled away, he said, "What makes you think I'm fool enough to leave?"

"I knew you was leavin' when you looked up and realized that it was Scrap Elliot ridin' in to see you. Once a Ranger, always a Ranger."

The morning light was starting to fade before Josiah had Clipper ready to go. He cinched the saddle one last time, and looked to the porch. Ofelia and Eva stood shoulder to shoulder, watching his every move. Lyle stood between them, stoic, doing his best not to cry. Goodbyes had already been said. Now they waited for the inevitable, for

Josiah to leave them all one more time.

Without any more dillydallying, or fanfare, Josiah climbed into the saddle and reined Clipper to a turn so his horse was nose to nose with Missy, Scrap's horse. Both beasts seemed to know what was happening, were comforted to be in each other's company again.

"Looks like we're burning daylight, Scrap," Josiah said.

"I'm waitin' on you, like usual, Wolfe. I'd be halfway to Austin by now if it was me and Missy here."

"Well, then, you best get a move on."

"Last one out of the county cooks dinner."

"You're on," Josiah said. He knew Clipper couldn't outrun Missy, but the race would keep him occupied until the little farm was out of sight.

"Let's go!" Scrap hollered, then urged his blue roan mare into a run.

Josiah followed after Scrap, waving, refusing to look back, to see what he was leaving behind.

ABOUT THE AUTHOR

Larry D. Sweazy is a multiple-award-winning author of fifteen Western and mystery novels, thirty-one short stories, and over sixty nonfiction articles and book reviews. He lives in Noblesville, Indiana, with his wife, Rose, and is hard at work on his next novel. More information about Larry's writing can be found at www.larry dsweazy.com.

The employees of Thorndike Press hope you have enjoyed this Large Print book. All our Thorndike, Wheeler, and Kennebec Large Print titles are designed for easy reading, and all our books are made to last. Other Thorndike Press Large Print books are available at your library, through selected bookstores, or directly from us.

For information about titles, please call:
(800) 223-1244

or visit our Web site at:
http://gale.cengage.com/thorndike

To share your comments, please write:
Publisher
Thorndike Press
10 Water St., Suite 310
Waterville, ME 04901